VICTORIA WALTERS has always loved creating stories. Her first book was handwritten when she was sixteen years old, and was closely modelled on the *Sweet Valley High* series. Victoria studied sociology at Warwick University and has since worked for a business publisher and as a Waterstones bookseller. She lives in Surrey with her cat Harry (named after Harry Potter, not Harry Styles). This is her first novel.

You can discover more about Victoria – and find pictures of Harry the cat – by following her on Twitter at @Vicky_Walters or by visiting her blog at: www.victoria-writes.com

By Victoria Walters

The Second Love of My Life

Digital Novella

The Summer I Met You

VICTORIA WALTERS

The Second Love of my Life

headline
review

First published in paperback in 2016 by
HEADLINE REVIEW
An imprint of HEADLINE PUBLISHING GROUP

2

Cataloguing in Publication Data is available from the British Library

ISBN 978 1 4722 2932 8

Typeset in Plantin Light by Avon DataSet Ltd,
Bidford-on-Avon, Warwickshire

Printed and bound in Great Britain by CPI Group (UK) Ltd,
Croydon, CR0 4YY

HEADLINE PUBLISHING GROUP
An Hachette UK Company
Carmelite House
50 Victoria Embankment
London EC4Y 0DZ

www.headline.co.uk
www.hachette.co.uk

For my mum, Christine. For everything.

Prologue

Four years earlier

'Goodnight, future Mrs Wood.'

I wave to my soon-to-be to be mother- and father-in-law, Gloria and Graham, who follow the last of our friends as they weave down our path somewhat drunkenly into the night. I close the door and look down at the sparkling solitaire diamond ring now adorning my left hand. As someone who has never worn much jewellery, it's going to take some getting used to.

'I'm not sure I like the sound of that,' Lucas says into my ear, wrapping his arms around my waist.

I raise an eyebrow. 'Changed your mind already?'

'Never.' My new fiancé twists me around so I can see him. His familiar tousled fair hair, tanned skin and wide, bright blue eyes greet me. He gestures to the painting hanging in our hallway of the beach just à stone's throw away from our house. He lingers on the signature in the corner. My signature. 'You might be a rich and famous artist one day; you can't change the name on your work.'

I chuckle, leaning into his chest. 'I don't think we need to worry about that.'

'You never know.'

'Are you serious? You want me to keep my name when we get married?'

'As long as we're married it doesn't really matter, does it?'

Lucas has always been the biggest fan of my art. Probably because we met in art class at school, all those years ago. My mum used to say Lucas was a keeper when we were just teenagers; she was always right. I reach for his lips, unable not to kiss him again. He feels like home to me when our lips meet. He has always felt like home.

I can't pretend that his proposal took me completely by surprise tonight. I've felt certain we would end up together for a long time now, but we're still young, and I wasn't sure it would happen this soon. He kisses me back enthusiastically and pulls me by the hand back into our small living room, which just minutes ago was crowded with all of our favourite people. Lucas had wanted them here to be part of our special moment. He loves that our family and friends have always been part of our relationship; we live in the small town we grew up in and everyone is so excited that we're getting married. But even though I love Talting as much he does, I'm pleased we now have the rest of the night to ourselves. The two of us alone together in our house is always my favourite time of the day.

We curl up on the leather sofa in our usual position, Lucas sitting up and me leaning against his chest, my legs curled up beside me. Lucas brushes back a stray hair from my cheek and looks at the mantelpiece in front of us lined with photographs from our life together. 'I wish I could have asked her.'

'Asked who?'

'Your mum. I always thought I'd ask her permission – well,

her blessing, because I wouldn't have taken no for an answer. I wish she was here,' he says, murmuring his words into my hair. I look at the photographs, moving past the one of us on a beach in the Caribbean to one with his parents when we were younger, then the one with Emma and John, our best friends, and last of all the one of me with my mum in the house I grew up in. 'I wish she was too. But you know she would have been so happy for us, I think she loved you even more than I do.'

'She just knew I'd always look after you.'

I feel in danger of crying so I look away from the picture and into Lucas's eyes. He always steadies me. 'Did you choose the ring by yourself?' I ask him.

He chuckles, his chest moving under me. 'It's quite annoying that you know me so well. Emma actually demanded to come with me and she dragged John along too. We went into Plymouth a few weeks ago. Seriously, we were there hours; she dragged me to every jeweller's. She told me you'd be wearing this forever so it had to be perfect. I kind of thought all diamond rings were the same . . . I'll never say that again,' he says, shaking his head at the memory. I can imagine Emma making a very impassioned speech as to why that was definitely not the case. Secretly, I agree with Lucas, but I'd never have the guts to tell her that.

'Well, I love it, so you chose well,' I tell him.

Lucas turns to me, his eyes serious. 'This is what you want, isn't it?'

'Well, I'm still waiting for Brad Pitt, but as it's unlikely he'll ever come to Talting . . .' I tease, leaning in to kiss him on the nose.

'Ha ha,' he says sarcastically. 'I just want to make sure

you'll never regret just being with me your whole life.'

We haven't been back long from our travels. Instead of going to university, we had taken the opportunity of being young and free and headed off to see the world. Emma had actually thought that Lucas would propose whilst we were away. 'Imagine all the romantic places he might be thinking of doing it in,' she said as we shopped for clothes for me to take. But I didn't agree with her. Our home town has always been the soundtrack to our relationship – we were born and bred here, and we want to grow old here. I knew he'd want to mark this special moment here somehow.

I think about his speech earlier. How he got down on his knee, holding out a blue velvet box. I couldn't hear the gasps around me or see the smiles; all I could focus on was him – my Lucas. My best friend, my partner, my soulmate.

My everything.

'I can't wait to walk towards you,' I say. 'Do you know how lucky we are? Because sometimes I look at other people and wonder how we got so lucky to have each other. We just fit.'

'Like Ross and Rachel?'

I shake my head with a smile. He has always been obsessed with *Friends*. 'You do realise planning this wedding is going to be a nightmare, though?' This will be the news of the year here, and I know everyone will want to be involved.

'It's going to be fun,' he disagrees. 'We're going to get married in the church then have a big party. You know you won't have to do anything – Mum, Emma, Joe, they'll do all the organising. All you have to do is wear a white dress and show up.'

I groan. 'Oh God, a white dress.'

'You can do it, I believe in you.'

I nudge him in the ribs. 'Hey, you chose an un-girly girl, it's your own fault.'

He turns serious again. 'I chose perfectly,' he says.

I roll my eyes, unused to all of this. Lucas and I are usually the 'we know we love one another so we don't need to say it all the time' couple. 'Tonight has made you impossibly romantic.'

'Don't worry, tomorrow I'll just be impossible again.'

'Good.' I lean in for a lingering kiss and then relax back in his arms. I'll never get tired of Lucas holding me.

'We're going to be together forever,' he promises then, as if he can read my mind. I sometimes think he can, actually. There is not one doubt in my heart he's right.

I was blissfully unaware in that moment just how short our forever would end up being.

Chapter One

Now

They say that everyone is famous in a small town.

In my home town of Talting I had always been known as an artist.

The Last Painting?

I stare again at the bold headline on the front page of the *Cornwall News*. 'This might be your last chance to own a painting by renowned local artist Rose Walker', reads the opening line of the article.

'Why are you reading that again?' my best friend, Emma, demands as she comes to sit opposite me in the booth. 'Who left this here?' She looks around the room accusingly. It's been two weeks since the article was printed and I'm still haunted by its words.

Joe, our boss, comes over then, guilt flashing in his eyes when he sees the paper. 'I thought we agreed to get rid of them all,' he says.

'I just can't forget it,' I say, thinking back to the young journalist interviewing us all in this very bar a few weeks ago to publicise our town's annual Easter Fair, which takes place this Saturday.

Emma snatches the paper from my hands. 'I still can't

believe the nerve of him,' she says.

I don't need the paper in front of me to remember the words: 'Ms Walker hasn't painted anything new in two years and it looks unlikely we will see any work in the future by this talented woman, so head for her stall at the Fair and grab an original Walker before it's too late.'

'I'm sorry, Rose,' Joe says for the hundredth time, looking at the paper fearfully. 'I only wanted him to know how proud I am that you're taking part in this year's Fair with everything that you've been through. How proud we all are.'

'He twisted everything you said,' Emma says indignantly, trying to console him. I know how bad he feels about the article. She screws up the paper in her hands. 'We are all really proud of you. This article doesn't change that.'

Two years ago, my world changed forever.

I was no longer known in Talting for being an artist. Instead I became known for being something I could have never imagined: a widow at the age of twenty-four.

It's April and the weather is beginning to warm up, which means Talting is beginning to turn from an inconspicuous coastal town in Cornwall to a busy tourist destination, thanks to our stretch of golden sand and, more importantly, waves ripe for surfing. Our Easter Fair used to be one of my favourite events here but I missed last year's, unable to think about attending without Lucas by my side. It would have been my first time there without him in ten years and I wasn't ready to accept that. I'm still not sure if I'm ready to face the Fair alone, but I need to sell my last few paintings.

The remaining pieces of my past life.

It's the only way I can start to get some of myself back. I used to love these events and I'm determined to take part again. This is what living in Talting is all about, and I've never wanted to live anywhere else.

Although the past two years have severely tested that resolve.

The door to the bar swings open and a group of tourists come in, talking loudly and drawing our attention to them. Thanks to the forecasted warm weather this weekend, the Fair is going to be packed, and Talting Inn and our various B&Bs are already booked up for it.

This group are almost certainly here for the waves. I'd guess they are city types, working in banks or similar and here for a break to blow off steam. Their outfits are trying to be surfing cool but look expensive. Maybe they won't even get out to the sea, just take photos of it to brag to their Facebook friends.

'Here we go again,' Mrs Morris mutters as she walks over to collect her bag and coat from next to me, her eyes narrowing at the newcomers to the bar. She has displayed my paintings in her café since I was a teenager, but she's having it refurbished as it gets so packed during the tourist season and there won't be room for them. It gave me the perfect opportunity to free myself of them. 'I'm always relieved when it's all over,' she adds. Everyone in Talting calls her Mrs Morris. She's about seventy but we don't know her exact age, as she doesn't ever seem to have a birthday. She has one daughter who moved up north when she got married, but her granddaughter Amanda lives with her here.

'It'll be a busy few months,' I reply non-committally. Mrs Morris exemplifies a typical Talting view. We like to moan to one another about our town being invaded each season, even though we'd all sink otherwise. It's just one more eccentricity

I love about this place. I don't actually mind that we'll be seeing tourists now all through the summer and into September. Anything that occupies my mind is welcome.

'It'll be over before you know it,' Joe consoles her, with a wink at me. I know exactly how much his profits are boosted during the summer months. Joe is Emma's uncle, so I've known him all my life. He's past sixty now with a mop of unruly hair and a round belly that Emma constantly pokes fun at. I've worked for him for eight years and he likes to think of himself as my surrogate father. He has taken to popping by my cottage to 'fix things' – and check up on me. It's almost impossible for me to stay upset with him about the article; I just need to put it behind me and hope that he and Emma are right that it will mean a sell-out of my stall. And keep quiet about the main reason I can't be mad at him: I'm worried the journalist will be proved right – that these will be the last paintings I ever sell.

'Right, we better get to work then,' Emma says, linking her arm through mine as we go out to the back to put on our Joe's Bar aprons. Her heels clip-clop against the wooden floor, her chestnut, shoulder-length curls bouncing as she walks.

The bar is pretty small but we have a few booths at the back and a terrace with outside tables, although it's too cold tonight for them to be occupied by non-smokers. The décor is rich dark wood and creams, from when Emma and I spruced the place up when we started working here as eighteen-year-olds. Joe's only acknowledgement that the summer brings tourists, mostly young ones, is to play music in the bar. And usually it's the Beatles at a very low volume, but he thinks it makes the place seem hipper. He doesn't need to worry, though, as apart from the Inn, which is more expensive, and the fish restaurant on the beach, it's the only place serving alcohol in town, so we're pretty much guaranteed customers.

The place soon fills up and Emma and I circulate the room taking drinks and food orders whilst Joe mans the bar. I don't know how Emma wears heels all night; my feet are already aching, and I'm in ballet pumps. What I love about this place is how central it is to life in town. I always know everything that's going on. Of course, it can be negative when you're one of the news items, but apart from some extra warm smiles and sympathetic looks when I serve people, which I used to get a lot, the conversation is easy and light.

The group of tourists quickly start to cause annoyance, though. They are drinking quickly and heavily and getting louder and more obnoxious with each round.

I reluctantly go over to clear their table when they've finished eating.

'You live here then, darling?' one of them asks. He's about my age with short hair and is wearing a white shirt, open to show off his chest hair. He half lunges at me as he speaks but the drink has made him too uncoordinated to reach me.

Then his friend nudges him. 'I wouldn't bother, check out her rings,' he says, slurring his words. They all gawp at my left hand. I follow their gaze; my fingers tightening around the glass in my hand and making my knuckles turn white.

Then I shake my head. 'Because you'd have really been in with a chance otherwise.'

'Ha ha, mate, she's got you there,' another one of them cries out with loud laughter. They continue their tasteless banter as I empty the table and hurry away. Emma is beside me in an instant, taking one of the glasses from me even though I can carry six without breaking into a sweat.

'They tried it on with me earlier too,' she says, propelling me into the kitchen and sweeping the glasses from me, crouching down to put them in the dishwasher, whilst I lean against the counter and take a deep breath. 'Can you imagine what John would have said if he'd been here?'

Emma's husband John is the most good-natured person I know. I squeeze my eyes shut for a second then open them. 'Take her off my hands?'

Emma stands up and beams at me. 'Precisely. But are you okay?' Her eyes sweep over me as if checking for signs of hurt. She has always done this. We met at primary school when she sat next to me on the first day and stared at me for a full minute before telling me I had weird hair. She tugged on one of my bunches then laughed. 'I like it that you're not cool,' she said matter-of-factly, then pulled her hair into bunches too. We've been best friends ever since. I watch her take in my long, blond hair pulled into a topknot as usual when I'm at work, my blue eyes which have dark circles under them thanks to my restless nights, and my tall, lean figure which has got a hell of a lot leaner these past two years. She frowns slightly and I wonder how much of the girl she used to know has faded away.

'I'll be fine,' I promise, looking away and shifting my feet, uncomfortable with her assessment. I used to just stare back when she did this, confident that she'd find nothing wanting, but now I fear the study because I know how different I am.

Everything I've experienced since Lucas's passing has changed me.

'I'll serve them for the rest of the night,' she says with a wave of her hand which always means no arguments. 'Take five.' She breezes out through the double doors, a true force of nature. Logical and forthright in comparison to my head-in-the-clouds creativity. A perfect team, she always said, but lately our dynamic has become skewed as my creativity has become a burnt-out flame.

I follow her out five minutes later, annoyed that I let those jerks get to me. I sweep the bar for more empties and when I glance at their table I see that they're getting up, ready to leave. I breathe an inward sigh of relief. I'm proud of my comeback but I dread the questions of strangers. At least I don't have to explain anything to the people who live here, a perk of small-town life. It's the worst moment when you have to tell someone what happened. You look into their eyes and you just see one thing overwhelm them.

Pity.

It still hasn't got any easier to deal with seeing that.

The guys take their time in leaving. They are completely wasted and even pulling on their coats is a massive effort, but finally they make it to the door, calling out thanks and good-byes to the whole place, which are met with eye rolls and shaking of heads. I check their table as I usually do when a group leaves to make sure they have taken everything, and I look up as the door starts to close on them. That's when my eyes focus on something in one of their hands. A flash of silver and black. A glint of light.

I've only experienced this sensation twice in my life. A cocktail of sudden heat and ice-cold washing over me. Feeling like my heart has stopped beating. Time standing still. Horror sinking in with reality.

Car keys. Seeing them in his hands sends me straight back to that night.

Hearing a knock at the door and opening it to PC Thomas. I've known him all my life too. I remembered the talks he had given at my school showing us pictures of the damage drugs could do to you. I had never done anything to warrant his attention apart from serving him drinks in the bar on his nights off, so I was confused when he appeared at my door, but not unduly concerned. Until I saw the look on his face. And I knew then that something terrible had happened.

This time though I might actually be able to do something. I shake off the memory of the worst night of my life and take off at a run. My legs move automatically as I push through the door and try frantically to find out where they are. I hear someone call my name but all I can think about is stopping them. My heart in my throat, I spot them across the road opening the car doors, laughing and talking loudly, utterly oblivious to the danger they are about to put themselves, and others, into.

This is my fear coming true. Ever since the night PC Thomas told me what had happened, I have dreaded being confronted with this. I thought about leaving the bar. Emma and John thought I should. But I needed the money to supplement the income I made from painting, and jobs in Talting are hard to come by, plus I couldn't cope with any more change. When your world is ripped apart, you cling to familiarity. Right now, though, I feel like I made a huge mistake.

'Stop,' I yell, anger boiling up under my skin at their stupidity. I was safe with people in town; they would never even consider it after what happened. But this bunch of idiots haven't got a clue about what kind of damage they could do. They look over but just laugh. I move closer to them and hear footsteps behind me. Emma calls my name but I continue moving into the road.

'Did we forget something?' the one who tried to flirt with me before asks, looking confused.

I grab hold of the car door so he can't shut it. 'Yeah, how much you've drunk.'

He laughs. 'Oh, I'm fine, I always do this.'

'You selfish prick. You could kill yourself or your friends but you could also kill an innocent person,' I shout at him. In my head I'm screaming at someone else, I realise that, but I couldn't stop him and I can stop this.

'Let's just go,' one of them says.

'You are drunk, you can't drive,' I tell him, planting myself closer to the car. They can run me over for all I care.

'This is getting boring, get lost,' the driver says, starting to raise his voice back at me.

Then we're not alone. Emma and Joe arrive with a couple of other men.

One of them steps forward. 'She's right,' he says in a cool, deep voice. I glance at him and recognise him from the corner seat in the bar. He had been nursing a beer all night. I haven't seen him here before.

'She's crazy,' the guy says to him.

'Give me your keys.'

'No way.'

The guy grabs them from his hand. The man starts to protest but Joe steps in between them. 'Enough. There's no way I'm letting you drive after what I've seen you drink tonight. You can walk to the Inn from here.'

'Walk?'

'You have two legs, use them,' Emma says, putting her arm through mine.

'I'm staying there too, come on. You can pick up your car in the morning,' the guy from the bar says, pulling one of them by the sleeve of his coat. They look at one another, then their drunken good humour returns and they shrug and laugh and set off with him. He tucks the keys in his pocket and glances back, lifting his hand in a quick wave to the rest of us before turning the corner and disappearing from sight.

I slump against Emma. 'Jesus.'

Joe sighs. 'I knew they'd be trouble, bloody bankers. I'd ban them all if I could.'

'You girls okay?' the other guy asks, who I now see is Steve the postman.

'We're okay,' Emma says, pulling me closer. 'I think we should call it a night, though.' I see her exchange a look with her uncle.

'Definitely. Home now, both of you. And well done.' He briefly touches my arm before nodding to Steve. They both walk back inside the bar. I let out a shaky breath.

'You did good,' Emma says. 'I didn't even think . . . I'm glad you were here.'

I touch my wet cheeks. I didn't even know I was crying. 'I just can't believe they thought they were okay.' Just like I couldn't believe PC Thomas telling me about a man called Jeremy Green. A drunk driver who ripped my world in two. It only takes a second to make a bad choice but the consequences of his choice that night will be with me forever. 'I'm glad I was here,' I say, thinking about what she just said. That had been hard, but if I saved someone else . . .

'You want to stay over tonight?'

'I just want to sleep.' I let her walk me home as I sense there's no point in arguing with her about it. I stayed with Emma and John after it happened as I couldn't bear to be in our house without Lucas. To be honest I stayed with them too long. I'll never be able to repay their kindness to me. They never once even hinted that I should look for somewhere else and were both shocked when I said I was going to move out on my own a few months ago. But it was time. I needed to start to build some kind of life for myself alone. I needed a fresh start. A place I could find myself again.

I was also hoping it would become a place I could paint in again. But that hasn't happened yet.

'Ring me if you need me,' Emma says, giving me a hug outside my front door, lingering a little as if she wants to say something else but isn't sure what or how.

'I will,' I promise, just to get her to leave, and watch her walk away. I let myself in to my cottage, weariness enveloping me from head to toe. It was like I had a burst of adrenaline and now it's all seeped away, leaving me drained.

Walking upstairs in the dark, I ignore the closed door of the second bedroom. It's the room I set up to paint in. I thought having a room just for painting would awaken my muse, but the door has remained shut so far.

In my bedroom, I climb on to the bed in my clothes, too exhausted to get undressed. I curl up into a ball and press my face into the cool pillow. There are moments now when I don't think about it constantly, moments when I can smile and live in the present, when happiness feels within touching distance, then something happens to bring it all back so vividly, so painfully, it's like it happened yesterday.

17

Tonight has done that. I'm right back there.

When there was a knock on my door. When I was told that my husband Lucas had been in a car crash. When I discovered that a drunk driver had hit his car head on. When I learned that the man I thought I'd be with forever had been killed. He had died instantly.

Two years ago, when I lost the man I loved, my childhood sweetheart, my everything.

I lost myself and, without him, I have no idea how to get me back.

Chapter Two

I wake up at three A.M. to the sound of my heartbeat racing in the dark, silent cottage. I realise it's been a few weeks since I last awoke like this. After the accident, I could barely sleep at all. The bed felt so empty. When I moved in with Emma and John I hoped being somewhere else would help, but I would still roll over, reaching out to touch Lucas, clutching only the sheet in my fist. The ache of being alone felt so piercingly strong it was a struggle to breathe, let alone sleep.

I sit up, trying not to think about my dream. Lucas had been there, walking across the sand and heading out towards the sea, and I was behind him, running, trying to catch up, but I couldn't. I'd called his name but he didn't hear me and he was getting closer and closer to the water before I woke up. I don't think I ever used to have significant dreams, they were all just silly or mundane, easily forgotten, but dreams about Lucas stay with me for days.

I look at the clock, wondering if there will come a time when I don't regularly see three A.M. I won't miss it. I lie back down on my pillow and look up at the ceiling.

I wrap my fingers around my engagement and wedding rings, holding on to them, and to Lucas, for dear life, wondering if it will ever feel possible to move on from the love we had.

*

It's mid-morning when I finally emerge into the fresh air, catching the scent of the sea in the distance. I glance back at the small white cottage that I bought after leaving Emma and John's. I lived close to the beach in a town house with Lucas, as he loved having a sea view, but I had to sell it. The only way I could contemplate living without him was to find somewhere completely different to the home we had together. Somewhere that was just mine.

It's set back from a quiet road, and you can only just see it through a gap in the oak trees that surround it. I like how private it is. My garden is full of rose bushes and the cottage has a mock thatched roof, making me feel like I live in another time.

It's the kind of place I would have painted in the past. I think Lucas would say it suited an artist. He would be shocked, though, at how tidy it is. It was a standing joke between us that I was the messy one and he was the neat freak. I think it was because when faced with two prospects, painting or housework, painting always won. Now I have a lot of time to clean.

I pretty much always knew Lucas. For years he was just another annoying boy at school, but when we were fourteen we were sat next to one another in art. Lucas couldn't draw. Not even stick people. I looked over at his attempt at a tree one day and burst out laughing. He leaned over to look at my picture, ready to mock me right back, but instead he looked up at me with his big blue eyes and grinned. 'One day you're going to draw a building and I'm going to build it and we're going to grow old there.'

How does a fourteen-year-old girl respond to such a lofty claim? 'You want to build an old people's home?'

Then it was his turn to laugh. 'Not what I meant exactly.' I remember blushing at missing his point and we lapsed into embarrassed silence, but we started sitting at the same lunch table and Emma became his friend too, and Lucas's friends became mine.

It was at the park one night that we kissed for the first time. I'd like to say it was special, but we were tipsy on cheap cider an older boy had bought for us, surrounded by half the school, and there was far too much tongue involved, but he asked me to be his girlfriend and I said yes without really knowing what it meant to be someone's girlfriend. And I never found out because I was only ever *his* girlfriend. That's the worst part. I only know how to be with Lucas. We were a pair for so long, I never learned how to be on my own.

A group of seagulls fly overhead, bringing me back to the present. I'm walking towards Talting Inn, where I'm meeting Emma for a late breakfast before we head over to start setting everything up for the Fair. I pass the long line of multi-coloured beach huts which are flung open to sell food, drinks and all sorts of wares to visitors. I slow down to peep inside Mrs Morris's café at the painters carrying out the refurbishment. The walls are being painted cream and look bare without my paintings hung up there. It feels like the end of an era.

Mrs Morris spots me and comes out to the front door. She always wears a long skirt and blouse, her neat grey hair tucked behind her ears and a long beaded necklace hanging around her neck. 'Rose, dear, are you going to the Inn? I've heard there's an art collector staying there; he's come to town just for your sale.'

'Really?' I'm a bit stunned – my work has been popular with tourists wanting to take home a piece of Cornwall with them, but I've never been sought out before. 'Are you sure?'

'He told Mick he's here just for your work; he saw that horrible article in the paper by all accounts.' There's no point my asking how she knows all of this; nothing that happens here escapes her notice. She leans closer and drops her voice to a conspiratorial level. 'Apparently he's very well spoken and polite, good-looking too . . .' She ducks back inside then and I hear her shout at one of the painters.

I shake my head and carry on walking to the seafront. I can't really understand why an art collector would be here for my sale; probably he's just interested in art and happened to be coming here for a visit. Still, at least that newspaper article has drummed up some publicity.

I've always liked to draw and paint. My mum was talented and encouraged me, saying I would be better than she ever could be. She was a teacher and taught me every chance she got. We used to sit at our kitchen table painting to music. Sometimes Lucas would come round to watch us. He was always amazed at my ability to create things.

My mum told me I should go to art school in London but I didn't want to leave our home or Lucas, and then she got cancer. I was only sixteen when my mum died. I never knew my dad. He was just passing through town one summer.

It has never got easier, missing my mum, but I feel as if she's always with me. We shared so much and we were so close, just the two of us together.

It was money from selling my childhood home that let me

buy a house with Lucas, and then my own cottage. Sometimes I sit at my kitchen table and wonder whether, if my mum were still with me, she'd be there painting beside me, Lucas smiling at us lost in our world of art. But this new cottage will never know either of them.

I feel another bout of melancholy coming on and look out towards the sea. Talting's stretch of beach is golden sand rolling out to the deep blue water; in the distance is a curve of rugged coastline, a cliff where you can see for miles if you walk to the top. The waves are crashing against the shore today, the sea sparkling from the sun high above it and the beach is peppered with walkers, although soon it will be packed and everyone who lives here will try to avoid it. I have painted this scene a hundred times, sitting on the beach with my sketch pad, Lucas taking his surfboard in the sea, his wet-suit showing off the muscles and year-round tan he got from labouring on building sites, coming to join me for beers as the sun started to set against the horizon. When you grow up by the coast, it is your playground and then your sanctuary.

Lucas and I had travelled to some of the world's most famous beaches but it's this one that will always have my heart.

I pause briefly to take in the view and then trace the curve of the beach towards Talting Inn. I walk a hell of a lot more than I ever used to. I never learned to drive. Lucas drove if we wanted to go anywhere, and within Talting, everything is so close. The irony is, now he's gone, I could do with having a car, but his car took him away and I'd never want to learn to use the thing that snatched him from me. I have been in a car, and on a bus, in the past year but I'm nervous about it now. I never used to be.

Emma is waiting outside the Inn in a black maxi-dress with large red flowers on it, with her hair billowing out from the sea breeze. I wish I had worn sunglasses as a look of dismay crosses her face when she sees me, although she quickly pulls on a smile and hugs me. I must look like crap. She doesn't have time to ask about it, though, as someone clears their throat behind me. I turn around and my stomach drops as two of the guys from the bar last night walk up to me. They're both in sunglasses and look worse than me. I hope they have hangovers from hell. Beside me, Emma puts her hands on her hips.

The one who was going to drive last night clears his throat again. 'I just wanted to say I'm, um, sorry about last night. I drunk way too much and . . . uh . . . thank you for stopping me.' He glances at his friend, who gives an encouraging nod. 'We're leaving later today but I couldn't go without apologising.' He takes his sunglasses off and meets my eyes. 'I'm really sorry.'

'It wasn't your life she was worried about saving, it was other people you could have hurt,' Emma tells him sharply.

I wince a little at her words but she's right. 'I just hope you think in the future. I lost someone because there wasn't anyone to stop a drunken idiot from getting behind the wheel,' I say, my voice breaking at the end. I look away from them.

'We really are sorry,' the other guy says.

I hear them walk away and I let out a breath. Emma touches my arm and I nod to let her know I'm okay. Hopefully they won't do anything like that again. I look over my shoulder and watch them walk back to the Inn.

'Well, I'm glad they're going,' Emma says. 'Come on, they're not worth thinking about anymore.'

She takes my arm and steers me away. We step up on to the terrace and sit at the table Emma has already commandeered for us.

Emma is bossy, she always has been, but I don't know what I would have done without her by my side. Her family took me in after my mum died. She let me share her room for two years, becoming a second sister and part of her family. Once I was eighteen, I used the money my mum had left me to put a deposit on the townhouse for Lucas and me. I took the job at Joe's to pay for art classes at college, and Emma joined me. She said she didn't want to go away to university without me. She hadn't done that well at school but she could have gone somewhere. She met John on holiday in Devon a couple of years later and he followed her back here, so, like me, she's never lived anywhere but this town.

Despite living in the same place all my life, I've had a fair few homes, and I sincerely hope that nothing else happens to make me have to leave another one.

Mick, the owner of the Inn, bustles outside with a pot of tea and two glasses of orange juice on a silver tray for us. Mick is Joe's age, with thick grey hair, and is wearing his usual smart grey suit. He runs the Inn with his wife Joan and has done for as long as I've been alive. He gives us both a big smile. 'Well, well, I finally have you here for breakfast,' he says, only slightly joking. He knows we've always gone to Mrs Morris's café if we're having breakfast out, and there's more than a bit of rivalry between them over who does the best full English. Most of us stay wisely quiet when asked for our opinion. 'That refurbishment of hers is really boosting our trade. Now, Rose, I'm glad you're here, have you heard about my new guest?' Mick says, casting a quick check over his shoulder to make sure no one's there.

I see Emma raise her eyebrows at me. 'Mrs Morris just said something . . .'

Mick rolls his eyes. 'Of course she did. Well, he checked in yesterday and apparently he's come to Talting just to buy art from the sale at the Fair. I said, "Do you mean our Rose Walker's work?" and he said he did. What do you think of that then?'

Emma claps her hands. 'I think it's bloody brilliant. He's come here just for your work.'

'He can't have seen it before, though.'

Emma sighs. 'When will you get some self-belief, for goodness' sake? He must have seen that article – there were two pictures of your paintings in it – plus if he's an art collector I'm sure he's heard about you before. I think you should put your prices up for the sale.'

Mick nods. 'You should listen to Emma. Right, I'll be back with your food,' he says, not even bothering to check what we want, and disappears back inside.

I think about it, wondering if I could make more than I'd expected. 'I guess I could use the money; I think the cottage needs a new boiler.'

'Or you could do something fun with it. How about a holiday?'

Emma has been trying to get me to go away for ages. She thinks I need a change of scenery but I just want to stay where I'm close to Lucas.

'There's nowhere I want to go.' It's not like I've never left Talting. The six months that Lucas and I spent travelling before we got engaged was really fun and we saw a lot of the world, but we both felt like there wasn't another place that could be our home. We were content here. No, happy. We were happy here. I need to believe I can be happy here again. I just wish the thought of being happy without him didn't fill me with both fear and guilt.

'Can we talk about something else now?' I ask hopefully, picking up my orange juice and taking a long sip.

'Fine. Actually I do have some news – John might be getting promoted,' she replies.

'Oh, that's great, Em.' John is an accountant in Truro. He's been with Emma for six years now although he still finds it funny that he's referred to as a newcomer here. It took him a while to be accepted by the town after he followed Emma back here after their holiday romance, which still amuses him. He became Lucas's best friend and the four of us were always together.

Lucas's death affected us all. Emma and John went away for the weekend three months after the funeral and came back married. They had seen first-hand how fragile life can be and they didn't want to wait. It is hard sometimes seeing their happily married life knowing that I lost my own, but I always feel guilty for thinking like that. Because they so deserve it. And I know how happy Lucas would have been for them too.

'Yeah, we were thinking that if he does get it, then, well, it might be time to . . .' She trails off as Mick emerges from the Inn carrying two plates for us. I understand Emma shutting up – you have to be so careful in Talting of saying anything private in public. I know Emma so well, though, I can guess what she was going to say. It has been in their plans for a while to try for a baby, and a promotion means money for a family. It's something Emma's always wanted.

I'm actually relieved that Mick has arrived. It gives me time to think about what to say. I have to support her. It's just that I always thought it would be Lucas and me who would have a family first. I hate the selfishness of that thought.

'Here we are,' Mick says, putting our plates down with a flourish. I look down at the huge pile of bacon and eggs in front of me. I have almost double Emma's portion. What is it with this town and keeping an eye on my eating habits?

Mick suddenly leans down, pretending to check my teapot. 'It's him,' he hisses in a stage whisper. He turns around to smile at the man stepping out from the Inn on to the terrace.

Emma nudges me with her leg under the table. It's obvious what she's thinking. He's tall, definitely over six feet, wearing chinos and a black polo shirt. He runs a hand through his dark hair and I can't help but watch the movement before quickly looking away, instantly feeling guilty at agreeing with Emma that he's good-looking. It feels disloyal to Lucas.

'Rose, can I introduce you to the guest I was telling you about? This is Robert,' Mick says, waving Robert over to our table. 'Robert, this is our renowned local artist – Rose Walker.'

I meet the stranger's eyes and I feel a jolt of recognition. The man who helped me to stop the drunks from driving last night is the man who's apparently here to buy my paintings.

Chapter Three

'It's a pleasure to meet you properly, Rose. I didn't get a chance to introduce myself last night; everything happened rather quickly,' he says in a deep, cultured voice, his lips curving into a gentle smile. I frown, wondering how he'd known who I was last night, and then remember the photograph of me taking up far too much space in our local newspaper. I don't think I'm ever going to be able to put that article behind me. Robert holds out his hand and I shake it, relinquishing it quickly but not before some of the warmth from his skin transfers to mine. I introduce him to Emma. 'Thank you for your help last night,' I say.

'We've had two of them apologising just now,' Emma says with a scornful look.

'Good, you deserved an apology.' Something flashes in his eyes and I instantly sense that their apology was on his suggestion. 'Well, I'm glad I'm getting the chance to meet you before the Fair. I'm sure you're going to be very busy there,' he says, smoothly changing the subject.

'I told you the article would be good publicity,' Emma says to me. 'So, do you collect art?' she asks Robert, giving him a rather blatant look up and down.

'Not officially, no. I've just bought a flat, so I've been on the lookout for some pieces to hang there. I saw the ones in the article and thought you had really captured this place; your work is beautiful. I knew it was what I've been looking for. You're very talented, Rose.'

'Thank you,' I stutter, embarrassed by his praise. I always suspected the people who bought my pictures did so because they thought they were pretty and wanted to take souvenirs of Cornwall back home with them, not because they knew anything about art.

'How long will you be staying in town for?' Emma asks, picking up her knife and fork.

'I'm not sure yet, a few weeks, I think,' he replies, keeping his eyes on me. 'It depends how long my father will let me have off work.'

'What do you do?' I ask him.

'I'm a lawyer, back in Plymouth.'

'How did you see the article about the Fair if you live in Devon?' Emma asks him.

'I keep track of local news for my clients. It's useful to know what's going on,' he replies.

'You don't expect a lawyer to be interested in art,' I say, speaking my thought before I can stop myself.

He smiles and doesn't appear to be offended by my comment. 'I suppose not. It was my mother who taught me; she did art history at university and took me to far too many galleries when I was growing up.' I suppose you could say I inherited my appreciation of art from her. He glances at our food. 'But enough about me. I should let you two finish your breakfast. It was lovely to meet you.'

'You too,' I reply, returning his smile. Mick goes back inside with him and Emma breaks out into a grin.

'Sorry, but that's the fittest art freak I've ever seen.'

'You've met so many art collectors, of course,' I say with a roll of my eyes.

'Okay, fine, but you're going to make a killing out of this guy this summer. You are going to put your prices up, right? He looks rich,' she says, her mouth full of bacon.

'He looks rich?'

She nods. 'Sure, his job, his clothes, his voice . . . trust me, you know I can spot one.'

I laugh. 'You should add that to your CV.'

'I think I will.'

I shake my head and have some of my eggs before asking Emma if John will be in the bar tonight. 'I feel like I've hardly seen him lately.'

'Yeah, he's persuaded some guys from work to come. They seem to want to sort stuff out after work over drinks lately and it's always in Truro, but if they give him more money at the end of it all it will be worth it.'

'It's so weird you have such a career man,' I tell her.

'Hey, he's with me for my mind,' she protests, at which we both snort. Neither of us ever really had any grand career plans. I was happy painting and Emma wanted to raise a family. Lucas preferred more practical pursuits. And yet John fitted in with our group as soon as Emma brought him here.

'Remember when we went for breakfast at Mrs Morris's the first time you two met John,' she says, 'and he dropped his plate and all the food went on to the floor because he was so nervous?'

I smile at the memory. 'Well, you told him you couldn't be together if we didn't approve; he was scared stiff.'

'I told him Lucas knew karate. He soon worked out what a softie Lucas was, though.'

I nod, thinking about how Lucas would make me take spiders out because he was so scared of them. Once I chased him around the room with one in my hand. He always pretended that had never happened.

'I told him we should buy a guard dog as he would probably welcome the burglars in.'

Emma shakes her head. 'He actually probably would have. I don't think he would have liked your cottage; he would have said it's creepy, too.'

'It's peaceful, not creepy. And you just pretend to hate it because I moved out.'

'Sometimes I wish you were still with us. I hate you not being in town.'

'I am in town.'

'Barely.'

'I couldn't live with you forever,' I tell her quietly.

She looks at me sadly for a moment then grins. 'I know, poor John was starting to realise that I love you more than him.'

I smile back and eat another mouthful of scrambled eggs. I don't think she'll ever realise how much she cheers me up some days. I look out to the beach as a wave rolls in and wonder what Lucas would make of the flashy newcomer wanting to throw his money at my work if he was here having breakfast with us. I hear his voice in my head whisper, 'Milk him for everything, babe, I think I'd suit being a kept man.'

After we've finished eating, Emma drives me back to my cottage to pick up some of the supplies for the Fair. Everything save the paintings, which will have to wait for the actual day to be taken over and are currently stacked up in my supposed painting room waiting for me to pull them out. I've been putting that task off for days now. I know it will be painful to look at them again and remember where I was when I painted them, so many with Lucas by my side.

As we drive towards the green where the Fair is held each year, he surfaces anyway. It's strange how some days I search for memories – I actively think of him and try to remember things he said or the way he held me – whereas other days I try desperately to shut them out, certain that if I think about him I'll break.

As the vast expanse of green comes into view, I think about how the Fair has always played such a role in our lives. I can't help but smile at the memory of when we were fifteen, sneaking off hand in hand whilst everyone we knew was there, so we could both lose our virginity.

It was naturally awkward but I wasn't nervous because I was with Lucas. He had this way of making me feel safe but fearless at the same time.

The green is full of activity as Emma drives over the bumpy, muddy grass towards the centre. I take a deep breath to try to feel that way again – safe but fearless. I imagine Lucas giving my hand a reassuring squeeze. I can do this for him. I can do this because of him. He loved taking part in this Fair, and I owe it to him to continue our tradition of being here.

Emma pulls up outside the tent marked for me and we start unloading the supplies from the boot.

'Need some help?' Joe strides over with a couple of boys from town and they help us to lift out the easels and large corkboard which will be displaying my paintings, and three chairs for Emma, John and me if we need them. Emma has also made a large sign with my name on to hang at the front of the tent, and I need to make some cards with prices on later, once I decide what to sell them for. Maybe I should listen to Emma and mark them up slightly. If these are the last paintings I might ever sell, I need to make as much as possible.

I want to believe that I can paint again, though. I need to believe it. I feel like I've lost so much of my identity since losing Lucas, I can't give up this as well. I just need to find a way out of my block.

'How the hell do you put this up?' Emma demands, bringing my attention back, and I chuckle at her struggle with one of the easels.

'That one is always tricky,' I say, remembering cursing it myself when I first got it, Lucas coming into the room to find me on the floor with it collapsed on top of me. He laughed about it for months. The curse of someone not practical being married to someone annoyingly so. 'I know a trick,' I tell her, taking it and managing to put it up. I had to learn to do a lot of things by myself – changing a light bulb for the first time, for instance, involved fusing all the upstairs lights one night in the cottage.

'Where do you want this?'

I look behind me as Robert follows Mick across the grass carrying a large sign. I wonder what he'll think of my paintings at the Fair; I hope he likes them. I think back to my teacher at college saying my work was 'technically good' but she always seemed disappointed in what I produced, as if it was lacking something.

'Mick is roping his guests in again to help, I see,' Joe says, following my gaze.

Emma comes over to watch Robert too. 'I could watch him lift that all day.'

I shake my head. 'You're crazy.'

'So are those muscles,' she says, nudging me in the back. I can't help but glance at his arms beneath his shirt and silently agree with her.

'I think we're all done,' Joe says, taking our attention away from Robert. I look at the easels and board all set up, ready for the paintings, and feel the beginnings of excitement. I've never seen all my work together like this, never sold it myself like this, and there are butterflies starting to flutter in my stomach. I am saying goodbye to the past with this sale, goodbye to my old work, and hopefully setting up a blank canvas for something new in the future. The sun starts to peep out from behind the clouds, lifting the green with its light, and promising a better day for the Fair.

It feels like a sign of possibility and I'm determined to embrace it.

'It's going to be great,' Emma says next to me.

I hope she's right. We head back towards her car and I steel myself to perform the final task for the stall – collecting the paintings. Which means going into the room I've avoided since moving into my cottage.

Chapter Four

When I lived with Lucas in our town house close to the beach, I used the top floor for my painting. It had three large skylights that I would open all the way even in the winter to let in the sea air and the light, and sometimes I'd be up there for hours on end, unaware of time slipping by. On dry days I'd paint outside in front of the landscapes I wanted to capture on canvas, or in our small garden at weekends with Lucas, sipping beers and barbecuing burgers at sunset, but the rest of the time that room was my sanctuary and I loved being in there.

When I looked around my new cottage, I instantly liked the smaller second bedroom, which faced north overlooking the pretty garden, and I imagined the wonderful light that would stream in on summer mornings. It took me back to that third floor of my old house and I had a hope-filled moment that I could rediscover some of my old fervour. I filled the room with my paintings, easels, paints and brushes, ready for me to be inspired once again.

It's still waiting for me.

I look at the staircase and take a deep breath to steady my nerves. I move slowly up, gripping the wooden rail until I reach the landing and stand outside the closed door. I hover outside, chewing on a fingernail.

It's so stupid to be scared of this room. But it holds so much of myself inside it. The woman who had dreams and passions and love, who wasn't scared about the future, and who wasn't alone.

I cling on to that girl as I push open the door and look at the paintings propped up around me. I am instantly drawn to two of Talting church. It sits on a slight hill overlooking the town – a small, grey stone building surrounded by lush grass. Bluebells line the path to the large oak door in the spring, which is when I painted these. I sink to the floor on my knees in front of them. I have avoided the church since Lucas died. It's where we got married. And it was also the place his funeral was held.

There is no other building that holds both the happiest and worst days of my life.

I feel tears start to prick behind my eyes as I remember our wedding there. It was the wedding I always knew we'd have – the whole town showed up to see us get married. The white lace dress hadn't felt as uncomfortable as I had imagined it would, and when Lucas's eyes lit up I knew it had been the perfect choice. Lucas's dad Graham walked me down the aisle. He's always felt more like my father than my father-in-law. He and Lucas's mum Gloria were so proud watching their son get married. Since I had no parents of my own, they embraced me as part of their family and were so happy for us.

We both agreed it had been a perfect day.

But his funeral is an event I never want to think about. He had his whole life ahead of him. We had planned to spend that life together. Then it was ripped away from us. We were supposed to have forever but we'd only been married for two years when he died.

A sob catches in the back of my throat and the tears flow

freely as I prop my knees up to my chest so I can lean on them and let out all my grief. Seeing the painting of the church makes it all raw again. I've tried so hard to not think of him like that – inside the polished wood coffin next to the altar we were married in front of. But his funeral will be forever burnt on to my soul. I didn't think I could bear to go but his parents begged me to, and I couldn't let them down. They had lost their only child. I owed it to them to be there. They wanted me to speak too but I just couldn't do it. I felt like I had disappointed them, although they were so kind about it, saying they understood. I couldn't face talking about Lucas in the past tense. I couldn't face saying goodbye.

Gloria asked for one of my paintings of him. She had it propped up at the altar. It's still in their house but I couldn't keep any of the other ones I painted of him. It was just too hard to have them around me. I sold them just a few weeks after his death. There weren't many, considering all the years I had to paint him. Lucas would never stay still long enough for me to capture him; he was always doing something, always talking. The only time I could paint him was to watch him do something when he didn't know I was watching. He would always act so surprised when I showed him a picture of himself, as though he couldn't believe I could find him an interesting subject to study.

And now all the rest will be gone too. All purged. A life in paintings surrounds me and I marvel at the power images have. The power to make you feel things. It's why I grew up loving art, why I wanted to create it myself, and why now I'm terrified of it.

I haven't been back to the church since. On the first anniversary of his death, Gloria and Graham asked me to come to his grave with them but I couldn't get out of the car. I hated not being able to be as strong as they were that day – laying flowers and saying a prayer for their son, whilst I was a wreck. I will never forget how brave they were.

I wipe my eyes and stand up, brushing away dust from the floor that I've neglected to clean. Emma will be picking me up soon for our shift at Joe's, so I tear myself away from the paintings and the memories they wrench from me. I check the time and wonder what to do with myself. That's one thing I discovered after losing Lucas. Grief makes you both restless and listless. It's as if I forgot what I used to do to fill my time. It stretches out endlessly sometimes, making hours feel more like days, whereas before my life moved at a rapid pace.

I move downstairs and curl up on the sofa and look up at my mantelpiece. All the photos from the town house I shared with Lucas are still packed in boxes hidden in the cupboard under the stairs. I haven't been able to put them up here.

I think back to when I first lost Lucas. Emma suggested I should go to see a therapist after staying on their sofa in my pyjamas for what felt like months. I snapped at her, not seeing how far away from myself I was. I went into the bathroom and looked into the mirror and didn't recognise myself. I thought about Lucas being able to look down on us all and I knew how devastated he'd be to see me like that. I ran a bath straight away. It was a small thing but having a bath and putting on clothes did make me feel a bit better. And that's what it's been like really – a slow climb back to feeling human again after almost self-destructing.

I thought maybe I'd be able to handle grief better the second time around, having lost my mum after her year-long fight to stay with me. I even started seeing a therapist then on the school's insistence, but I only went a couple of times. They didn't know my mum. I felt better being around people who knew her, who missed her like I did. And I'd known it was coming. I had prepared as best I could. Everything had been arranged.

But Lucas's death was so sudden by comparison. There had been nothing to prepare me for it.

Somehow with my mum, it was about the past. I mourned for all the moments we'd had together, everything she had taught me, the times she had comforted me when I was sad or ill, the advice she'd given me about Lucas. With Lucas, I mourned for the future. The seemingly empty black hole stretching ahead of me after all of our plans went up in smoke.

It was the second anniversary just a couple of months ago. I still didn't want to go to his grave, so Emma, John and I went to his favourite surfing spot. We took blankets and a picnic and drank his favourite beer, toasting him on a chilly but sunny February afternoon. It was so sad that he wasn't with us but we managed to smile, talking about the times we'd had as a foursome and silly things that had happened. It was good to remember the happy times and talk about him with them. I realised that however hard it is to think about him, it's better than not thinking about him. That was a step in the right direction. I went back to work at the bar, moved into the cottage and was planning the Easter Fair sale, and for the first time in a long while, my mind was occupied with more than just the loss of him, although my heart was still full of it.

Is still full of it.

The grandfather clock in the corner announces a new hour. Gloria and Graham gave it to me as a moving-in present, although they haven't been to see the cottage yet. I think it's still too hard for them to see me living somewhere without Lucas. It's been in Gloria's family for generations and it makes me feel as if I've stepped back in time when it jingles loudly in the silence. Time is a strange thing.

The doorbell chimes soon after the clock. Emma puts her hands on her hips when I open the front door to her. 'It's still weird to have you answer the door,' she says, stepping into the hall. She smiles when she sees the paintings. 'I've always loved this one,' she says, pointing to one of the beach.

'What do you mean, it's weird?' I ask, pulling on my jacket and picking up my bag. It's so annoying when she drops in a comment like that then moves on like you weren't supposed to have heard her say it.

'You never used to let me in. You'd usually be painting with that hideous country music you like so much at ear-splitting volume. I stood outside for half an hour once. I had to call Lucas in the end,' she says, looking guilty for having mentioned it.

'There's nothing wrong with country music,' I say, opening the door and leading us out. I used to love getting lost in the music as I painted. I realise I miss it. It feels strange to miss something other than Lucas. But it's another example of other things I lost along with him.

I lock the cottage behind us and follow Emma to her car. It's still light outside, the days getting longer as we creep towards summer, and the promise of a new season surrounds us as we drive to work and I smile, because I've always loved summer in Talting.

That's one thing that hasn't changed.

And somehow that makes me feel more hopeful than I have in a long time.

Chapter Five

'Look who's back,' Emma says under her breath as we walk into Joe's. I glance behind the counter where Adam is serving drinks. Adam is at university in London but stays here most holidays to work for Joe.

Adam looks over as we walk in and a big smile takes over his face, which, when added to his mop of light brown curls, makes him look like an adorable puppy. 'How are you, Rose?' He gives me a look full of scrutiny and I shift uneasily.

Emma rolls her eyes. 'Hi, Emma. Hi, Adam,' she mutters as she walks into the kitchen. She thinks he has a crush on me. I can't believe he does; I'm five years older than him, after all, but he does have an annoying habit of always being around me.

'I'm fine. How's university going?'

He grins. 'I'm loving it.'

I smile politely and turn as Joe pokes his head out of his small office and says he needs to see me. I go over and he shuts the door behind us. There's just room for a desk and chair in here, so I stand by the door, waiting for Joe to speak.

'Are you sure you're okay to work tonight? I'm fine if you want to take the night off.'

I shake my head. I didn't work for almost six months after Lucas died. I can't take a step back by shying away from it tonight. 'In a way I'm glad I was here to . . . stop them. I didn't know if I wanted to work in a bar again, you know that, but I helped stop something that could have been . . . well, we know what can happen, and that felt, not good, but like a piece of justice for Lucas. Does that make sense?'

'It does. I've put up a poster in the bar about drink driving, to raise awareness and remind people there are other ways to get home. I don't want you to have to deal with it again. And you're sure? Because you promised to let me know if things were too difficult for you to work when you came back, remember?'

I sigh, a little frustrated that he doesn't trust me with this. 'Will you let me decide for myself, Joe? I don't understand why people think I can't make decisions anymore.' I instantly regret snapping at him when his face falls. I suck in a calming breath. 'I don't want to sit at home alone, I want to be here.'

'I'm just trying to look out for you. We all are. Lucas would have wanted us to, right? He would have killed me if I stood back and did nothing,' he says, trying to lighten the mood.

'He wouldn't have hurt a fly,' I say.

'I don't know, he could be pretty fierce when it came to you. Remember those drunks trying it on one summer and Lucas throwing them out?'

'I forgot about that,' I say, thinking back to how he reacted when one of them climbed over the counter to the bar where I was and tried to feel me up.

Joe gets up and slings an arm around me. 'Come on then. Emma will not be happy if we leave her out there alone at our busiest time.'

I lead Joe out into the bar where Emma waves at me from

the CD player, a grin on her face. Taking advantage of Joe being out of the way, she has replaced the Beatles with Taylor Swift, the only artist in my collection that she ever tolerated listening to with me.

I haven't listened to this album in two years. It was my favourite and I used to play it all the time, making Lucas listen to it too, rolling down the windows of his car and singing along loudly, much to his amusement, as I really can't sing at all. I'm probably one of the few people who prefer her country sound to her newer songs.

'Rose,' she cries, grabbing my hands and pulling me from my spot. I have to laugh as she waves our hands in time with the music. This song is just impossible not to dance to and I feel my hips moving almost by themselves. God, I have missed this.

'What is this?' Joe demands from behind us.

'This is real music,' I tell him, laughing as Emma spins us around. My eyes meet Robert's across the bar. He's just walked in and is smiling at us.

Emma finally drops my hands. 'When I hear this song, I always think of you,' she says to me, out of breath from our attempt at dancing. Joe turns it down a bit and she pokes her tongue out at him.

'I'm happy to be known as the town's country fan,' I tell her.

'What got you into that music?' Robert asks, looking amusedly at us both, as I lean against the counter to get my breath back. Joe slides him a beer across the bar.

'Well, my mum loved the old stuff like Patsy Cline. She'd play it endlessly. And then I started to bring home newer artists and we were both hooked by it. I love the stories. It's

44

amazing how they tell a story in like three minutes. It's always been my painting music. I'd like people to look at something I've painted and see a story in it.' I flex my fingers. They haven't held a brush for so long.

'It's amazing the power that music can have,' Robert replies. He looks at me as if his whole focus is on me in this moment and I feel myself staring back at him, giving him the same courtesy. The bar around us slips into white noise.

'So, what kind of music do you like?'

'My favourite band is Coldplay but I like anything really. Except jazz.'

'Why not jazz?'

He swirls the beer around in his glass and then reaches up to run a hand through his hair. 'It's my dad's favourite. Have you been to many concerts?'

I don't miss the sudden attempt to change the conversation. I wonder what the story is with his dad.

'Not many. A few years ago, Lucas took me to see Taylor Swift for my birthday. I think he screamed louder than me.'

That night was so much fun. I listen to the song playing behind me and remember being awed by her singing it with just her guitar a few feet away from us, Lucas's arm around me, his deep voice singing along in my ear. It was a small concert at the start of her career and it felt like a special moment for all of us.

I leave Robert to serve drinks, letting the music heal a piece of my soul I didn't realise I had let slip away. I feel an itch to go home and listen to more of my favourite songs, something I haven't done in a long time. I'm grateful to Emma for playing this tonight.

I don't want to lose anything I love because I lost him.

★

The hours pass quickly as the bar gets busier and busier. Robert perches on one of the bar stools chatting to some regulars, and halfway through the night John comes in with three guys he works with and sits down at the booth Emma kept empty for him. John is completely different to the guy I thought Emma would end up with, which I think is exactly why they work. He and Lucas were great friends almost from the start, each of them easy-going and laid-back. They used to say they had both picked alpha women. John comes to the bar to get the drinks and kisses me on the cheek. 'Beers all round, Rose.'

'Sure. This is Robert,' I say as he's standing next to Robert's stool. 'He's in town for the Fair.'

'For Rose's paintings,' Robert corrects with a smile. He and John shake hands.

'You have good taste then,' John says, giving me a smile. 'You're staying at the Inn?'

'That's right. I think I'll be staying for the summer.'

'I wish I could get the summer off from work,' John says wistfully, handing me money for the drinks.

'Well, I work for my father and he's never given me any time off, so he couldn't really refuse me,' Robert says. His eyes move to the beer in his hand and I notice his knuckles turn white.

'What do you do?'

'I'm a lawyer,' he says, taking a swift gulp of his drink. He looks across at me like he can feel me watching and gives me a small smile that doesn't reach his eyes. I catch a glimpse of sadness in them. Maybe I'm more attuned to it these days.

'I think I was born to do it; I don't have a creative bone in my body,' he adds ruefully.

'I bet you carried a briefcase to school, didn't you?' I say, trying to cheer him up.

'Actually I did,' he says, letting out a small laugh. 'It was a requirement at our school.'

'Not St James's?' Emma asks, coming over.

'Yes, you know it?'

Emma shakes her head. 'We hated you at our school. You beat us once for the district football cup and we never got over it. What did we call the kids that went there?'

'I don't remember,' I lie, wishing she would shut up, but when I look at Robert he's smiling at her.

'Oh, yeah, James the lames,' she says, laughing. I can't help but join in, remembering the chant we used to sing about them.

Robert raises his eyebrows. 'I didn't think I'd be mocked at this age. I thought school was over?'

'In a small town, school is never over,' Emma replies. 'Oh God, you were Head Boy, weren't you?'

I see his neck turn a little red. 'Um, I don't remember.' He winks at me, though, so I know she's right.

'Anyway, I remember you crying because you didn't get to be a prefect,' I say to Emma, nudging her hip with mine.

'Nope, no recollection of that,' she replies breezily, walking off with a toss of her hair.

'She bosses me around like she's a prefect,' John says, picking up his drinks.

'What will you give me not to tell her you said that?'

He pokes his tongue out at me but retreats quickly in case I do tell her. Robert shakes his head. 'I'm quite glad I'm not

47

still friends with my schoolmates; I'd rather forget what I was like then.'

'Actually, I like having friends I've known forever, they know me and I know them – we can just be ourselves,' I tell him, hating the tightening in my chest that follows my words. I turn away a little, wishing our group hadn't had to diminish.

'That sounds nice,' Robert replies quietly.

Adam comes over then. 'When can I see your new work, Rose? I'd love to come round and take a look,' he says, like he's always popped round to see my paintings. He never has. Is it my imagination, or is he standing up straighter than usual, as if he wants to look taller? I see him glance across at Robert to make sure he heard him.

'There's nothing to see,' I say shortly, moving to the side to see if anyone needs another drink.

'Why not?' Adam asks, not catching that was an 'I don't want to talk about it' answer.

I sense both their eyes on me. I start to feel hot. 'I don't have anything ready to show people.' I look around hopefully for Emma to step in and save me from this, but she's on the other side of the room with John.

'That never bothered you before, you've shown me things half finished,' Adam says, although I can't actually remember doing any such thing. Maybe that's because I've tried to forget all about my art. I grip the counter, feeling a little unsteady. 'She shouldn't be precious about it, should she?' he says, bringing Robert into the conversation.

Robert watches me for a moment. 'I think when you're as talented as Rose is, you should share your work with as many people as possible.'

'Well, maybe my talent is all used up,' I snap back at him.

'You don't know anything about my art.'

'I know it's beautiful,' he replies, maddeningly calm.

'You don't know anything,' I tell him. The room feels too hot. 'I need some air,' I tell them, pushing past Adam and hurrying out of the door, drinking in the breeze lifting off the sea.

It's dark now and the stars are out above me. I hug my arms across my chest as I look up at them, trying to slow my heartbeat down. I know it's not their fault. I hear someone behind me and I sigh, knowing I was rude back there but not knowing how to shake off the anger I feel. Anger at them. Anger at myself. Angry at whatever force took Lucas from me and changed everything. Angry at him for leaving me. I never had a hot temper before, but now it feels as though anger is constantly bubbling up under my skin, ready to erupt at the slightest nudge.

'So that newspaper article was right about you struggling to paint again?' Robert asks in a gentle voice behind me. 'It seems like a real shame.'

'And what do you know about it? You just arrived here, you don't know anything about me and you haven't got a creative bone in your body, as you put it,' I say, not turning around as I feel like I might burst into tears.

'I envy your talent. I think you could do so much more with it. I'd hate to see it all go to waste. You're right, I've only just got here, but that doesn't mean I'm not right about this.'

I pull my arms tighter around myself. 'It's not as simple as that. I just can't paint,' I choke out, my voice mingling with the wind.

I feel him step closer to me. 'Why not?'

'I just can't.'

49

'Have you tried?'

'Yes.' I think about it. 'No.'

'Why not?'

I brush a tear from my cheek. Why not? My heart won't stop thumping inside my chest. 'I'm scared,' I whisper. The thought of letting out what I'm feeling in my heart on paper is too terrifying to contemplate. I'm scared of what would come out. I'm scared that once I started I wouldn't be able to stop. I'm scared of what I would paint without him. I don't want to paint without him.

I'm scared I can't do any of this without him.

'I became a lawyer because my father is a lawyer,' Robert tells me. 'He always expected me to join the family firm. He even set up a local office for me to run for him. I was too scared to even consider doing something else. I sat in the office one Monday morning and wondered how I got there. That's why I came here. To find out.'

I turn around then. 'You didn't ask me why I'm scared.'

'Everyone is scared of something,' he says. 'You just have to find what fear you can overcome. If you want to paint again, then you can.'

'You make it sound so simple.'

'No, it's not simple. Nothing is simple, Rose. God, I know that. I . . .' He breaks off and shakes his head. 'I just see that you have a gift and I don't want you to let it go. I can see you don't either. You wouldn't get so angry, so upset, if you did.' He walks back into the bar, a burst of noise and light coming out as he swings the door open and extinguishing just as suddenly after he closes it behind him. I stay outside for ten minutes, thinking about what he said over and over until my head feels like it might combust.

The Second Love of My Life

When I go home later, I walk past my painting room and pause. Before I can talk myself out of it, I open the door and leave it halfway open as I hurry past it to my bedroom. I feel better when I lie down in bed. I think about what Robert said. What scares me most? Painting or not painting? I don't have the answer yet, but leaving the door open will remind me that I need to find that answer soon.

Chapter Six

Saturday, the day of the Fair, dawns light and bright. I'm awake early, the sun just beginning to rise as I sip black coffee at my kitchen table and try to keep my nerves at bay. I decide I need to go for a walk to clear my head before Emma and John arrive to help me take my paintings to the field. I slip on jeans and a hoodie and head for the beach.

I can't avoid seeing the row of town houses on my route where Emma and John live, and beyond them the one I used to share with Lucas is just visible as I step on to the beach. A young family live in our house now. I do miss living by the beach on mornings like this, as there's rarely anyone here apart from joggers or dog walkers and you can be alone with your thoughts. But I had to make a home without him. And I still have all this on my doorstep.

I think you can live beside the sea and never get bored because it's constantly changing and always reminding you that you are just a tiny cog in the wheel of the world.

Nature always used to inspire my art. I loved to try to replicate it on canvas, to try to capture the feel of the sun on your face as you walk across the sand and look out to where the sea meets the sky. I trace the path I have walked so many times in my life.

I remember the days I spent here as a kid running into the

sea with my mum chasing me and laughing, and then as a teenager with Lucas picking me up and threatening to drop me into the water, and getting distracted when I kissed him. A place with so many traces of the people I love it's amazing that the ghosts of them don't appear right in front of me. But they don't need to – they are cemented on my heart.

Today is going to be so hard without them. Losing my mum was heartbreaking but it felt like I still had a family because I had Lucas, and now I'm facing a future alone. This feels like the first step in accepting that. The first time I'll be going to the Fair without one of them, and I hope I have the strength to make it through the day.

I sit down cross-legged on the sand for a few minutes watching the sun rise up into the clear blue sky, tilting my face towards it. I think I come here more now than ever. I used to walk past it coming to and from our town house but now I live further away, I take time to drink it in, to appreciate it more. That's the flip side to grieving, the way you want to cling on to the good things in life in case they leave you too. I bury my hand in the cool sand, letting it run through my fingers, reminding me it's still here.

I'm still here.

'It's a beautiful morning,' a voice breaks into my musings. I look up to see Robert walking across the sand towards me.

Seeing him transports me back to the last time I saw him – outside the bar last night – and I inwardly cringe at my outburst. 'You're up early.'

'I was just having a walk before breakfast. Mick tries to make me have five courses.'

'This town loves to feed,' I say, wishing I were as calm as he seems today. I notice he's wearing something more casual this morning – a polo shirt and jeans – and his hair looks less gelled. He is holding his shoes, bare feet in the sand, and the relaxed look suits him better somehow.

'Especially if they think you're not eating properly, I imagine,' he says, giving me a quick look that gives me the uncomfortable feeling that he sees so much more than I want him to see. 'I don't mind, I'm used to just cooking myself beans on toast. I'm a true bachelor cliché.' He grins but seems to shift uneasily as if he's embarrassed by what he's said. 'And why are you here so early?'

'Having a quiet moment before today's madness, I suppose.' I find myself twisting my rings around, a habit that helps to displace my nerves sometimes. I see him glance at my hand in the sand, my diamond ring and wedding band catching the morning sunlight, and I feel self-conscious about touching them. 'I didn't mean to get so upset with you at Joe's, it's just . . .'

'You can't paint without him?'

I stare at him in surprise then shake my head. 'That article was bullshit, okay? He twisted what Joe said to him,' I snap, then I sigh. 'I mean, I have been struggling, but it's more than my grief, I feel like I should be doing something different now, something more. I guess that doesn't make any sense. Not much seems to make sense right now. It's like there's this huge . . . block.'

'That's completely understandable, you know. You've been through something so . . . tragic. You're just finding a way of, not dealing with it, but coping, maybe. If you can make your way through this block, then you will find inspiration again, I think,' Robert says softly.

I wish it were that simple.

'You know, it's good that I ran into you. What time do I need to get to the Fair to make sure I can snap all your paintings up?' I sense he's trying to lighten our suddenly dark conversation and I'm relieved. It's hard enough to talk about it with people I know, let alone someone who will never know Lucas.

'The Fair starts at eleven but I doubt there will be a rush on my stall, so you should be fine.'

'I wouldn't bank on that.'

I squint up at him, the sun rising above him and getting in my eyes. 'You really are a fan of my art, aren't you?'

He chuckles. 'I shall prove it to you today.' He turns to walk back to the Inn. 'See you later, Rose.' His voice seems to linger on my name a little, then he heads off back down the beach, strolling across the sand, his shoes dangling in his hand. I watch him for a moment, wondering why a guy wants to stay in our small town for the whole summer. It seems a strange destination for a single man. I caught the bachelor reference. He obviously has money too – wouldn't he rather be in an exotic location instead?

I look in my bag and find my earbuds and plug them into my iPhone. I need to drown the world out for a couple more hours, and nothing used to help more with that than music. I start my favourite playlist and lean back on my hands gazing out to the sea. Carrie Underwood fills my ears.

The world around me fades into the background and when I eventually realise the sun is fully on my face, I check the time and see that the morning is well underway, so I start to walk back across the sand towards town.

'Rose!' a voice calls, interrupting the music. I turn and frown a little as I see Adam jogging towards me. Ever since he'd started working in the bar in the holidays, Emma had maintained that he had a crush on me. Then Lucas had joined in the teasing, asking if I was going to leave him for a toy boy. I never took them seriously, but I must admit lately even I have noticed that he likes me, and I'm really not sure how to handle it. He's wearing shorts even though it's a crisp morning, a sure sign he's Talting born and bred – we're all pretty hardy when it comes to the elements. He breaks into a wide smile when he sees me and I lift my hand slightly to acknowledge him. I carry on walking, wishing he'd just jog on by, but, of course, he slows to a walk beside me. Annoyed, I pull out my earbuds, which I thought were a universal sign for 'I don't want to talk to you' – but obviously not to him.

'So, today's the Fair . . .' he begins, fiddling with the edge of his white T-shirt. I wait for him to continue. 'Well, I was wondering if you wanted to go, to the uh, evening thing together?' He kicks the sand with his foot and avoids my eyes as his question hangs in the air between us.

God. I panic for a second. I don't know how to deal with this. Being with someone since I was fourteen meant I never had to go on a first date or turn anyone down. I can feel my palms start to sweat. 'Adam, I'm there to sell my paintings, I might not even get to watch the band, I don't know . . .'

'But if you do you'll go with me?' he asks eagerly.

I stop walking. 'I can't,' I choke out.

'Oh. I'm sorry. Is it . . . is it too soon for you?' he asks quietly, turning to face me.

Is it? How do you know when it's not? All I know is, this doesn't feel right. Not now, not with him.

Like me, he looks confused and lost. 'Do you think I'm too young for you?'

'No . . . yes.' I clench my hands into fists and wish I could just sink into the ground. 'I'm sorry.'

'I just thought—'

'Please, I'm just not ready for this,' I cut in, losing patience with him. I don't see why I have to explain. This isn't what I want. 'I have to go. Sorry.' I break away from him and walk back up the beach towards town. The backs of my legs start to ache as I try to put as much distance as I can between us.

I walk briskly back to my cottage, my cheeks burning. I haven't ever shown any interest in him – why would he think I'd want to go on a date?

As I let myself in, I wonder what Lucas would have made of the incident. 'I think it's flattering other guys appreciate how gorgeous my girl is,' I imagine him saying to me. I don't feel flattered, just embarrassed and annoyed, but I try to push it aside as I hurry upstairs to have a shower and get ready.

When Joe and John turn up with the van they've borrowed an hour later, my nerves about the Fair have taken over any thoughts of Adam. I'm in jeans, a shirt and ballet pumps with a grey scarf covered in butterflies that Lucas bought me a few years ago. It's still one of my favourites and I thought it might be lucky today.

'No need to be nervous,' Joe says as he picks up a painting ready to put into the van. 'You already have one customer, remember.'

'They look great,' John assures me as he looks at one of them propped up by the door. I take a deep breath and follow them out, the cottage looking empty now all my work has gone.

The blue sky and sunshine seem to be holding up and the

field is already swarming when we drive across it towards my tent. Emma is already there with plastic mugs of coffee for us as we haul the paintings out of the van and on to the stands.

'How did you walk across the grass in those?' I ask, pointing to her four-inch heels.

'I can't possibly reveal my secrets,' she replies.

'I dropped her here,' John says, which earns him a glare. I laugh, glad they're here with me to keep my nerves in check.

I arrange the paintings in the order they were painted, each one bearing my small signature in the corner, and stick a small price sticker on the frame. I couldn't bring myself to charge more than I usually would, despite what Emma said. It's never been about the money for me, and I don't want it to be now.

'Okay, tell me what you think,' I ask the three of them as I step back to join them at the tent opening.

'They look great,' Joe says, putting his arm around me. 'It will be a sell-out, I know it.'

'It's perfect,' Emma agrees. 'Although you've charged too little, as always.' She wraps her arm through John's. 'This was the right thing to do.'

John turns to me. 'Lucas would have been proud of you.'

I swallow the lump that has formed in my throat. I feel the sun warming the back of my neck and my scarf ruffles in the light breeze sweeping past us, and for a second I close my eyes and imagine that he's with us too as he should be. He would have been proud; I know that John is right about that. I'd like to think he's looking down on us right now. 'You got this, babe,' I can hear him whispering in my ear, ever confident about my talent.

And I'm determined to prove him right.

Chapter Seven

Soon the Fair is underway. The field is now crammed with tents and stalls, some selling local crafts and jewellery, others with games for the kids to play. A band is getting ready to play on the stage at the back. The smell of food starts to envelop us – onions being fried and popcorn being popped. The hive of activity is an attack on the senses, a far cry from the usual empty, vast green space every other day of the year.

There are people everywhere. All the surrounding towns turn out for this. I spot Mick and Joan leading a group across the grass, no doubt all the guests staying at the Inn. It would have been mandatory for them to come today. I spot Robert easily in the middle wearing light trousers and a polo shirt, Ray-Bans covering his eyes and his arms already looking tanned from the sun. He says something to Mick and leaves the group to head towards my tent. Emma comes to stand beside me and lets out a low whistle as she watches his approach. I shake my head and tell John over my shoulder that he has some competition.

'I made sure I arrived as early as I was allowed to,' Robert says as he comes over. 'Wow, it's heaving already.'

'The highlight of the year around here,' Emma says, only half joking.

'I think I've been here before. My family came here once

when I was little,' he says. He glances at me and smiles.

'I would have thought you were more the Caribbean type,' Emma says.

'Well, I have been . . . but you know what, I prefer it here.'

'Seriously?' I ask. I know that it's home for us but it's hard to believe that someone from Robert's kind of background would take to it so much. Then again, with his skin glowing from the sunshine and a relaxed smile on his face, I think perhaps this place is going to be good for him. Talting is slow-paced and sometimes you need slow-paced. I imagine it's a world away from his law office. And maybe that's what he was looking for this summer.

'It was one of my favourite holidays because my dad didn't work, my mum was calm, which is rare, and they actually spent time with us. That meant more than any of the fancy holidays we went on.'

'Us?'

He looks at me. Through his sunglasses I can't see his eyes. 'My brother.' He looks away again, telling me he doesn't want to elaborate on him right now.

'My sister ran off to join the circus,' Emma declares somewhat dramatically.

Robert turns to her with eyebrows raised. 'Seriously?'

'It's not a circus – it's a dance company,' I tell him.

'I still don't believe a dance company needs to travel as much as they do. Anyway, this one's more like a sister than she is,' she says, gesturing to me. I know she gets hurt about how little she sees her sister, though. She has the wanderlust we never felt.

'Friends are the family you choose,' John chips in with a sage nod. Emma and I roll our eyes at him.

Robert chuckles. 'That is very true. I must admit that I'm enjoying being away from my family this summer.'

I sense his flippant tone is masking the sad truth. I wonder what the story with his family is – and if I'll ever find out.

'So, what do you think?' John asks, gesturing to my work, and I'm pulled away from my musings.

Robert dutifully steps forward to look at the paintings. Emma and John move back next to me and we watch as he looks at each one in turn, slowly taking them in as if they're hanging in an art gallery somewhere. I find myself chewing on my lip as the silence ticks on. I haven't been so nervous to find out what someone thinks of my work for a long time. I realise I want his approval, and I'm not entirely sure why.

Finally, Robert turns around to face the three of us. 'I love them, as I knew I would. I'll take them all.'

I stare at him and then look at Emma and John, who seem just as stunned. 'All of them?' I repeat, to check I heard him correctly.

'Yes, all of them, and you've underpriced them. I'll pay double,' he says, pulling out his wallet. 'You prefer cash, I presume?'

'Um . . .' I seem to be unable to do anything but watch as he counts out the notes in his hands and then holds out the bundle. There must be about two thousand pounds there. John lets out a long whistle and Emma digs her finger in my back. I stumble forward. 'This is too much,' I tell him, but he shakes his head, takes my hand in his and transfers the money into my palm, closing his fist around it and shaking on it. 'Are you really sure?' I raise my eyes to meet his.

He meets my gaze for a moment and then smiles.

'Absolutely.' He lets go of my hand. 'I wonder if Mick will let me keep them in the Inn until I can arrange for them to be taken to my flat.'

'I can't see why not, and I still have the van, so we can drive them over now,' John says, sweeping him away to find Mick and Joe.

'Oh my God,' Emma says slowly once they've gone. 'Did that just happen?'

I stare at the money in my hand. 'He's actually serious, isn't he?'

'Of course he is. Um, why don't you put the money away? I trust most people here, but . . .'

I nod and put the money safely in my purse in my bag. 'Well, looks like my tent is closed for the day.' I meet Emma's eye and we start giggling a bit hysterically at the turn of events. When John, Joe and Robert come back, we put the paintings back in the van and I watch them climb in and drive across the grass towards the Inn in wonder.

Just who is this guy who's swept into town and bought all of my work?

Emma rushes off to fill the town in on the news. I watch her find Mrs Morris and tell her what's just happened. The Fair will be buzzing with the story in no time.

I go back inside the now-empty tent and sit down on the grass to look around the blank space. I did it. I have no art left. I feel like a weight has been lifted off my shoulders, but at the same time scared that the empty space will never be filled again.

When Emma comes back, she pulls me up and we go for a stroll around the Fair. It's packed now and it's difficult to weave our way through the crowds, especially when people keep congratulating me. 'Did you make the announcement over the loudspeaker?' I hiss at her.

She grins. 'Good news travels fast.'

'You mean bad news.'

'Well, any news in Talting really.'

'Unfortunately, true.' I see John and Robert walking towards us, and we wait for them to catch us up. 'That was quick.'

'Mick said to leave them in his van and he'll drive Robert into Plymouth tomorrow to his flat. He wouldn't take no for an answer.'

'Sounds like Mick,' Emma replies. 'So, now we don't need to man your tent for the rest of the day, let's all have a look around.' She puts her arm through John's and starts walking again, leaving Robert and me no choice but to follow them.

I feel unsure what to say to Robert, still feeling surprised and a little embarrassed about him buying all my paintings like that. Thankfully, we don't have to walk very far before someone grabs our attention.

'Fancy a game, guys?' Dan calls out from his games stall where you shoot tin cans off shelves. He runs it every year, but on the other days of the year he's a butcher. The two things could be related, I don't know.

'I'm up for it if you are?' Robert says to me.

'You're on.'

'Good luck,' Dan says with a smile at me.

I've been playing this for years. Lucas taught me how to play it when we were teenagers, being typically patient with me as I missed the cans by miles my first few tries. He also taught me to play pool when we were old enough to go to pubs and, most importantly for him, he taught me how to surf. I shoot and knock all my cans off. Robert's eyes widen as he watches, then he tries, lifting off his sunglasses and concentrating so hard I want to laugh. He only manages to knock down one.

'Bad luck,' Dan says, handing me a giant panda teddy bear. 'Well done, Rose.'

'I feel like I've been hustled,' Robert complains as I take the big bear from Dan and wonder how I'm going to carry it around all day.

'We should have placed a bet on it,' I say, turning around and realising that Emma and John have melted away in the crowd. Huh. I hover for a second awkwardly, unsure if Robert and I should stay together now or not. I see one of the kids from the town walk past and offer the panda to her, which she accepts with a shriek of delight. Robert watches the girl walk away with the panda and gives me a funny look. 'What's the Farm?' he asks, looking away from me to the sign ahead of us.

'Ah, this is cute,' I say, leading him over to it. There is a pen covered with straw and filled with various small animals – a goat, a pig, some chickens and sheep. The kids are allowed in to pet and feed them. 'Do you have any pets?' I ask as we lean on the fence to watch.

'We have a dog called Bertie, he's a Labrador.'

'I always wanted a cat when I was growing up but my mum was allergic, and Lucas and I spent so much time doing up our house, we never really got around to it.'

'What is it about cats you like?'

'I guess they are calming, plus easier to look after than dogs. I liked the idea of one curled up beside me whilst I painted.' I try to smile. 'Emma's always saying my house is too lonely, so maybe I should get one.'

'Is it lonely?' He looks at me with those searching eyes of his and I hear the unasked question – are you lonely?

'It's peaceful, quiet – I like that. But I guess it would be nice to have someone there when I come home.'

Robert reaches out to pat a goat on the head. He seems to hesitate then glances across at me. 'Is it ever hard living here, you know, with all the memories of him? Of Lucas?'

I pause in patting the piglet snuffling at my feet. 'Sometimes. We came to this fair every year together. But sometimes it's nice too. I'm still close to him here. Mostly, I can't imagine living anywhere else.' I pull myself off the fence, feeling that this conversation has become too sad and too deep for me to deal with right now. Robert follows me. 'Do you think you'll always live in Plymouth?'

'I don't know. My father lets me run our South West office whilst he looks after everything in London. To be honest, I think he set up a local office just for me to run. He knows I hate the city. I'm still working for him, though.'

'You don't enjoy that?'

'I'm only just starting to decide what the answer to that question is. So, how about a ride on the Ferris wheel?'

'Sure.' I'm curious as to why he doesn't want to talk about his family but then I remember how hard it is sometimes to talk to people about Lucas. Especially at the beginning. We try to avoid pain if we can. Plus I mustn't forget that we've only just met. I'm so used to being with people I know inside out. I wanted to enjoy today, not open up wounds, and I should respect that he probably feels the same. So even though I'm burning with curiosity, I queue with him for the Ferris wheel, climbing into one of the swinging chairs when it comes to a stop in front of us.

The wheel moves slowly and the view we get as we climb up to the sky is amazing. The wheel freezes for a few minutes at the very top. Everyone on the grass below looks tiny and it feels like we're flying over them in our own private bubble.

I look out at Talting below us and marvel at how different everything seems up here. For a moment I wish I could stay here, far away from any pain, with the sun on my face, and then everything would be okay again. Then Robert's leg brushes against mine for a moment, bringing me back to reality. 'I wish I could paint this feeling right now.'

'How do you feel?' he asks me in a soft voice. I feel his eyes on me again but I carry on gazing at the light, fluffy clouds hanging above us in the blue sky.

'For the first time in a long while, I'm starting to feel like the world is full of possibility again. Does that make sense?'

'Yes,' he whispers. 'I feel it too. I'm glad I came here.'

With a start, I realise I'm glad he did too. I look across at him and he holds my gaze steadily with his own. Everything around us seems to fade for a moment, as if the world is on mute except for us two. My heart starts to speed up inside my chest. I wonder if he's one of the possibilities.

Then with a lurch the wheel starts moving again and the moment, whatever it was, is broken.

I don't know whether to be disappointed or relieved.

Not until the wheel touches back down and Robert has taken my hand to help me climb out, does my pulse slow to a normal pace again.

Chapter Eight

'Are you hungry?'

A delicious waft of burgers and onions reaches my nose and my stomach rumbles on cue. I realise my shorts are starting to fit snugly on my waist now, when last summer they were hanging off me. 'Sounds great,' I reply to Robert.

We each get a burger and can of Coke from the stall and then find a spare patch of grass to sit down on to eat. A folk band is playing on the stage near us and their music suits the sunshine, making it feel as though we're at a Californian music festival rather than an English town fair.

I bite into my burger; the greasy goodness tastes amazing and I murmur appreciatively, earning a raised eyebrow from Robert. I let out an embarrassed laugh and dribble ketchup on my chin. He leans in and wipes it off with his napkin. I freeze and he pulls away quickly like he just realised what he was doing. We exchange shy smiles and I polish off all of my burger in record time. It's another thing I lost after Lucas – my enjoyment of food. I am relieved that it's slowly returning.

'There you are,' a voice calls out. I squint in the sun to look up and see Emma and John picking their way through the people sitting on the grass to join us. I give her a look that tells her I was not amused they ditched us, but she cheerfully ignores me and asks how Robert is enjoying himself.

'Rose is an excellent tour guide.'

'I bet she is.' Emma winks at me and I want to throttle her. John saves me by talking about the band and we relax into the afternoon. The grass fills up with people coming to listen to the music having spent too much on the games and stalls. I lean back on my arms, stretching my legs out, and look around us. I feel how I always feel here – part of something special. It's rare to live in a tight-knit community like this nowadays.

I had dreaded today and Lucas hasn't been far from my mind for most of it, but I think he would be proud of me for coming here, for doing something I've always loved again, and for my sale being such a success.

I'm glad I came here. I feel as if I've taken a big step forward. It's as I said to Robert on the Ferris wheel – I can taste possibility again. As though the wind has slightly changed direction.

A future without Lucas still scares the hell out of me, though.

Emma and John move closer and he wraps his arms around her. I watch them, and I can't help but think that's how Lucas and I would be sitting right now. A sharp pang hits my chest. I realise I ache to be held like that again. I wonder what it would be like to hold Robert's hand. Guiltily, I raise my knees to my chest and wrap my arms around them to make sure I don't reach out to him. Not that I know he'd want me to. I may have dreamt that moment between us on the wheel. Plus he's just here for the summer. He likes my art, that's all.

And that's all I want.

I think.

The band starts playing a love song and I close my eyes to

listen to it. I never thought I would ever be with anyone but Lucas. But I am attracted to Robert. That much is clear. I'm not sure how I could not be. I think even Emma is. Hanging out with him today has been really fun and more relaxed than I could have imagined. Adam wanting to come here as my date freaked me out, but being with Robert doesn't. And I don't know how to handle it.

'Are you okay?' Robert's voice asks, close to my ear.

I touch my cheek, surprised to feel the wetness of a tear there. Robert hands me a tissue. 'Just the music, you know,' I say, wiping my cheek with it, wishing I wasn't such a slave to these crazy emotions. I have so many highs and lows in one day it's draining.

'Do you want me . . . do you want to go home? I can walk you.'

I nod gratefully and tap Emma on the shoulder. 'I'm tired, Robert's going to walk me home.'

'Are you sure?' Concern immediately flashes across her face.

'I'm fine.' I give her a hug and she tells me to text her when I get home. John kisses me on the cheek and shakes hands with Robert and then we set off, stepping around everyone sitting on the grass, the sounds of the band fading as we walk away.

Dusk has fallen and I shiver a little, wishing I had brought a cardigan with me. The sky above us has darkened and clouds have appeared. I wonder if everyone will make it home before it rains.

'I had a great time today; you guys really know how to put on an event,' Robert says when we reach the main road together.

'I'm glad you enjoyed it.'

'It's really a great place to live. I can see why you've stayed here.'

'We have a few events like that through the year. It livens things up, especially when the tourists leave.'

'Is it weird having all these people around just for a couple of months?'

'I'm used to it, I guess. It's part of living here. We need the visitors to survive.'

'You've never thought of going somewhere else to sell your art?'

'I make good money from the tourists,' I say, nudging his shoulder.

'That's true. I actually pass by a gallery in Plymouth every day on my way to work; they're always looking for new artists.'

'I don't think I'm good enough for a gallery. Besides,' I say, looking at my feet, 'I haven't been able to paint for a while, remember.'

'I don't think it's something you can just give up; you just need to be inspired again.'

'Maybe. We'll see. You seem to know a lot about it.'

'When you have no talent yourself, you tend to notice when others do, that's all.'

'Being a lawyer doesn't require any talent?'

'Maybe for arguing,' he replies with a grin. We walk into my road and I point out my cottage to him. He stops to look at it. 'It's exactly where I pictured you. You know, when you said you lived in a cottage. It's a real artist's home,' he says, babbling a little as if he's nervous.

'What's your place like?'

'It's a modern flat, very open-plan, lots of white walls, which is why I wanted your paintings.'

'I hope they brighten the place up.'

He turns to me. 'They will.'

'Thank you for today. For buying my paintings, obviously, but also for being with me at the Fair. It was the first one that I didn't go to with . . . someone,' I tell him quietly, hoping he knows how much I appreciate the day we've had.

'It was my pleasure,' he says with a small smile. He steps closer to me, closing the small distance between us. My breath hitches at his closeness and the serious look on his face. I'm acutely aware of how alone we are and how much time we've spent together today.

'Actually, Rose, there is something I wanted to say to you,' he says, running a hand through his hair.

There is a rumble of thunder in the distance. I jump a little at the sound.

'What is it?' I ask, my voice coming out as barely a whisper. I glance back at my cottage, wondering if I can flee there. What if he tells me he likes me? What if he doesn't? I don't know what I want him to say.

'It's not easy . . . but, Rose, I . . .' he says haltingly, looking across at me biting my lip. He pauses. I hold my breath for what he's going to say. And then there's a flash of lightning, followed by a louder clap of thunder. This time we both jump.

He steps back from me and I let out my breath. 'I think I better go,' he says, looking away from me with a pained expression.

I guess my hesitation has made him change his mind. 'Robert . . .' I begin, wanting to make things okay between us but not sure how to when I don't know that I want to hear what he was going to say.

The rain begins in earnest then.

'Go inside, Rose,' he says, speaking loudly over another rumble of thunder. He turns away from me.

'Wait . . .'

He shakes his head, ending the conversation. 'You should get inside. I'll see you soon. Goodnight, Rose.' He's walking away from me then.

Confused, I wait for a moment until the rain thickens into sheets that make it impossible to see him anymore. I realise that I'm getting soaked so I hurry inside. The rain pounds on the roof of the cottage. I shut the door and go upstairs to take off my wet clothes. My hair has plastered itself to my face.

I look out of my window and I think I see a figure at the top of the road. I strain to see him through the rain but then he fades into the darkness. I lean back.

What did he want to say to me?

I wonder if I should have let him tell me. I think back to that moment before the thunder started and remember how close we were standing, the look in his eyes as he spoke to me. It was a charged moment and I can't believe that it happened.

My phone rings, making me jump. 'Emma?'

'We're soaked. We all had to run into the church. Did you get home in time?'

'Just. It was a bit weird really, Robert just kind of ran off.'

'How come?'

'He said he had to tell me something but then the storm started and he changed his mind . . . then he just left.'

'He likes you,' she says instantly, speaking the words I was worried about.

'I thought that too, maybe, but . . . then why did he leave?'

'He was nervous. He didn't know what you would say.'

I nod, even though she can't see me, knowing that he saw my nerves. 'I don't know what I would have said.'

There's a few seconds of silence. 'It's okay, you know, Rose. He seems really nice and he's pretty hot. Sorry, John. Oh, John says to tell you he likes him too, and you know how picky he is. What we mean is, don't freak out about this, okay? It was a lovely day, and that's all that matters.'

'So, don't overanalyse it?'

'Exactly. Which I know is easier said than done, but it's late. Go to bed and have sweet dreams.'

I smile into the phone. 'I'll try. And get home safe, okay?'

'Bloody English weather. Goodnight.'

'Night.' I hang up and slip into my pyjamas and dressing gown, shivering still from the sudden downpour. The rain is still thrashing against the windows and I wonder if Robert has got back to the Inn yet. He will be drenched by the time he gets there.

I climb into bed, my body warming up instantly under the covers. I wonder if he was going to tell me that he likes me. Maybe it's better that he didn't say anything. We hardly know each other. It feels like it's been a very long day and I'm exhausted. I can't decipher anything right now, especially my own feelings.

I run my fingers through my damp hair and curl my legs up. My eyelids start to droop and I yawn, burying my head into my pillow. I have no time to worry that I might not sleep tonight, because I drift off instantly.

And I sleep through until morning.

Chapter Nine

Sunday morning dawns and I wake up feeling better than I have in a long time. I take a long, relaxing soak in a bubble bath and then head into the kitchen wearing leggings and a long shirt, my hair pulled into a messy bun. I am due to go to Gloria and Graham's house today for lunch.

Lucas and I used to go to his parents every Sunday for lunch and after he died, they continued to invite me there. Sometimes it's a comfort to do something that we always did; after all, they are practically my parents too. Sometimes the absence of him at the table hits the three of us hard and silence descends whilst we sink into our memories of him. Sometimes Emma and John come with me and keep up a lively conversation, or Emma's parents will pop by on their way to the pub and drop off a bottle of wine. When you have no family, Sundays feel like the worst day. Things are closed around here and you sit inside thinking about everyone else eating their roast dinners and the loneliness builds to an impossible crescendo. I tried it a couple of times, thinking it would be preferable to going to their house without Lucas, but it wasn't.

Also, I think he'd like the fact that the three of us carry on the tradition. Maybe it won't – maybe it can't – last forever, but for right now, I want to do it.

The Second Love of My Life

I decide to bake a dessert to take with me. It's been a long time since I baked anything. Baking has always relaxed me. I don't need to think about anything apart from the recipe. Painting always required concentration, my whole being in the moment of painting, whereas baking is just fun.

Turning on some music, I roll up my sleeves and start to make an apple pie. Tapping my feet to The Band Perry, I lose myself in making the pie, and wonder why I waited so long to do this again. My mum taught me to bake when I was little and we used to make fancy cupcakes on rainy Saturdays, eating cake mix out of the bowl and making a mess of our kitchen.

Whilst the pie is baking, I slip on my ballet pumps and have a cup of coffee in my garden. The weather is slowly getting warmer and my small patch of grass is a suntrap. Lucas would have probably already been surfing by now, but the sea is still a bit too cold for most people. I think back to my first surfing lesson when we were teenagers. I swooned at the sight of him in his wetsuit and made a poor attempt at standing up on the board, but I got better with his help and we used to surf together some mornings in the summer, although he was always ten times better than I ever could be. It was as if he was one with the board. He was so at home in the sea. I think sometimes it's what I miss most – walking to the beach and watching him out there riding the waves and having the time of his life.

I haven't been in the sea since his death.

I wipe away a stray tear. Going to his parents' house always makes me think about him. How we should be walking there together, my hand resting on his waist, his arm slung over my shoulders. I can't imagine how hard it must be for them to open the door just to me. I check the time and realise I'll be late if I don't leave now. I take the pie out of the oven and put it in my cake tin so I can carry it there. I grab my bag and keys and head to their house.

Gloria and Graham live on a pretty, tree-lined road right in the centre of town in the house they bought after they got married almost thirty years ago. I push open their front door, knocking as I do, the smell of roast beef hitting my nostrils instantly and making my mouth salivate. Gloria is an amazing cook.

'Rose, you look lovely,' Gloria says, peeking around the kitchen door at me. I think that's a bit of a stretch, especially as I probably pinched this shirt from Lucas at some point, but I thank her anyway. Gloria is always immaculately turned out with a dyed-blond bob and today is wearing a pretty green dress. I lean in to kiss her cheek, getting the same jolt as I always do when I look into her blue eyes. Lucas has her eyes.

Had her eyes.

'I brought this for us,' I say, quickly moving past those eyes to put the tin down on the counter.

'You're going to make me fat, Rose,' Graham says, lifting the lid to sniff the apple pie appreciatively. 'And I really don't care.' He puts an arm around me. 'Now, we have been reliably informed that we need to crack open that bottle of wine as there's something to celebrate.'

'We heard about you selling your paintings at the Fair,' Gloria says, bending down to look through the oven door.

Graham nods. 'We're really proud of you,' he says, giving me a squeeze. 'Who's the man that bought them?'

'He's a lawyer in Plymouth who's staying here for the

summer. He bought the paintings for his flat, and he paid much more than they're worth.'

'Nah. He just has very good taste.'

I watch Gloria's back, wondering why she's being so quiet. 'It certainly was a surprise. Can I do anything to help, Gloria?' I ask her.

'No, I'm fine, you both go through.'

Graham grabs a bottle of wine and steers me out into their small dining room. My eyes automatically go to the two pictures on the sideboard. One is of Lucas and me at our school prom. His sandy coloured hair is too long and flops over his eyes. His arm is around me, his tuxedo complementing my long black silk dress. We're both smiling at the camera but we look a bit awkward as only teenagers can. The next one is of us at their wedding anniversary party at Joe's. Lucas is wearing jeans and a black shirt and I'm in a long skirt, my hair is shorter and layered and we're looking at one another, laughing about something. I look at my eyes so lit up and happy. I wonder when, or if, I'll feel that happy again. And whether it's okay to want to feel that way again one day.

'We went to the service this morning,' Graham says, drawing my attention from the photograph. He pours us both a glass of wine as I sit down next to him at the mahogany table. Gloria and Graham have always been regular church-goers and I admire their faith, even though sometimes it's difficult to understand it in the face of what happened to Lucas. 'We put some daffodils on his grave.' His voice wobbles slightly on the word 'grave'.

'If I had to pick a flower to describe Lucas it would be those – sunny, happy and smiley.' I feel my voice wobble too, this time on his name. He always feels so present when I'm here.

Graham squeezes my hand briefly. 'I completely agree.'

Gloria bustles in then. I wonder if she heard us. 'Here we are,' she says, placing the roast beef down on the table. Her eyes meet her husband's as he starts to carve and he gives her a reassuring smile. I feel a pang that I will never know what it's like to be with the same person for as long as they have been together. She leaves again and comes back with more dishes. 'I can't remember if you like carrots?' she asks, her voice sounding unusually bright.

'I do,' I say, aware she knows this full well. She seems to be acting strangely and I can't think why. I know they wish I would visit the grave with them, but they said they understood why I don't want to. I never know if I'm right or wrong with the way I handle things sometimes. Maybe it's because there is no right or wrong way to handle it. There's no manual for grieving after all. Sometimes I wish there were.

She sits down and has some wine then seems to draw in a big breath. 'It really is good news about your art. Lucas would have been so proud of you.'

I smile at her, pleased that she thinks so. It's always some-how comforting to be with people who know what Lucas would think or say or do, what he was like, who he was. It means I will never lose that knowledge myself.

'So, what is the man like who bought them all?' Graham asks, cutting into his meat.

'Mrs Morris already gave us a detailed account,' Gloria snaps at him.

I look over at her, seeing her frown at her husband. I'm confused. 'I'm sure you'll both meet him soon. Maybe at the café opening?' I suggest. There's a small silence and then Graham starts talking about his golf club and Gloria and I fall quiet. I'm a bit lost as to why there's an atmosphere in the room. Lunch is a quiet affair as we all seem to be frequently wallowing in our own thoughts.

They have always felt like my own family but it's as if we're still trying to find our rhythm without Lucas. We never used to struggle for things to say when he was here, and I felt as if I could talk to them about anything. But today it seems as though the three of us are treading on eggshells.

I'm relieved when dessert is over and I get up to leave. I refuse Gloria's half-hearted offer of coffee and let Graham lead me to the front door.

He leans towards me and speaks softly so his wife won't hear. 'We heard about those boys at the bar. Mrs Morris told us Robert helped you stop them. I think it just brought it all back . . . how no one stopped . . . well, you know. And Mrs Morris was very gushing about him, so Gloria . . . well, it was a bit difficult for her to hear about him buying all your work like that too, that's all.'

It all clicks into place as he shifts uneasily. Gloria is worried about this good-looking, wealthy newcomer with a passion for my art. And when I think about him standing in front of me last night, my cheeks turn pink because I don't know if she's right to be worried or not. I say goodbye to Graham quickly and walk away, breathing in the early evening air, hoping it will cool my flushed cheeks down.

I walk home feeling as though I've done something wrong.

Lucas and I never had a 'what if' conversation about our mortality. We were too young, I suppose. Maybe if we had, though, I'd have some clue about how he would want me to navigate all of this. Although all the words I can guess that he would have said to me – 'I'd want you to be happy, I'd want you to live for the both of us, I'd want you be loved' – which I would have said right back to him, wouldn't actually help me now.

You can't make someone grieve the way you wish they would. You don't have a choice in how you handle it. You just feel the way you feel.

Chapter Ten

Adam finds me alone in the kitchen on Tuesday getting ready for my next shift at the bar. 'So, I heard you had a good time at the Fair?' he says in a bitter tone, brushing past me to hang his coat up.

'I can't believe Robert bought all of my paintings,' I reply, thinking that's what he meant.

He spins around to glare at me. 'That's not all he did, though, right? It's all over town that you spent all of your time there with Robert. You supposedly weren't ready to go on a date but it was fine to be with him?'

I lean against the counter for support. 'I didn't go with him, it wasn't a date; after he bought my paintings, we just hung out. With Emma and John as well. Not that it's any of your business, Adam.' Even though what I've told him is true, I know that hanging out with Robert felt okay whereas the thought of doing the same with Adam felt very wrong. I'd thought I was worried about it being too soon to spend time with another man, but maybe it was just the thought of being with Adam that had worried me. Because being with Robert didn't make me feel that way. I don't want to make things worse by telling Adam that, though. And I do feel bad that he seems so upset. I never meant to upset anyone.

'Whatever, Rose. You could have just been honest with

me,' he replies, marching past me again and out into the bar. I sigh. I hate that he's pissed off with me but I can't make it better because there will never be anything between us. And he has to accept that.

Emma breezes in then. 'What's with Adam?'

'He's annoyed because he thinks I went to the Fair with Robert when I said I wouldn't go with him.'

She rolls her eyes. 'So what if you did? You don't have to go out with him if you don't want to. Blimey, has he never been rejected before?'

'Rejected? Oh God, have I been a bitch to him?'

She touches my shoulder. 'No, of course not. You know the truth about what happened. Besides, it's none of his business anyway. Just because he likes you, doesn't mean you owe him anything. I know I've teased you about his crush but seriously, he needs to get a grip. And I'll tell him that.'

'He also said it's all over town that I was with Robert. Is it?'

'Of course not. Everyone was so happy to see you there, that's all.'

I give her a sceptical look; I know what people are like here. But maybe I shouldn't have been there with Robert. 'It's too soon after . . .' I trail off and bite my lip. 'What must everyone think of me?'

'Stop torturing yourself. I promise you no one has even mentioned it to me. It's no one's business anyway who you hang out with. The man paid a fortune for your art, the least you could do was have a burger with him, right?' I have to smile at that. She pats my arm. 'Rose, you haven't done any-thing wrong, I promise. But you know what, even if you had gone on a date with Robert, that would have been okay too.'

I sigh, wishing I could stop the nagging tug of guilt pulling on me. 'I don't know about that. I feel like I don't know anything right now.'

'You need to stop being so hard on yourself.'

I wish it were that easy.

Joe comes in then, putting an end to our conversation, with invites to the grand reopening of Mrs Morris's café now that the refurb has finally been finished, but still the whole shift passes with Adam throwing me filthy looks and me worrying that I've done something wrong. Because if Robert had asked me to the Fair like Adam did, I'm not sure what I would have said. That makes me feel guilty not just about Adam but Lucas too, and more confused than ever about having such a good time with Robert.

I think back to Robert wanting to tell me something that night and Emma thinking he was going to tell me that he likes me. Suddenly, I'm grateful that he left before saying anything. I couldn't handle having to form a response to anything like that right now.

I take a deep breath and focus on pulling a pint, because if I give Greg the Grocer too much foam on his beer, he'll never let me hear the end of it.

I don't see Robert for a few days. Mick says he left him in Plymouth to sort out my paintings and get them hung in his flat, as well as catch up on some business. Apparently he has the penthouse apartment in a flashy high-rise building on the edge of the city. I can't quite picture him there. Although I have to remind myself that I don't really know him. And he is a corporate lawyer after all.

It's warm on Friday afternoon when I walk with Emma

and John into town for Mrs Morris's reopening party. As we walk there, I congratulate John on his promotion being confirmed, which I know because Emma had texted me about it the day before. They walk hand in hand, beaming, and I can't help but think about her plan for them to try for a baby now he'll be making so much more money. I wonder when it will happen, but I don't want to ask her because I'm scared of how I'll react to her answer.

The whole town has turned out for the event as expected, and most of the tables inside and out have already been taken by the time we get there. We go to the door to peep in and the place looks brighter with extra tables and booths, the walls now bare of art with just a blackboard of specials hanging up. The new colour scheme is cream and light blue and works really well for a seafront café. My paintings would have cluttered the new space although it's sad not to see them up there. I was just seventeen when Lucas arranged for Mrs Morris to hang one in here as a surprise for my birthday. My paintings sold consistently after that, but she always refused to take any commission for displaying them for me.

Amanda, Mrs Morris's fifteen-year-old granddaughter, appears with a tray of free coffees and we grab one each.

Mrs Morris joins us. 'Well, what do you think of the place?'

'It looks fantastic, Mrs M,' Emma says. 'They did a great job.'

'I had to keep a close eye on them, that's for sure. I'm glad you like it, I need my regulars back. Now, love, have you asked her yet?' She looks at Amanda, who shakes her head, blushing and glancing nervously at me. Mrs Morris turns to me. 'She has an art project to do for school that she wondered if she could pick your brains about. What do you think?'

I hesitate, not knowing if I can help when I'm so stuck myself, but Mrs Morris has always been good to me so I find myself nodding. 'Sure. Do you want to talk about it now?'

'Go out the back, we can handle things here,' Mrs Morris says, taking the tray from Amanda and giving it to Emma, who gives me an amused look. I follow Amanda through the café into the kitchen and we sit down on the stools by the counter. I ask her what she has to do for the project. She explains the assignment is to capture something you love. 'Do you have any ideas?'

She explains that she wanted to choose the beach but her teacher said she had to put herself into the picture. 'I'm not sure how.'

'Well, how does the beach make you feel? Does it make you remember anything? You have to make it feel personal to you, not just a beach scene that could be anywhere, you know?' I remember my own art teacher telling me that a beach scene I drew didn't make her feel anything. I think about the mother and daughter I saw building a sandcastle together the other day and how it reminded me of doing the same thing with my own mother, and I realise now that I know what she meant back then.

I wonder if I'll be able to take my own advice and paint something really personal.

I leave Amanda thinking over some ideas and go outside to find Emma and John, when I feel a hand on my back and I turn to see Robert. 'You're back,' I say stupidly.

He grins. 'I am. Your paintings look perfect on my walls,' he says. 'I'm very happy to own some Rose Walker originals.'

'I'm glad you like them. You've given me some faith in my artistic skills.'

'You should have faith. I know you'll paint again, Rose Walker; the world can't lose a talent like yours.'

'It's strange, I never really thought of myself as talented. I loved to paint, that's why I did it. At college, there were so many other better artists than me, I struggled to compete with them.'

'There's no point in trying to compete, you should just be yourself.'

I like how Robert sees me. He makes me feel more confident, makes me have hope that one day I'll get my painting spark back.

But will I ever be able to do what I've always struggled with: to put my emotions into my art? How do I even start?

My fingers itch a little with the need to paint. I feel more positive than I have in a long time. If I paint again, it needs to be something from my heart. I know that now. The only way I can be an artist again is to be a completely new one. Everything has changed for me, and my art needs to change with me.

'Oh, look, Gloria and Graham have arrived,' Emma says, interrupting my thoughts and nodding in their direction.

I look over at them greeting Mrs Morris. I feel Robert follow my gaze in their direction. He seems to tense up behind me. 'That's Lucas's parents,' I murmur to him. 'I'd like them to meet you,' I say before I can stop myself. And it's true. I want them to meet him even though I'm not sure yet what is between us. But if there is something, I don't want to hide it from them anymore.

'I can't,' he says quickly, turning away so he has his back

to them. 'Um, no, I'm sorry but . . . I just remembered that I need to call . . . a . . . a client.'

'Now?' I ask, surprised. 'Didn't you just get here?'

'I'm sorry, I completely forgot about it. I was really looking forward to catching up. Are you working tonight?' he asks. I manage to nod. 'Great, I'll come in to the bar later then,' he says over his shoulder as he hurries off.

'What's up with him?' Emma says, watching him go.

'That was weird, right?' I shake my head, confused. He obviously didn't want to meet Gloria and Graham. I understand, though, that he'd feel awkward about it. I will too when it happens, I think. Emma pulls my arm, reminding me that Mrs Morris is going to make a speech. I follow her, not knowing whether I am more relieved or disappointed that Robert left without letting me introduce him to Lucas's parents.

I am starting to understand why so many artists pour themselves into their work. My emotions are so all over the place at the moment, I could do with several canvases to try to sort them out on.

It's a terrifying prospect, tapping into my feelings and painting them for all to see, and yet I feel as if I want to try. I have so much building up inside me that I want to get out.

Right now, though, it feels like an impossible mountain to climb.

Chapter Eleven

On my next day off, I decide to walk to Hampton, a neighbouring town, to look around. Emma is having lunch with her mum and rings me in the morning to invite me along but I decline, as I'm sure she'll want to talk about all her plans for her and John and I don't want to put a dampener on things. I walk alongside the beach, passing the Inn terrace, which overlooks the beach. I see Robert sitting at one of the white iron tables, with a cup of coffee and newspaper. It's a cool morning, which I'm guessing is why he's the only person sitting out on the terrace.

He waves me over, so I walk up the sand towards him. 'Are you always up this early?' he asks as I approach.

'I've never been good at sleeping in late, even as a teenager. I like to be doing things. What about you? You're supposed to be on holiday.'

'Used to being in the office early, I guess. What are your plans today?'

'I'm heading over to Hampton,' I say.

'What do they have in Hampton, then?'

'Well, it's a slightly bigger town than Talting and they have some good shops, but it's a really pretty walk there, which is why I like it so much. And it looks like the rain will hold off today.'

'My dad called earlier,' he tells me. 'I had to have a meeting with him about a client when I went back to Plymouth and he doesn't think I'm doing enough on the case. He doesn't really grasp the concept of a holiday. I could do with a walk before I start work on it, though, if you fancy the company?'

I hesitate, Adam's words echoing through my mind, but this doesn't count as a date either, right? He's just tagging along to somewhere I was already going to and he's never been there before, so it would be nice to show him.

It'll be good not to be alone.

'I'd like that.'

We leave the terrace and start walking towards Hampton. It's about a half-hour walk past fields and trees and I just love how peaceful it is. Robert strolls beside me, looking as comfortable as I feel. He sees me looking at him and smiles across at me. 'You're right, this walk is beautiful. I have done twelve-hour days in the office for so long, I forgot what the sky looks like, what grass looks like, how it smells outside.'

I wrinkle my noise. 'Right now, I can smell manure.'

He nudges me. 'You know what I mean.'

'I'm glad you like it. I can't imagine not taking time to get outdoors.'

'That's because you have all this on your doorstep. Plus, you're an artist, you're always looking for inspiration.'

Hampton comes into view then. There are hanging baskets outside each shop in the High Street, full of vivid colours. There are a few cute gift shops here for the tourists who visit the stately home that stands at the end of the road plus a second-hand bookshop that I love to browse in.

'I love bookshops, there are so few left,' Robert says, spotting it.

'I love the smell,' I agree as we walk over to it. 'I sniff books, is that weird?'

Robert grins. 'I'm saying nothing.' He holds the door open, which jangles merrily, and we step inside, that deliciously musty old book smell enveloping us. I can get lost in a bookshop; there are so many worlds to discover in the pages of a book, so many stories for you to dive in to. Actually, Lucas was always bored when I came in here and would wait for me in the coffee shop rather than traipse after me. He was never a reader; his attention span was too short.

'Hi, Marie,' I say to the woman who hurries out of the back office on hearing the bell. The shop has been in her family for eighty years.

'Rose, how lovely. And who's this?' She peers over the top of her glasses, her thick red hair moving across her face.

'This is Robert, he's in town for the summer,' I say, moving over to the Classics section. 'Anything new in?'

Marie looks Robert up and down, then follows me. 'Someone brought in some lovely hardbacks of Dickens,' she says, showing me. There's a couple I don't have and they look in excellent condition. 'I knew you'd like them. And what can I interest you in?' She goes over to Robert, who's looking at the crime section. 'This is new,' she says, showing him a book and leaning in closely.

Robert steps back, looking alarmed at her proximity, and backs into a stand of books. As if it's happening in slow motion, the stand wobbles before falling backwards with a loud crash, sending the fifty or so books on it flying everywhere. Robert looks horrified, his face turning pink as Marie gasps and covers her mouth with her hand. I can't help it, I look at the mess and Robert looking so ruffled and I burst out laughing. My laughter breaks the heavy silence and Marie joins in, with Robert finally breaking into a smile.

It feels good to really laugh and once I start, it's hard to stop. I have to lean against a bookshelf for support as I'm finding it hard to breathe.

'I've always been clumsy,' Robert admits sheepishly. 'I'm so sorry,' he says to Marie and goes over to start picking the books up. It's kind of reassuring to see him looking so embarrassed, his polished exterior shattered. Marie pulls herself together to help him lift the stand back up and I take a deep breath and grab some books to put back on it. I hiccup loudly and Robert grabs my shoulders, making me jump. 'A scare stops them,' he protests when I give him an annoyed look.

'No, you have to drink water,' Marie says.

'I think I just have to stop laughing.'

When we've finally cleared up the mess, Robert and I both buy a bunch of books each, trying to make up for it. Marie gives us both a hug goodbye, Robert's cheeks turning slightly pink again, and we leave the shop promising to come back soon. Outside the sky has turned grey and a breeze ruffles my hair.

'I need a coffee after that,' I say, rubbing my bare arms, which are pricked with goosebumps.

'Good plan. That was so embarrassing.'

'Sorry about laughing so much.'

He looks across at me. 'No, you're not, but I'll let you off; most people laugh at me.'

'It happens a lot, then?' I ask, trying not to laugh at him again. I lead us in the direction of the stately home, which has a lovely café in the gardens.

'Once I knocked over a statue in this really posh hotel when we were on holiday, and my dad didn't speak to me for the rest of the holiday. He thought I did it on purpose. Sometimes I just don't see things.'

'You're worse than Bella Swan.'

'Who?'

I shake my head. 'Why doesn't it surprise me that you don't know who that is?'

'Have I met her, then?'

'Doubtful.' We walk into the grounds of Hampton House, which is a tall, imposing stone building surrounded by manicured lawns lined with rose bushes. 'I used to come here a lot as a kid; they'd have things like Easter egg hunts and people dressed like the men and women who lived here when it was built.'

'I've always loved to imagine how people lived back then,' he says, gazing up at the house as we walk past it.

'Me too. Like, was this a happy house or sad, you know? What kind of things happened here? It's so fascinating.'

'Is this a good time to tell you I'm a member of the National Trust?'

'They let you be a member under the age of fifty?'

'Hey, history is interesting,' he argues.

I lay a hand on his arm. 'I'm only joking. I love looking round houses like this. My mum and I used to visit a stately home or castle every summer. My favourite was Chatsworth House.'

'It's stunning,' Robert agrees, holding open the café door for me. It overlooks the gardens and we find a table by the window so we can look out. Robert buys us coffee and a slice of cake each. 'I can't believe you like carrot cake.'

'Victoria sponge is so boring,' I say, pointing to his plate. 'My favourite is lemon drizzle, I make possibly the best one in Talting. You know, in my humble opinion.'

'I'll have to try it whilst I'm here.'

'You can help me bake one.'

'You'd let me loose in your kitchen after what you witnessed today?'

'Hmm, good point. I quite like my kitchen.'

Robert sighs. 'Discrimination against the clumsy, I might start a club.'

'If we get T-shirts, I'm in.'

'What would a club be without T-shirts?' He grins across the table at me and holds out his fork to me. I clink mine against it with a roll of my eyes. We are just starting to tuck into our cakes when my phone rings.

'Hello?' I answer through a mouthful of cake.

'Emma is threatening to make dinner, can you please come round?'

I let out a laugh when I hear John's voice. Let's just say that Emma is not the most talented cook. One Christmas she tried to serve still-frozen turkey and we had to have grilled cheese sandwiches, so we all agreed I'd do Christmas dinner from then on. She and John either eat out or have takeaways or pasta with a jar of sauce, which she has managed to master. 'What is she trying to make?'

'A lamb casserole. I'm scared, Rose,' he hisses, as though he's hiding our conversation from her, which it's likely he is. 'She has a cookbook out.'

'Okay, I'll come round and make sure she doesn't put sugar in it or something.' I glance at Robert, who mimes a protest he's never done anything like that. I shake my head to indicate I'm not sure I believe him.

'Is there someone with you?'

'I'm having a coffee with Robert.'

There's a short pause. 'Well, why don't you bring him too? That way it won't be so obvious that I invited you to help save dinner.'

'I don't know.' I glance at Robert, who's sipping his coffee. Would it too much after today? 'I could ask him.' He raises his eyebrows at me.

'Text me to let me know, and come round at six so it won't be too late to avert disaster.' He swiftly hangs up.

'That was John. He wants me to come over for dinner to try to save him from one of Emma's creations – she doesn't have good precedent, shall we say. He actually wondered if you wanted to come too?' I say it casually, because I'm nervous about it sounding like a double date.

He thinks for a moment. 'Well, it would save me from another burger at Joe's,' he replies, not quite meeting my eyes. 'If it's okay with you?'

'Emma will be so busy trying to find out everything about you, I can keep an eye on the dinner,' I reply, keeping things light, but I feel a slight flicker of butterflies in my stomach and I'm not entirely sure why or whether they are good or bad ones.

'I'll do my best to distract her,' he says, giving me one of his smiles that light up his face and making it impossible not to smile back.

Chapter Twelve

The closer to six the clock ticks, the more nervous I become. I sit at the kitchen table scrolling through photos on my phone, thinking how strange it feels to be having dinner with Emma and John and someone who's not Lucas. I pause at a photo of the four of us at our house crowded round the camera, arms wrapped round one another, pulling stupid faces. It's one tiny moment in the years we had together, a moment that passed so quickly we didn't even think about its significance at the time. But the problem with moments is when you know you won't have any more of them, they become infinitely more significant. In fact, everything Lucas and I did or said has become significant now. I wish I had treasured the moments more at the time but that's the problem with moments, you never know when you are about to have your last one.

Our last moment together was in the morning *that* day. Lucas was about to head out for a building job and I was due at the bar late morning. We had breakfast together, which wasn't rare but wasn't an everyday occurrence either. We had tea and toast. There was no bacon or eggs or pancakes or something fancy, just plain old tea and toast, sitting around our tiny pine kitchen table with Radio 1 playing in the background. It was a nondescript day, really, not too cold, not too hot, with a slight trickle of sunshine coming through the light grey clouds. Lucas was in his work gear, tatty jeans and T-shirt, his hair still messy from sleeping, and I was still in my pyjamas, my hair piled on top of my head.

'What time will you be home?' I didn't beg him not to go to work; it wouldn't have even entered my head. I had no way of knowing it would be the last time he went. I wish I could go back in time and make him stay at home, but who knows whether that would have kept him with me or whether he would have been taken some other way. When your time is up, is it up no matter what?

'Probably about seven. I'll get changed and come to the bar,' Lucas said. He often came by to see everyone and then walk me home once my shift had finished; he'd probably eat there as well. I nodded and he got up, putting his things in the sink and leaning down to kiss me on the cheek. He smelt of our magnolia shower gel and winked as he grabbed his car keys from the counter. 'See you later, babe.'

We didn't say 'I love you'. I guess some people say it every time they leave or hang up the phone, but we didn't. We knew it through and through; our love was wrapped around us but we didn't say it all the time. It used to haunt me at night, the fact that I didn't tell him I loved him on that last morning, but I know in my heart he knew that I did and he loved me right back. Neither of us could have been aware that it was our last opportunity to say it.

You never know when the last time to say 'I love you' is coming.

I still wish I had told him it more often. I was lucky to love someone and have him love me back. I shouldn't have taken it so much for granted. If I ever get lucky to have love again,

I will grasp it tightly because I know how it feels when you lose it. I don't think love is about letting go; it's about treasuring it whilst you have it in your life.

I come out of my photos and lock my phone. It's almost time to leave.

A knock at the door startles me and when I pull it open, I see Robert standing there. He's in a black shirt and trousers and runs a hand through his hair as he greets me. 'I thought we could walk over together?'

Pulling on my denim jacket and picking up my bag, I lock the door and we set off for Emma and John's. I try not to think about this feeling even more like a date now we're going together. I know it's not a date and so does he. I think he does, anyway. I steal a glance at him, thinking he's quiet too. Maybe we're both nervous.

It's a cool evening with the sun low in the sky, and the town is still dotted with people who made the most of a dry day at the beach. Emma and John live right in the centre of Talting close to the High Street and you can see the beach from their bedroom window. It's a three-floor town house like the one that Lucas and I used to live in. John throws open the door to us with a wide grin.

'Thank God,' he says, pointing behind his back. 'She's already in the kitchen.' He kisses me on the cheek and shakes Robert's hand, thanking him for the red wine he's brought. John pushes me towards the kitchen and leads Robert into the living room.

Their house is brimming with things. They are always collecting more knick-knacks and have photos everywhere, lots of cushions and a strange abundance of clocks. The walls are white and the floor polished wood but everything else is cluttered. The house always smells of Emma's perfume and tonight that's mixed with the smell of lamb cooking. I push open the kitchen door. 'Hey hey.'

Emma turns round. 'He just invited you so you could help me cook, didn't he?'

I burst out laughing. 'You listened to his phone call again, didn't you?'

She shrugs. 'Have to keep an eye on him. Wine on the table. So, I think it's okay but the recipe makes no sense. This is why it's not my fault that things go wrong; they make recipes impossible to follow. In fact, is it written in French?'

I pour us both a glass and go over to the oven. I turn it down straight away as she has it set so high the lamb would have burnt for sure. I take the dish out and peer inside. It all looks okay, if a bit watery. I stir it and thicken it up, adding some more wine and herbs before putting it back in the oven. I reassure her it's fine and agree not to tell John it would have burnt without me, and then we go into the living room to join John and Robert.

'Everything okay?' John asks, glancing at me hopefully.

'Jesus,' Emma says, elbowing him in the ribs. 'I'm not that bad. Am I, Rose?'

'It's going to taste great,' I say diplomatically, sitting down next to Robert on the opposite sofa to them. I take a sip of my wine and realise that Emma didn't bring hers in. She is asking Robert about his job but their voices are muted suddenly. I remember that photo of the four of us I looked at back at home, some of that night coming back to me. The conversation about a girl we went to school with who we'd just found out was having a baby. 'We should get pregnant at the same time,' Emma had said. 'You two can't do anything on your own,' John said. 'I think our baby would be cuter than yours,' Lucas had added with a grin.

I jump up and excuse myself, rushing to the bathroom. I have to get over this. I have to support Emma, but if she's trying for a baby then it's real. We won't be pregnant together.

I choke back a sob and wash my face over the sink. I can't lose it with them all out there. I feel like such a crap friend. A gentle knock makes me jump. Emma pushes the door open and I curse myself for not locking it. 'Rose?'

'I'm fine, just felt a bit hot, that's all.'

'I always know when you're lying, remember?'

I look up at the mirror, watching her reflection behind me. She looks so worried; guilt pinches me. I don't want this to come between us. 'You're not drinking, are you?'

'I've heard it can help.'

'You haven't talked to me about it.'

'No.' She perches on the edge of the bathtub. 'I see how you react when I mention anything close; I just thought you didn't want to talk about it, you didn't want to know. And I understand, you know. I really do.'

'We always talk about everything,' I say in a small voice. I hate that this could come between us but I don't know how to make sure it doesn't. I don't want to be jealous of her. I don't want to resent her for anything. None of this is her fault. And I know that, but it's so hard to talk myself out of the way I feel.

I turn around slowly. 'I guess we should go back in.'

Emma bites her lip then stands up. 'Will you tell me if I can talk to you about this?'

'When, not if,' I promise, hoping I will find the strength soon, for her.

Emma touches my shoulder then ducks out of the room. I pat my face dry, take a deep breath and go back in. I can feel Robert watching me and I wonder what he sees. I drain the rest of my wine and try to focus on the here and now.

'My father didn't even consider I wouldn't want to work with him,' Robert is saying to John. 'He's a difficult man to refuse. But it did make sense after university to go into the firm; he pays well but he expects a lot. And not just at work.' Bitterness clouds Robert's voice. I hear real pain in his words, yet what he's saying is alien to me; my mum was always supportive and encouraging, never pushy.

'Doesn't he want you to be happy?'

Robert turns to me. 'I don't think he'd ever think of happiness . . . I'm not sure I have, either. But this summer is making me wonder about how happy I am and what would make me happy.' His eyes lock with mine and I suddenly see how unsure he is about everything. I thought he was polished and confident, even a bit intimidating, but right now in this moment, he just seems like a lost boy.

'You'll figure it out.'

'I hope so.'

The oven timer sounds, making us both jump. I look at Emma, who exchanges a look and smile with her husband before heading out to the kitchen. Confused for a minute, I jump up and follow her, my cheeks still flushed from Robert's piercing gaze.

The four of us eat in their small dining room, our elbows practically touching around the round table. The men and I drink a lot of wine and all four of us have seconds of the stew and mash. Emma realises she forgot about dessert and she tells me off for not bringing cake after I admit that I took a pie to Gloria and Graham's. But I can see how pleased she is that I'm baking again. Then John finds a box of chocolates in the back of the cupboard, which we have with brandy and coffee. With a buzz of alcohol, Robert and I leave past midnight with him offering to walk me back. Emma and John shout goodbyes and wave until we are at the end of their road, and then we head for the cottage, a pool of moonlight guiding our way.

'I had a lot of fun tonight,' Robert says, breaking the comfortable silence.

'I'm glad.' I wobble a little as I step up a kerb. I have drunk way too much. 'Can I ask you something?' He nods but looks a little worried. 'How come you came here all alone? I mean, it's not a typical summer plan for someone like you.'

'Someone like me?' He touches my arm to steady me and I put my arm through his, leaning against him gratefully.

'Hmmm . . . single, good-looking, rich?'

'Oh, I'm good-looking, huh?' He grins at me.

I wave my hand airily. 'Come on, you know what I mean.'

'If you're asking why I'm not with anyone then I don't know. I was with a girl through university, it was over three years, and I guess at one point I assumed we'd stay together and get married. Then I came home and she lived in London and we just drifted apart. Looking back, it wasn't love. We would have made it work if it was.'

'But why here?' I press, still confused why he wants to be here for his summer.

'How did you know that Lucas was The One?' he asks softly, ignoring my question.

'I don't know if there's a One, a soulmate; it sort of sounds so final. All I know is Lucas was my best friend and I loved him. We were together for a long time and I never imagined that we wouldn't be.'

'I'm really sorry, Rose.'

We walk down my road, my cottage standing there ready to welcome me home. I stumble again. 'I need some lights,' I mutter as we reach my gate. I push it open. 'I had fun tonight.'

'That's good,' he says. 'Will you be all right getting in?'

'I think so. Rob, do you think you get one shot at love?'

Robert thinks about that for a moment. 'No, I don't. I think if you're capable of love, you can always be loved in return.' He leans in and my breath hitches in my throat. I freeze, unable to move, scared about what he might do, but then he brushes my cheek with his lips. 'See you soon?'

'Yeah, I'll see you,' I choke out, my head swimming with confusing thoughts and my heart thumping with confusing emotions.

'Sweet dreams, Rose. You deserve them.'

Chapter Thirteen

A couple of days later, I let myself into Emma's parents' house. They never asked for their key back after I moved out to live with Lucas, telling me that I should always think of it as my home. When I step into the hall, I push the hood of my parka down and shake off the rain. I take off my coat and hang it up on one of the hooks by the door. I still use the same hook I used during the two years I lived here.

This house was so lively back then – Emma and I would play loud music and Emma's sister would be dancing in her room. Their parents would have to yell up the stairs to call us for dinner and then we'd all crowd around their kitchen table talking about our days with the TV in the background, even though we mostly ignored it.

This house helped to heal me after my mum died. It looked after me when I needed it the most.

Today, the house is much quieter but I still feel the same security envelop me now as I did when I first arrived, torn by grief, needing a home and family and receiving both with open arms.

'Rose, darling,' Emma's mum Sue says, rushing into the hall and pulling me into a big hug. Emma is the spitting image of her mum, even though neither of them believes it; they could be sisters. Sue had Emma when she was still a teenager so they are close in years as well as looks. 'How are you? Thank you so much for coming to help. I told Emma not to bother you as I know it's your day off, but she thought there would be some of your things up there too. It's unbelievable how much stuff we've accumulated. Mind you, it has been over twenty years,' she says in her usual quick-fire way. She propels me up two flights of stairs into the loft, which they converted then left as a storeroom. They've finally decided to use the room, so it needs clearing out. They're still arguing about what it will be, though. Emma is sitting on the floor in the middle, surrounded by boxes.

'Where's Gary?' I ask, wondering why her dad isn't here too.

Emma looks up and grins at me. 'He went to make tea.'

'I've just come from the kitchen and he wasn't there,' Sue says crossly. 'I'll kill him; he's gone to the pub, hasn't he? Leaving it to us as per bloody usual. Right, well, I'm not having it. I'll be back. Thanks again, Rose darling, you look great.' She disappears before I can utter a word.

'Has he really gone to Joe's?'

'Definitely, she's driving us both mad. Come here, look at this.' I cross my legs on the floor and take the small shoebox from her, full of photographs. 'When we used to take our films to Boots and get actual photos back.'

I flick through them, chuckling at Emma and myself dancing around in her room pretending to be the Spice Girls. 'That was not a good hair year,' I say, showing her one of the two of us with slightly mad frizzy locks.

'I still say straighteners were the best invention ever.'

'Is that mine?' I pull a box over, seeing my name on it. I open it up and pull out a poster of a bare-chested boy band star. 'God, I had this stuck to the wall.'

'Don't remind me, that used to give me nightmares.' Emma leans over the box too. 'Look, our friendship bracelets.' She grabs a stack of bracelets that we bought from a past Talting Fair and takes half, sliding them on her wrist. 'Remember all those late night conversations we used to have in our room about whether we'd stay friends or not.'

I pull on the other half of the stack, a lump forming in my throat. We were always worried about growing apart.

'Twenty years of friendship,' I say, lifting my wrists next to hers. I swallow the lump down and look at my best friend. 'Tell me, Em, I want to know.'

Emma takes my hand and holds it. 'I've come off the Pill. It feels like the right time for us. It's bloody scary, though. I don't know how long it will take, but you know how much I've always wanted a family.'

When we were teenagers, we were always fearful of getting pregnant. Sue drummed into us how much she wished she could have waited, even though she loves Emma with every fibre of her body; she felt too young when it happened. She always said that we should know who we are before we take that plunge. In our teens, Emma began to say how much she envied me for having Lucas. It's hard when your friends are at a different stage in life to you. I can see why she felt like that now. When she met John, she began to talk more about wanting to have a family. I suppose it changed from wanting a baby to wanting *his* baby. And I know what a great mother Emma will make. I nod for her to continue. I look down at our hands and squeeze hers, unable to find any words just yet.

'But it's hard. I am excited as well as being bloody terrified and I hate seeing you upset. I wish I could take your pain away. I wish we could be doing this together. I always thought . . . I always thought we would.' Her voice breaks and when I look up she's wiping a tear away.

'It's okay,' I say quickly, squeezing her hand again and feeling a tear trickle out of my eye too. 'I always thought we would too, but you know . . .' I have to stop and find my voice again. 'I always imagined that Lucas and I would have a family; he loved kids and it was just assumed between us, you know? And when you used to talk about it, I could see it. I could see the four of us with our kids going to the beach and the Fair, our kids being friends and playing together and . . .' I wipe away another tear and she sniffs. 'But now Lucas isn't here, I don't have that pull.'

'What do you mean?'

'I mean, I can't see it. I don't have that need like you do. Not yet. I assumed we would have had a baby but I wouldn't have been ready yet, not like you are. I just don't know if it's something I will want or not. And when I knew you were going to start trying, I was jealous, because I'll never have that with Lucas. I'll never have a piece of him with me, but, I don't know, maybe that's okay, because how could I have raised his child without him?' I let out a sob then and she pulls me into her arms.

'I'm so sorry,' she says into my hair.

I pull back a little to look at her.

'I'll never have a family with Lucas and that's always going to hurt, but I never want to make you feel bad for being able to make one with John. Lucas would have been so happy for you guys too. And I am. I promise, I am.'

'Rose, you are my best friend,' she says, brushing back a

strand of my hair and smiling through her tears at me. 'You are so strong and brave, you know? You deserve to be so, so happy.'

'God, you're going to make me cry again.'

Emma wipes a tear from my cheek. 'I just feel so helpless sometimes, I don't know what to do to make things better for you.'

'Just having you with me helps.' I take a deep breath. 'It hurts . . . I don't know if "less" is the best word, but maybe it's more like the pain is becoming bearable. I'm starting to think about the fact that I will have a life without Lucas. You know that I will never love anyone the way I loved him, but now I feel more able to face the future without him. Does that make sense?'

Emma nods. 'Lucas would have wanted you to build a new life, a new future, without him. He always wanted you to be happy and he is up there somewhere rooting for you, Rose. I just know it.'

'Do you really think so?'

'Of course I do. He would never have wanted to hold you back in any way. You guys had something really special and nothing will ever change that, okay? And John and I will always be here for you. I promise.'

I smile at my best friend. 'Friends forever?' I say, remembering us promising that in this very house when we were twelve.

She smiles back. 'Friends forever.'

We lapse into a contemplative silence and sit up here for what seems like forever, holding one another, until her parents suddenly walk in and we pull apart.

'Everything okay?' Gary asks. He's just retired from his

sales job and is finding it hard not having anything to do. He refuses to take up golf or fishing, so he and Sue are going to a salsa class next week.

'We're fine,' I say.

'We haven't done a lot, though,' Emma admits.

Sue lifts her hands up. 'Let's just leave it, we can't even decide what to do with the room anyway. I'll make us all lunch. Come on, Gary.'

Gary winks at us and follows his wife out. Emma looks at me and chuckles and I smile back. Sue is well known for her sudden changes of mind and I love how we have all learned to just go along with her.

'We must look like crap,' I say, taking out an elastic from my pocket and pulling my hair into a ponytail.

'I'm starving. Crying makes you hungry, I swear.' She pats my arm. 'Thanks for listening to me. And you know, you just have to take things one step at a time. Things will carry on getting easier.' She pulls me up off the floor with her. 'And maybe one day you'll fall in love again . . .'

I shake my head at her. 'No match-making. Ever. Deal?'

She holds up her hands. 'Fine, fine. But just don't close yourself off to anything, because you never know.' She gives me a significant look before following her parents out of the room and I just know she's got herself carried away about Robert. It's written all over her face that she's wondering if something might happen there. I have no idea if she's right or wrong to be wondering that. Or whether it's okay to be wondering it myself.

How will I know if and when the time is right?

I follow Emma downstairs and we have cheese sandwiches

and mugs of tea with Sue and Gary, who banter like the old married couple they are and take the piss out of Emma a lot, reminding her of all the silly things she did as a kid. I listen and smile, the familiarity of them helping to chase some of my melancholy away. It's been hard to adjust to never having the prospect of a family with Lucas, but I won't let that stop me from supporting Emma and John. I actually feel better for telling her that I'm not sure I see a family in my future, like it was a secret that I needed to let out. I don't know if it's disrespectful to Lucas somehow to feel differently about things now he's gone to how I felt when he was here, but I think I need to accept that losing him has changed everything, especially me. And it's okay to think about what I might want now I'm having to live without him.

When we leave her parents' house, the sun is setting and we look up at streaks of orange and red criss-crossing the sky in a blaze of natural beauty. I stand still and wish I could capture the colours nature has produced on canvas. 'Sometimes I feel so lost not painting,' I tell Emma as we start walking again.

'You'll paint again, I know it.'

'I think it's that I don't know what to paint anymore. Like I want to paint something different to what I did before but I don't know what.'

Emma tilts her head. 'That actually sounds exciting. It's not that you're stuck, you're just waiting until you know what you want to do.'

I like the way she sees it.

We walk past Talting Inn and glance over at it, the lights flicking on as we pass. I wonder what Robert is doing in there right now.

'I have to tell you something,' Emma says suddenly when she sees where I'm looking.

'What?'

'Robert was only supposed to stay for a couple of days, he planned to leave after the Fair, but after meeting you when we had breakfast at the Inn, he upped his stay to the whole summer.'

I frown, thinking back. 'But when we met him we asked him and he said he was going to be here for a few weeks, didn't he?'

She nods. 'Exactly, he lied to us. He changed his mind after meeting you and spoke to Mick once we'd gone.'

'That's crazy.'

'Is it? The first time I met John I knew there was something between us. Robert had already fallen in love with your art and then he met the artist and decided he wanted to stay and get to know her, you.' We are nearing Emma's house now so we slow down a little. 'Maybe that night when he was trying to tell you something, that's what he was going to say.'

'You don't just make a decision like that as soon as you meet someone, there's more to it. I know he seems to have a difficult relationship with his father; I think he wanted to get away from him.'

Emma shrugs. 'Maybe, but it's still clear he likes you. We can all see it. The question is – do you like him?'

'Of course I like him.'

'You know what I mean.'

I pause by her gate. 'I'm not sure I *want* to like him, you know?'

She nods. 'I understand that. He's just here for the

summer, though. How about a summer romance, a holiday fling?' She grins at me as she pushes her gate open.

'Like either of us knows how to have a fling.' Emma had two boyfriends before John, both lasting over a year. We are relationship girls and she knows it.

Her smile fades and she gives me a more serious look. 'I just see how he makes you smile. It's a lovely thing to see.'

I reach over the gate to give her a hug. 'It's nice to smile again,' I admit. 'I just never thought I'd even look at someone else,' I say into her ear before pulling away.

'The thing is, you may want time to get your head around that, but sometimes life doesn't give you time. Does that make sense?'

I watch her walk into her house, her words ringing in my ears. I walk slowly back to the cottage, darkness falling over the town.

I think about Robert. I don't think he could be here just for me but I won't deny that I'm pleased he is staying. I want to spend more time with him and get to know him better. That moment when we said goodbye after the dinner at Emma's was charged with something. I just don't know if I'm ready for it yet.

My thoughts about moments flood back. I didn't know how many moments I would have with Lucas. We never know. Waiting could mean you lose moments that you will regret losing one day. Maybe we have to seize the moments when we can, when they are here in front of us, even if we're scared of them. I know better than anyone how easily time can slip away from you. How you can think you have forever but have it snatched from you. Maybe I shouldn't hide from whatever may be blossoming between Robert and me, because who knows when I may ever feel a spark like this again? A possibility like this again. A moment like this again.

Maybe our moment is right now.

I pause by my front door; I look up into the sky and wish for a sign from the universe to tell me what I should do. I wish Lucas could give me a sign. I wish I could talk to him about all of this. I wish we could have just one more moment together.

And finally, I wish that I didn't have to make these wishes.

Chapter Fourteen

Robert calls me and asks if I want to come with him to the beach for a picnic. It's a gorgeous day, quite out of character for England, and I'm itching to be outside. I head down to the beach at midday and spot him sitting on a blanket with an appealing-looking hamper beside him. He stands up and waves and I start laughing. 'What?'

'Look at what we're wearing,' I call back as I walk over to him. We both have on light blue jeans and a white shirt. 'You went into the wrong shop, didn't you?'

He grins. 'What can I say, I love women's clothes.' He gives me a quick kiss on the cheek. 'I'm going to concede that it all looks better on you.'

'I would hope women's clothes look better on me.'

'Look, this is a man's shirt,' he protests, trying to show me the label.

'I won't judge. What did you bring?' I peer into the open hamper.

'Mick did this for me, he was very excited. It looks like he packed enough for five.'

We sit down on the blanket and pull out the food. Mick packed Coronation chicken sandwiches, pasta salad, sausage rolls and strawberries and cream, plus a jug of Pimm's and lemonade.

'I have to hand it to him, this is amazing,' I say, piling up my plate. I lean back on the blanket. There are no clouds in the sky and the sea laps peacefully at the edge of the sand. I lean my face up to the sun, eager to feel its warmth on me.

Robert's phone starts ringing but when he sees who it is, he rejects the call. He must see my curious face because he sighs. 'My father. Again. He's getting very frustrated with me being here. He keeps pressing me to come home; he thinks I'm jeopardising my future by taking this break. He wants me to take over the whole firm one day and thinks it looks bad to the other partners.'

'Is that what you want, to take over?'

'I don't want to think about it until the summer's over,' he replies, taking a big bite of sandwich. This strikes me as slightly immature, putting off thinking about something, but then I think about putting off trying to paint again so I decide to stay quiet. His face brightens then. 'But I have some good news. When I went home to sort out your paintings, I had to have a meeting at the office and I passed that art gallery I told you about. I went in to see the owner afterwards, Heather.'

Putting my fork down, I feel heat creep up the back of my neck. 'Why?'

'I wanted to ask how they find their artists and tell them about one that I've found. She was busy but I left some photos of your paintings with her, and she called me yesterday to say she loves your work.'

I stare at him in disbelief. 'You showed her my work without asking me?'

He looks surprised at my tone. 'I thought you'd be pleased. She loves them. I told her you weren't painting at the moment and she—'

Anger bubbles under my skin. 'Why are you doing this? Why do you keep pushing me?'

'Because you should be painting,' he says, his voice rising to match mine. 'She said you need to tap into your feelings and—'

'You know nothing about my feelings,' I snap in frustration. 'God, we've only just met.' I jump up from the blanket, unable to sit still.

Robert stands up too and faces me. 'I just wanted to help you.'

'I don't need your help.'

He grabs my arm as I turn to leave. 'Heather said she'd love to see more of your work, this could be a real opportunity. What about your future? You need to think about it, Rose.'

I shake my arm free from his grip. 'Like you think about yours, you mean?' I fling back before walking away. It's quite hard to storm away on sand; my feet sink into it and I can feel the backs of my legs burn with my effort to get away from him as quickly as I can.

I reach the end of the beach and glance back. I can just make Robert out, standing where I left him. I don't get why he's so desperate for me to paint again. I'm not his pet project. He needs to look at his own life. It's obvious that he doesn't want to work for his father, doesn't want to take over the firm, but he won't face it, so why should I take his advice?

'Rose, there you are.' I groan inwardly as Mrs Morris rushes out of her café, followed by Amanda. 'Have you got a second to look at this?'

Amanda is clutching her sketchbook and smiles at me shyly as she holds it out. She bites her lip and I recognise the nervous look in her eyes. The way you're hoping someone likes what you've created but at the same time doubting your own abilities. Creative people always struggle with self-belief. I used to feel the exact same way about my work. I soften, not wanting to take my anger with Robert out on her.

Sucking in a calming breath, I take a look at the picture. I'm pleased to see it fits exactly what her teacher asked for. 'Oh, Amanda, it's really great. If your teacher doesn't give you an A for that, they don't know anything about art.'

'Oh, wow, thanks. And thanks for all your help.' She gives me a sudden hug.

'You're really welcome,' I say, hugging her back.

I glance at the picture again and experience a familiar pang. I love that sensation when you've created something, of pride and accomplishment; you feel satisfied and content, complete somehow. I miss that feeling. More than I realised. I leave them looking over her drawing, both so happy, and I feel good that I was able to help.

Why is it easier to help someone else and not yourself?

As I walk home, more slowly this time, I wonder if that's why Robert acted the way he did. Was he trying to help me because he can't help himself? Maybe helping me is a way of putting off looking at his own situation.

I stop at the top of my road as I see Robert walking towards the cottage. Sensing me, he turns around, so I go over, stopping a few feet from him.

'I didn't mean to upset you,' he says softly. 'I honestly was just trying to help. I think you're really talented and I'd love to spread the word about your work. But I should have asked you first, I realise that. Sometimes I get so excited about something, I don't stop to think. A bit like when I knock everything over in a bookshop without looking where I'm going.' He smiles tentatively.

It's very hard to stay angry at that smile. 'Look, I do get you want to help, I don't doubt your intentions, but it's hard for me right now, I'm really struggling.'

'I can see that. I'm really sorry. I thought it might, I don't know, spur you on to know that she really loved your work. She thinks you have real potential.'

That's kind of flattering, I have to admit. I haven't had any contact with anyone in the art world since I left college. I have never sought it, not thinking I was good enough. 'I've never been in that gallery before.'

'It's a lovely space, I really think she has a good eye. I . . .' He looks nervous again. 'I did give her your number . . .'

'You're a piece of work, Rob,' I say, walking past him. 'I need a drink.'

He follows me inside the cottage and stops in the doorway, looking around as I start pulling out things for tea then change my mind and go to the fridge and pour out a glass of wine. He watches me take a sip then steps inside a bit further. 'I've imagined what this place looks like inside . . . it's really you.'

I lean against the counter and close my eyes. 'What if I can't paint again?' I whisper.

'You can do anything,' Robert whispers back, closer than I thought he was.

My eyes flick open and there he is, just inches away, his eyes meeting mine, a small smile on his face. I swallow hard and he steps even closer.

'I . . .' I start to say something but I have no idea what, as my mind is suddenly clouded as if I've been covered in a thick mist. I try to move but the counter presses hard into my back and then I freeze, unsure if I do want to move. He reaches out to touch my cheek, which burns under his fingertips. I can't tear my eyes from his. My heart starts to speed up. I'm struck by indecision. Do I want to stop this?

I don't have time to work out the answer as he brings his face closer and, keeping his eyes locked on me, brushes his lips against mine. I let out an embarrassing gasp and his hand moves to my hair and he pulls me closer, giving me a longer, lingering kiss. My lips have missed being kissed. They return his touch eagerly, clinging to his lips, but they feel so different to what I'm used to. His kiss is gentle but passionate and I can feel some of his stubble brush against my chin. Lucas never really had stubble.

Robert pulls back before I make the decision to and his eyes search mine. I don't know what he sees there. I don't know what I feel. My fingers move to my lips, which still tingle from his. I grip the counter, feeling weak suddenly. I just kissed someone else. I have only ever kissed Lucas.

'I'm sorry, Rose, I shouldn't have . . .' Robert says, stepping back from me as if I've burnt him.

Is he sorry for kissing me? Do I want him to be? A sob escapes my throat. 'You should go,' I say, trying to disguise it.

He walks out quickly, shutting the door behind him and leaving me alone in my silent house.

I walk shakily to the table and sit down on a chair. I'm so confused. I don't understand the pull I feel towards Robert. It's as if he feels the same pull towards me, but then he looked so guilty after kissing me. Is it because of Lucas? Does he think it's too soon for this? The worst part is it felt good. I've missed kissing. And I liked kissing Robert.

I need to let all these conflicting feelings out somehow. It's as though they're stuck inside me and the weight of them is starting to squeeze my heart, making it hard to breathe.

I go upstairs and grab a sketch pad from my art room. I go into my bedroom and sit cross-legged on the bed with the pad in front of me. I pick up a pencil. My hand shakes a little as I close my fingers around it. There is an actual pain in my chest. I touch the pencil against the paper and start shading. I have to concentrate hard as my eyes start to build up with unshed tears. I press frantically into the paper, creating dark lines and rubbing at it. The eyes are formed quickly. I pour all my confusion into the paper, close to tearing through it. Then I gasp and drop the pencil, exhausted. The two almost finished eyes stare back at me.

Robert's eyes.

What is he doing to me?

But I can't deny it feels good to have drawn something. I think about what Robert said about the woman at the gallery saying I need to tap into my feelings. Clearly he told her about me losing Lucas. How can I even begin to put down all I've felt on to paper? It seems impossible, but just drawing Robert's eyes has steadied me slightly. He has steadied me. He says I need to get over my fear and paint again and I know he's right. I want to. I really do.

But how do I do it?

I'm tempted to ignore my phone as it buzzes beside me the following morning but I don't recognise the number and my heart instantly starts racing. I am still terrified by the possibility of hearing bad news. But when I answer it, a woman introduces herself immediately as Heather from the art gallery in Plymouth and my heart continues to pound in my chest for a different reason.

'The reason I've called you, Rose, is a friend of mine is running an art retreat in the first week of June up in Scotland. He is amazingly talented and there is a great group of artists going. I think you'd benefit hugely from being there with them. Your . . . friend . . . Robert, isn't it? He came into the gallery and showed me your work and I think you have great potential to create something beautiful at the retreat. Dan is very skilled at getting artists to put their emotions into their work. I don't think you could fail to be inspired by them and your surroundings there.' She tells me it's run by Daniel Smith, a British artist who I have admired for years. I have a print of one of his paintings hanging in my living room – of a woman lying on a sofa. I can feel the love he had for the subject as if it's burning through the painting.

I can't believe I'm being offered the chance not only to meet him but also to be taught by him. 'He is, of course, very selective about who comes on these retreats but trusts my judgement and will welcome you, I'm sure. What do you think?' Heather has a brisk way of speaking that makes me think she gets exactly what she wants from life. I feel a little in awe of her.

'Can I . . . can I think about it?'

'The group is at the maximum number that Dan usually allows so I would need time to convince him to let you join, so please don't take too long. This could be a real opportunity.'

Her words echo what Robert said to me. But I'm left lying in bed long after she has hung up, wondering if I'm ready for this opportunity or not.

I spend the rest of the day unable to think about anything other than Robert and my art. I'm relieved when it's time to go to work, as it might take my mind off things.

But as soon as I see Emma, I falter and drag her outside to fill her in on what's happened.

'Spill it,' she says, shaking a ketchup bottle at me.

I glance around to make sure we're alone.

'I . . . well, Robert he . . . we . . .'

'You slept with him?' she shrieks at a pitch that would send dogs crazy.

'No, of course not, but . . . he kissed me.' I bite my lip and hiss the words out. I sag against a table. 'He said he was sorry . . . I told him to go. And now I don't know what to think or how to feel about it,' I tell her in a rush.

She looks at me for a moment. 'Okay, let me ask this, did you enjoy the kiss?'

I close my eyes and feel Robert's lips on mine again. I swear mine are still tingling from his touch. 'Yeah, but—'

'But nothing. You guys kissed, so what?'

'But I haven't seen or heard from him since.'

'You will,' Emma says firmly. 'He's a good guy, he was probably worried about how you would feel about it. He'll be back, he really likes you.'

'Should I feel bad about it?' I ask her.

Emma shakes her head vigorously. 'No way. You, more than anyone, deserve to be happy and you should do what makes you happy. Robert is gorgeous, let's face it, and he's here for the summer, this doesn't have to be your next big love, Rose. Just see what happens. If you liked kissing him and you want to kiss him again then go for it, but if you don't want to, that's okay too. It sounds to me like he really cares about your feelings and won't do anything you're not comfortable with.' She pats my arm. 'It will never feel like the perfect time. You will always worry that it's too soon and you'll always think about Lucas, it's completely natural. But no new love you have in your life will take away what you had with Lucas, you know that.'

I nod. I do know that. 'You would have thought kissing a guy you like would make you happy, right?'

She smiles. 'It will make you happy. You just need to let it.' Joe comes out to find out what we're doing as it's time to open up, so I don't have time to tell her about Heather's offer yet.

The first person in the bar is Robert. He watches me from the doorway like he's not sure if I want him to come in or not. I smile almost involuntarily over at him and he smiles back, the relief clear on his face. He walks inside and I meet him in the middle of the bar. 'I'm sorry,' we both say at the same time.

Robert pushes his hair back. 'You have nothing to be sorry for, it was my fault.' I experience a pang of disappointment that he sees our kiss as a mistake, but then he smiles and adds, 'I shouldn't have left you like that.'

'I shouldn't have let you go,' I say softly, a little embarrassed. Feeling the need to change the subject from our kiss, I tell him that Heather phoned me and invited me to go on a retreat. 'I'm not sure what to do.'

'No one can tell you what to do, Rose. It's terribly clichéd, but I think you just need to follow your heart.'

Emma brings Robert a drink and I'm called to a table, so we part for now, but I feel his eyes on me from across the room and I sneak just as many looks at him. I think about his words most of the night.

Follow your heart.

I know what my heart wants, but the idea of doing what it wants is terrifying.

Chapter Fifteen

Robert and I spend a lot of time together over the next couple of weeks but he doesn't kiss me again. I am a bit disappointed but I enjoy his company and I don't want to rush anything anyway. I just hope he doesn't think it was a mistake. He calls to say he has a surprise for me and we arrange for him to pick me up later.

Before that, I head to Gloria and Graham's for my usual Sunday lunch. It feels strange to have this thing with Robert but not know whether they would want to know about it.

'You look really well,' Gloria tells me as I stir the gravy for her. 'I'm glad.'

I instantly feel guilty for keeping our communication just to the weekly Sunday lunches the past couple of weeks when before I'd usually call them as well. It's been so hard to know what to talk about without talking about Robert. It hasn't felt right to say anything. Not yet anyway. Because they'll always be Lucas's parents. But I hate feeling as if I'm keeping things from them, or worse, lying to them. 'How have you both been?'

'Well, actually we had a message on Lucas's Facebook page from one of your old friends. Sam?'

I picture Sam with his short, spiky hair and shake my head. 'God, Sam thought he was the ultimate ladies' man. He was very deluded.' I turn to look at her. 'So, you still look at his page?' I couldn't bear to log on to Facebook after Lucas's death. Emma said there were tons of sympathy messages on both of our pages, but I didn't want to see them and face the reality of him being gone, so she thanked them all for me. Sometimes I look back at his old statuses, smiling when he was being silly or looking at the photos of us on there and remembering when and where they were taken, but I haven't posted anything on my page for a long time. I haven't known what to say, I suppose.

'He wanted to let us know he's getting married and to say he would love us to come. He said he would have asked Lucas to be an usher. It was sweet of him to think of us.'

'I can't imagine him getting married.' They kind of lost touch when Sam left Talting for university and never came back, but they were close at school and I think Lucas would have wanted to go to the wedding. Sometimes you forget how the world is moving on around you when all you think about is the person you miss. 'But I'm glad people are still thinking about Lucas. It means he made a mark on the world in some way, you know.'

She takes my hand in hers. 'He made a very special mark on our world, and that's all that matters.'

A lump forms in my throat as I look into her eyes and I worry I might start crying. I'm so grateful to have known Lucas and she's right – what matters is that we knew and loved him. Graham comes in then to tell us an old movie they love is on TV later and Gloria turns away to check the potatoes. I go back to the gravy, glad to have something to focus on.

We dish up the roast and have some of my lemon drizzle

cake for dessert. I have kept half for Robert to try. Graham is keen to watch the film after we've cleared up and when I check the time, I realise I should get going.

Gloria follows me to the front door and opens it, watching me step down. 'What are your plans for the rest of the day?'

'Robert's picking me up from the cottage, he wants to show me something. It's a surprise, apparently.'

'He could have picked you up from here.' I nod but I imagine we would all have felt awkward if he had. 'The village seems quite taken with him,' she says evenly, not meeting my eyes.

'He's become a good friend,' I say quickly.

Gloria looks out at me for a moment then pulls me into a quick hug. 'Thanks for coming over, Rose, we do appreciate it.'

'Don't be silly, you know I love it here,' I tell her, returning her hug tightly. 'We're family,' I say, my voice breaking a little. I have thought of them as my parents too for so long and it's heartbreaking to think that they might worry things will change between us.

Gloria smiles. 'We love having you. Now off you go and have a lovely time.' She pats my hand and her eyes pause on my rings there. 'Take care of yourself.'

'You too.'

Robert is parked outside my house when I get there so I climb straight in to his car – a black BMW. 'So, where are we going?' I ask him.

'I told you – it's a surprise.' He winks at me and pulls away. A blast of air conditioning cools my warm legs and the radio plays softly.

I lean back against the seat, ready to enjoy the drive. I

actually love surprises. Even when I was young, I didn't ask for anything or hunt for my presents, I liked to see what people chose to get me. Lucas wasn't a fan of this, though; present buying wasn't really his forte. One year I remember he got me a tool kit. After that, Emma stepped in to help him. He was better at cards, picking ones that would make me cry and always adding a sweet message of his own to the soppy poem. It actually became his mission to make me cry with them, and I always did.

When Robert pulls off the main road and takes us down a gravel track, I try to crane my neck to see ahead. He just smiles. Finally, we get to the end of the lane and turn into a small animal rescue centre. I turn to look at him and raise an eyebrow.

'Do you remember what you said to me at the Fair?' he asks, parking his car outside. 'That you wanted to get a cat one day. I drove past this place the other day and thought you'd like to look around – what do you think?'

'You remember that?' I ask, marvelling that he can remember that early conversation between us. 'I'd love to look around,' I say, feeling excited already. We get out of his car and go inside the centre, paying a donation fee at reception and heading into the cattery building.

There are rows of glass pens for the cats, leading to small outside enclosures, and we walk slowly down, reading the notes about each cat and seeing the said cat either sleeping, sitting in the sun or staring back at us, some giving a meow in greeting to us through the glass.

'You just want to take them all home, don't you?' Robert says, smiling at one cat standing on his hind legs to try to get to him. 'I'm not allowed a pet in my flat, though, sadly.'

I pause by one cat that's sitting in the middle of his enclosure looking out at me. He's black and white with large eyes and he puts two paws against the glass, giving out a low meow. I stand in front of him and touch the glass with my fingers and he tries to swipe them, getting annoyed that he can't get to them. I laugh. 'Are you trying to attack me?'

Robert comes over to see. 'He's really cute, Rose.' He checks the information card next to me. 'His name is Taylor.'

'Really?' I check for myself. I look back at the cat that is now rubbing his head against the glass and is purring so loudly we can hear him out here. This cat is so cute and, although he's male, he has the same name as my favourite singer, who loves cats herself. 'It seems like fate.'

'I think he's chosen you, Rose,' Robert says, reaching out to touch the glass too.

'Let's go and speak to someone,' I say excitedly. We go back to reception and are shown into a small office where one of the centre staff gets me to fill out a form and asks me questions about where I live and goes through Taylor's background and temperament. I'm extremely relieved when she says I am a match for Taylor and she takes us to meet him in a small room kitted out for cats, complete with comfy chairs, scratching posts and an array of toys.

She brings Taylor into the room and he walks up to us, sniffing us curiously. 'He's a real character, this one,' she says with a smile. Taylor stands up and puts his paws on my knee. I stroke his head and he starts purring really loudly. 'Sounds like a train, doesn't it? So, what do you think?'

'I think it's a done deal,' Robert says, reaching out to stroke Taylor's back. Taylor rubs himself against him. I hope Taylor is a good judge of character.

'I'd love to take him home,' I say, smiling as Taylor tries to attack a toy on the floor.

After we've sorted the paperwork and I've paid the adoption fee, we go into the shop and I get Taylor a carrier, litter tray, scratching post and probably far too many toys. The lady brings Taylor out in his new carrier with the blanket he has slept on here and he gives a disgruntled meow at being stuck in the box. I peer in to try to soothe him and hand him a cat treat, which helps a little bit. The staff wish us luck and wave him goodbye, and Robert carries Taylor outside.

Impulsively, I lean over the carrier to kiss him on the cheek. 'Thank you.'

He looks startled but pleased. 'You're welcome.'

I climb into the back of his car to keep an eye on Taylor and we drive away from the rescue centre with one more than we came with.

Robert stops off at a pet shop so I can hurry in and buy cat food and I can't resist buying an igloo bed for him too whilst I'm there. With the boot loaded with cat things, we drive back to the cottage and I carry Taylor out into his new home. Robert brings in all the supplies as I take Taylor into the living room and place the carrier down, opening it up for him. The lady at the rescue centre warned he might be nervous and that it would be best to keep him restricted to one room today. He might not want to eat a lot, either, she said.

Taylor bounds straight out of his carrier to do a circle of the room, sniffing his new surroundings with interest. We put his litter tray, some food and water in the corner and Robert sets up his scratching post and bed near the sofa whilst I make us both a cup of tea. I bring two mugs out with two slices of my lemon drizzle cake.

When I sit down, Taylor comes straight over and jumps on my lap, sitting up and purring, staring at my slice of cake. 'Um, what do you want?' I ask, smiling at his ploy to get me to share my cake with him.

'Didn't take him long to settle in,' Robert remarks, coming to sit next to me. He tries some of my cake. 'Wow, you weren't lying when you said you can bake, this is delicious.'

'Thank you,' I say, pleased he likes it. I look at Taylor and shake my head. 'Fine, here you go,' I say, giving him a small piece that he eats enthusiastically, still purring.

'He has good taste,' Robert says, sipping his tea.

Taylor gives himself a quick wash then circles on my lap, flopping down with a yawn.

'It's been a big day for you, hasn't it?' says Robert. He gives the cat a scratch behind the ears and we watch as Taylor drifts off, curled up on my lap.

I realise then this is the first moment in a long time that I want to share. I carefully grab my phone from beside me and take a photo of Taylor asleep on me. I post it to Facebook with the caption 'Say hello to Taylor'. I watch it appear on my page and I feel an immediate sense of achievement at having taken this one step forward.

I don't realise I'm crying until I see a tear fall on Taylor's head.

'Rose?' Robert says gently, noticing it.

'Sorry, I was just thinking how happy I feel right now. It's been a long time since I felt truly happy.' I look over at him. 'I thought at one point I'd never make it out of the dark days. Thank you for giving me a day that's been full of light.'

He looks away and I can't make out his expression. 'You deserve every day to be full of light,' he says and I hear his voice break a little at the end.

The sun is setting outside as we talk in low voices whilst Taylor sleeps, until I hear my stomach rumble. 'Do you want to stay for dinner?'

'I'd love to.'

I lift Taylor off me on to the sofa, which earns me a cat glare, but he jumps up ready for action. I leave Robert playing with him whilst I go into the kitchen to cook us a stir-fry. I bring in two plates and a sachet of cat food for Taylor. We watch as he goes straight to the bowl to wolf it down. So much for him not being able to eat. I'm happy he seems to be settling in so quickly here. I curl my feet under me as I munch on the stir-fry. Robert pours us both a glass of wine and the room feels relaxed and cosy with the three of us here.

Robert takes a bite from his plate and watches in horror as a piece of courgette goes flying across the room. Taylor turns to see it land near him and races over to it, but after a sniff, he decides it's not as good as cake and goes back to his own food.

'I'm so sorry,' Robert says, rushing over to pick it up, his face a flaming red as I chuckle.

'I'm very relieved I didn't ask for your help in the kitchen,' I tell him.

'I really am a walking disaster, aren't I?'

And that sets me off laughing again.

When I've finished eating, I switch on some soft music in the background. It feels chilly so I light the wood-burning stove in the fireplace, which Taylor is immediately drawn to, stretching out in front of it.

'Top marks, chef,' Robert says, putting his plate down. 'Did you ever think about taking up cooking professionally?'

I go back and sit next to him, leaning against the sofa and tucking my legs up to one side. 'No, to be honest I only ever thought about painting. I enjoy cooking but it doesn't get into here like painting does,' I say, touching my heart. 'What about you? What did you want to be when you were growing up?'

'I was obsessed with space when I was little. I wanted desperately to be an astronaut. My brother told me that I had to be able to hang upside down for an hour to become one. So I tried it out. We managed to hang me upside down by my shoelaces over the banister. But my mum came in and thought I was trying to hang myself. She was hysterical and couldn't get the knots undone. Our gardener had to cut them with garden shears. Needless to say, I lost my passion for all things space after that.'

'She must have been terrified.'

'She was, I have never forgotten it. My brother was younger but somehow he was the one who teased me. I guess as we grew up, I took on the more protective role. I have always been the sensible one, I suppose.'

'So you gave up dreams of wandering in space for the law.'

'I think I just gave up dreams full stop.'

That sentence stings my heart. I look at this gorgeous and seemingly self-assured man and just see someone really lost underneath. And I don't know how to help because I feel just as lost too. I touch his hand with mine and he turns cautiously to me.

'Don't you deserve to go for your dreams?' I ask him in a voice barely above a whisper.

He hesitates before leaning in and brushing my lips with his. Our second kiss lasts for just a short moment but once again I feel warmth spreading through me at his touch. I lean my head on his shoulder and he wraps his arm around me, pulling me so I lie against his chest. I can hear his rapid heartbeat close to my ear. He strokes my hair and I close my eyes.

I open my eyes briefly to look at Taylor fast asleep on the floor in front of the fire and a contented feeling washes over me. I let myself feel it. I close my eyes again, thinking that my cottage finally seems like a home.

Chapter Sixteen

When I open my eyes, dawn sunlight streams in through the patio doors. Pain instantly hits me from my neck. I sit up and rub it as Robert moves his arm and groans from the stiffness after I slept on it all night. Oh wow, we fell asleep on the sofa together. We look at one another, startled. Taylor jumps up from where he fell asleep and comes over to us, stopping to stretch out and use his scratching post on the way.

Robert gets up quickly from the sofa. 'I'm so sorry, Rose. I should never have fallen asleep.' He runs a hand through his hair and I want to take hold of his fingers to stop him. I recognise his stress movement now.

'It's okay, don't worry,' I say, confused at his sudden panic. I reach down to stroke Taylor, who starts purring instantly.

'No, I shouldn't have, we shouldn't have . . .' He looks outside at his car. 'Everyone will know I've stayed here.'

I follow his gaze and know that he's right – this will be news, but I don't want to feel guilty about a man staying over. 'It's okay, we know what happened. I mean, it's not like . . . it's not like anything *did* happen.'

'I shouldn't have put you in this position, I'll go.' He turns to leaves me but I grab his arm. I hate to hear the pain in his voice. I don't want the loveliness of yesterday to be ruined like this.

'I don't mind that you stayed. We both fell asleep, we didn't do anything wrong.'

'Are you trying to convince yourself or me?'

Taylor meows at me so I bend down and scoop him up in my arms, his warmth and purring helping to calm my anxiety down. I wish Robert didn't look so uncomfortable. I thought this was what he wanted. I step forward and meet his gaze. I could look into his eyes forever and not get bored, I think. Electricity crackles between us. I don't want him to go. I reach over Taylor and lean towards him, searching for his lips. But he moves backwards and my heart drops. 'What is it?'

'This was a mistake. I'm not good for you,' he says, his voice gruff and unsteady.

'Please, Rob, don't say that. This is hard for me, this is the first time I've spent the night with anyone since . . .' I trail off, hoping I won't start crying. Taylor struggles in my arms so I put him down. 'You're the first person I've even kissed . . .' My voice breaks this time and Robert steps back towards me, looking pained.

'I don't want to hurt you,' he whispers, wrapping his arms around me. I lean into him as he holds me, remembering how good it can feel to be held.

'Then don't say it was a mistake,' I whisper back.

He runs a hand through my hair then pulls back, lifting his fingers under my chin and tilting my face towards his. He leans down and kisses me. My hands move around his neck and his pull me closer on my waist. This kiss is deeper and lingering; it touches me from my lips down to my toes and I don't want it to end.

All too soon his lips part from mine. He gives me a tentative smile.

'You are such a beautiful woman.'

My heart flutters a little. It's maybe the first moment I've actually felt like a woman and not a girl trying to grow up. Taylor meows at us so I go into the kitchen and bring out his breakfast. He skips in after me, eager to explore the kitchen, so I give him his food in here and put the kettle on. 'Do you want a coffee?'

'I should get going back to the Inn. I have some phone calls to make this morning, so I better go and have a shower, and Mick is no doubt wondering where I am, why I'm not out on the terrace for breakfast,' Robert says, speaking quickly as if he's nervous.

'It's okay to tell him you were here,' I say, not wanting him to think I'm worried about what the town will say about this. We haven't done anything wrong. Robert smiles and gives me a kiss on the cheek before letting himself out of the back door.

I sit down at the table with a coffee, watching Taylor wolf his breakfast down beside me. I don't understand why Robert freaked out like he did. If either of us should have freaked out, it should have been me.

I think back to him saying he's not good for me and I frown, trying to work out what he meant by that. Maybe he's nervous of being the first man I've been with since Lucas. I touch the rings on my hand, wondering what lies ahead for us. It all felt so promising yesterday coming home with Taylor. We seemed to fit together somehow. But today, it seems uncertain again.

All I know is, I am drawn to him and I am happy when I'm with him. He is making me feel things I haven't felt in a long time. He's made me feel alive again.

I wrap my hands around my mug, trying to make myself as warm as I was when Robert was holding me. Should I feel guilty about another man making me feel like this? It's only been two years since I lost Lucas; is it too soon to want someone else? Will it ever feel like the right time, though?

Taylor runs past me into the living room, jumping on a toy. I follow him and open one of the toys I got yesterday – a mouse on the end of a wand. I drag it across the floor for him to pounce on as my phone rings. I tuck it under my chin to answer Emma's call.

'Okay, Mrs Phillips from across the road told me Robert stayed over last night when I saw her in the Post Office,' she says without saying hello.

I sigh. 'We just fell asleep. That's all.'

'You don't have to explain anything. I told her off. I know we gossip, but come on.'

I murmur agreement but then I freeze. 'I can't believe I didn't think . . . What about Gloria and Graham?' I ask her.

'No one would say anything to them about this. I mean, they wouldn't, right?' She says it like a question. There are a whispered couple of words before John comes on the phone.

'We're all going to the bar tonight for a drink, Robert too, okay? There's nothing to be worried about.'

I wasn't worried before but now I feel a prick of guilt set in. I should have been honest with Gloria and Graham – I told them Robert was just a friend and now they might hear he stayed over from someone else. They will think it's much more serious than it is. 'But—'

'Tonight then,' he says cheerfully, ignoring my concern and passing the phone back to Emma.

'I hate it when John's right, but he's right. You know what

happened – that's all that matters, anyway – and everyone here knows you deserve something good. There was nothing mean about what Mrs Phillips said, I promise. People just want to look out for you.'

'The thing is, I don't even know what it is yet, it's so . . . new.'

'Of course it is. It's all going to be okay, I know it. We'll see you tonight.' She hangs up before I can say no.

Maybe they are right, though. I can't hide away because everyone knows Robert stayed over; that just says I feel like I've done something wrong and I don't think I have. Although I'm nervous about what Gloria and Graham will think. I don't want this to come between us. I should talk to them, but I don't know what I would say.

Emma and John pick me up on the way to Joe's bar, popping in to meet Taylor first. He received a lot of likes on Facebook. He basks in their attention, rolling on his back to show his tummy and play-fighting John when he strokes him there. Tonight is cold and grey, a perfect night to huddle in the pub close to the fire, but I'm nervous about this group date as I feel like all eyes will be on us. We leave Taylor to his dinner and head off to the bar, which is busy with mostly regulars making the trip on such a grim evening.

I'm met by a wall of hostility from Adam – the look he gives Robert makes it clear he still hasn't forgiven me for turning him down and he blames Robert for it. There are a couple of whispers about the four of us settling down in a booth with beer and wine, but I get a lot of kind nods and smiles, so maybe Emma and John are right that everyone here just cares about me. Not Adam, though; it's obvious he's heard about the two of us and every time I look up he's glaring at either Robert or me. I hate knowing I've hurt someone, even though I didn't mean to. The thought of going out with him filled me with dread, but with Robert it just came naturally.

That's not my fault, is it?

Robert is quiet and the conversation is carried on mostly by Emma and John. Joe brings us some food and joins us for a bit. I see him make an effort to ask Robert a couple of questions, and I know his opinion means a lot in here so I'm grateful he's being friendly towards him.

Adam comes to the table to snatch two empty glasses and I've had enough. I follow him behind the bar and ask what's wrong.

'Nothing.' He starts stacking the dishwasher, slamming the glasses down.

'You're making me feel like I've done something wrong. That's not fair.' I turn to go, wishing I hadn't bothered to clear the air, when he stops me.

'I'm sorry, I just . . . I just don't trust him.' He jerks his head to where the others are. 'And I know you'll think I'm just bitter about us but I'm not, I think you're vulnerable and—'

I put up a hand to make him stop. 'You didn't think I was that vulnerable when you asked me out.'

'I've known you forever,' he protests. 'You hardly know this guy.'

'If you genuinely like me, you'd want me to be happy.'

Adam leans closer and lowers his voice, as we've attracted some attention at the bar. 'I do want that but I don't think you'll get it from him. Who is he? Why is he here? I just don't get it.'

I shake myself free and go back to our booth, wishing Adam's words hadn't made any impression on me. I try to ignore what he said – he's jealous, after all – and believe that Robert's doubts come from worrying about me.

I take my mind off it by telling Emma and John about Heather and her offer for me to go on an art retreat. I feel Robert watching me nervously but I'm not as angry as I was about him going to see Heather. I understand him better now, maybe. I think he was genuinely trying to help me. He likes my art and he wants me to find success at what I'm passionate about, something I think he lacks. But I explain my nerves about going and the fact it would mean four weeks away from home, plus the fact that I could get there and not be able to paint anything.

'I feel like this is something you can only do if you want to,' John says. 'We can say it's a great opportunity and sounds amazing for you, but if you don't feel it then that doesn't matter.'

Robert squeezes my hand and I jump a little at his touch. 'You need to go at your pace. It might be too soon or it might be just the right time. Only you can know. I won't push you again.'

I'm not sure if he's talking about painting or us, though. I look at Emma, my usual voice of reason. 'It's up to you, hon.'

I nod and let the subject move on because I don't know what else to say about it. They are right, of course. This is my decision and mine alone. I find myself wondering what Lucas would have said if he'd been here. I don't think I could have gone away for so long without him. I would have been too scared. He would have encouraged me, though, he always did. I never felt any burning ambition for my art when I was with him as it felt like I had everything I could want or need. But now I wonder if I was limiting myself.

At the end of the night, Robert walks me back to the cottage. I do up my jacket and wrap my scarf tightly around my neck to block out the breeze. My hair billows out behind me. Robert takes my hand in his as we walk, his hands warming mine.

'You're quiet,' I observe as we reach my road, having walked in silence almost all of the way so far.

Robert turns and smiles across at me. 'Just enjoying the night. It's so peaceful here, I can see why you love it so much.'

'What's it like living in Plymouth?'

'Far busier. Obviously nothing compared to somewhere like London, but I'd never walk home looking up at the stars. This place really makes you think.'

'Think about what?' I realise how much I want to know him more. I'm used to people I know so well; it's refreshing but also a little bit frustrating how little I know about him yet. I've never understood why someone might be called mysterious before meeting Robert. He is mysterious. It both intrigues me and makes me feel anxious at the same time.

He shrugs but I can tell from his serious expression there isn't anything casual about his thoughts.

'What I want, I suppose. It's amazing how you can navigate the everyday, working long hours and just doing everything you have to do, without stopping for a moment to consider if what you're doing is actually what you want to be doing.'

We reach my gate then and pause to look at one another. A fluttering sensation in my stomach accompanies the meeting of our eyes. I swallow hard to try to extinguish it.

'Do you . . . do you want to come in?' I blurt out the words, unsure what I want his answer to be but liking the fact it's his decision to make and not mine. This time it wouldn't be an accident.

'I think I should let you sleep.' He leans in and brushes his lips against my cheek. 'I'm so glad I'm spending this summer with you,' he whispers into my ear. He pulls back and his eyes search mine for a moment before he leans in and meets my lips with his. It's over too soon and he steps back from me quickly as if another kiss would shake his resolve to go home. It would definitely shake mine. Even a small, gentle kiss like that has sent waves of heat rolling through my body. I'm not sure either of us could maintain any control if we gave in to a deeper kiss right now.

I watch him walk down the road and turn to go into my house, hating the empty feeling that his leaving has produced. Because I know that even if I don't go to this retreat, he will go back home at the end of the summer. There's no preventing our separation. This, whatever this is between us, was always destined to be fleeting.

Taylor rushes to greet me at the front door and he pushes away my sad thoughts. He follows me to the stairs, purring, and I call him up with me. When I climb into bed, he jumps on it and leans against my legs on top of the covers. His presence is both comforting and warming and I'm so pleased Robert helped me to find him.

This feels like the start of a new chapter for me and I know that the only way I can keep turning the pages and moving forward is to see if I could go on this art retreat. I need to know if I still want to paint. If I can still do it. It's time. I can't run or hide from it any longer.

Chapter Seventeen

The beach is deserted when I arrive, thanks to the already grey, cloudy sky. I'm clutching my sketch pad, my heart lodged inside my throat. I lay out a blanket on the sand as close to the sea as I can get without being touched by a lapping wave and sit down, propping the sketch pad on my knees. I hold the pencil in my hand and look out at the seemingly endless dark blue water. I start to shade the sea on the page as I've done so many times before, but I feel blocked again. I sigh and tap the pencil against the pad as the sky starts to move, patches of light blue appearing in the grey.

'I thought it was you.' A voice pierces through my frustration and I smile at Emma and John, hand in hand beside me. 'We just had breakfast at Mrs Morris's. Are you . . . are you drawing?'

'Trying. Sit with me for a bit?'

They join me on the blanket. Emma looks really radiant today in her maxi dress and John is wearing an open shirt and light trousers. They look like the perfect couple, but instead of that making me feel lonely, it inspires me. Apart from occasionally sketching people I know, I've mostly stuck with landscapes, and each type of art has been so . . . well, literal. I have always painted exactly what I could see. Not how what I was looking at made me *feel*.

John is telling Emma about an annoying client at work and as she looks at him speaking, I catch the look of love in her eyes and I suddenly get that spark again. I don't want to just draw things anymore. I need to say something with what I draw. The pencil hits the paper again and I start to sketch them facing each other on the blanket, hands entwined, and then I shade in Emma's eyes and the spark that I see in them. I start to shade a link between her eyes and John's as they watch one another. The drawing begins to take on an almost abstract element as I draw how connected I can see they are. I look beyond them as shapes and draw them as the people I know. I start to draw Emma's heart beneath her dress, even though I can't see it; I imagine what it looks like when she talks with her husband.

I feel a thrill I haven't felt in so long and I'm lost to everything but what I'm creating. God, it feels amazing. My pulse is rapid, I can feel adrenaline pumping through my body and I know I'm smiling even as my eyes screw up with concentration.

'Rose,' Emma's loud voice breaks through my focus.

I look up. 'Huh?'

'We need to get going. We didn't want to disturb you but we've been here for two hours,' she says with a happy grin. I can tell she's pleased I'm drawing again. 'Can we see it?'

'Not yet,' I tell her. 'I'm fine, I can remember it all.' I'm already looking at the drawing again. 'Talk to you later.'

I feel something on my shoulders: John has left me his jacket. I look up to say thank you but they've already gone. I look at the half-finished drawing and know it's better than anything I've done before. It could really be something. It's different. Maybe I've finally let feelings into my art. I bite my lip. It wasn't as scary as I thought. In fact, it feels like some of the weight I've been carrying inside my chest has deflated a little.

A drop of water lands on the page. I flick it away impatiently as I start shading. Then another drop smudges the corner of my drawing and I'm forced to look up. A drop lands in my eye and I realise it's raining. The sky above me has turned black and the beach is completely empty save for me. Crap. I hastily close the sketch pad and grab my bag and blanket off the sand as the rain starts to fall in earnest, pelting me with heavy droplets. I turn, thinking I need to make a run for it, when I look over at the terrace to the Inn, and see Robert standing on it watching me.

I wait for a moment, watching as he waves to me, and then head in his direction, breaking into a run as the rain becomes thick sheets, making it hard for me to see and plastering my hair to my face. When I reach him, he holds out a hand for me and we both dart inside the dining room of the Inn. It's empty in there and we laugh as we shake off the water and ease our fast breaths.

'I was wondering how long it would take you to notice the rain,' Robert says.

'How long were you standing there?'

'A while.' He smiles and pushes a wet strand of my hair off my cheek. 'I've never seen anyone that focused before.' He looks at the sketch pad in my hand. 'It was amazing to see.'

'I feel kind of alive right now,' I admit, the thrill from drawing still with me. I feel his gaze on me and it's like it's burning through my wet clothes and under my skin. I didn't really think people could actually give smouldering looks but Robert can.

'You look alive,' he says softly. He pulls me closer and gives me a soft kiss. I'm keyed up and I can't help but deepen the kiss a little. I run a hand along his chest, his wet shirt clinging to him and giving me a view of his defined abs. I wonder how see-through mine has gone.

Robert pulls back slightly. 'Rose, there are things you don't know about me,' he says seriously, searching my face for a response.

I shake my head. 'There are things you don't know about me but we can find them out.'

He hesitates. 'But . . .' I shiver and he brings his hands up to my shoulders. 'You're freezing. You should get out of those wet clothes. Do you . . . I mean, do you want to come up to my room to change? I can lend you something?'

'Well, we do wear the same clothes,' I say with a smile, pleased he seems to be relaxing again. He seems almost more nervous than me.

Robert picks up my things and leads me out of the room. My pulse beats faster as we walk through the hotel. Robert walks briskly and I guess he's hoping no one sees us. It's a cosy place decorated with wooden beams and log fireplaces, pictures and antiques dotted around in a hotchpotch way.

Thankfully, we make it through unnoticed, up the winding staircase to the top floor and to the only suite. I shouldn't be surprised that he's claimed it, although usually I'd guess only newlyweds would choose it. It's a reminder that he comes from a very different world, even though when his hand is entwined with mine like now it feels like nothing does or could separate us. Robert pushes the door open and lets me step inside first. I gasp a little, having never been in here before. It really is beautiful. There is a grand four-poster bed in the centre of the vast room and there are windows on each side, giving an impressive view of Talting. The room is decorated in rich red and gold, with heavy drapes framing the windows, a polished wooden floor is beneath our feet and an ornate mirror hangs in one corner reflecting us back.

Robert watches me walk around the room. I can feel him studying me as I look at the picture hanging above the fireplace and my eye is caught by his neat pile of clothes. In fact, the room is shockingly neat, although again I'm not surprised. The room is the Robert I first met all over – polished and together. I've had a glimpse that underneath he isn't nearly as intimidating as this room would have you believe, and I like that I know that, otherwise I'd turn and run right now.

'It's a lovely room, huh?' he says softly.

'It really is,' I say, turning round to meet his gaze. I see him glance at my wet top, which no doubt shows off my lacy bra, but then his eyes snap back to mine as if he doesn't want to look.

He runs a hand through his hair and I step forward and take his hand, holding it in mine. I see him swallow. I'm sure he must be able to feel this heat between us. I don't want to lose how good I'm feeling. I want to be held. I want to be touched. I want to lose myself in him and not have to think or worry about anything else. The decision emboldens me despite my nerves and I step closer to him.

'Do you want to get changed?' he asks.

I lift my arms above my head.

'Rose?'

I give him an encouraging smile and he reaches out to lift my top off. He throws it gently on the floor. I start to unbutton his shirt. He touches my fingers, holding them in place. 'We don't need to . . . we can slow down. Maybe we should . . .'

'Is that what you really want?' I ask. He looks conflicted. Moving away from his touch, I carry on unbuttoning his shirt. He closes his eyes briefly then opens them and shakes his head as if he's given up resisting. I smile. I push the shirt off his shoulders and it slides on to the floor next to mine. I can see his chest rising with shortened breaths, as though his heart is beating as rapidly as mine. I watch as his eyes flick to my mouth and the need for him to kiss me is unbearably strong. I can't wait for myself to stop this. I don't want to stop it. I step closer and finally his arms go around me. God, that feels good. You get so used to someone holding you, but when that disappears you forget how it feels. Robert's arms are strong but gentle and I feel safe as our lips meet. He touches them only briefly before trailing kisses down my neck and on to my shoulder. I shiver when they touch my collarbone and he moves my bra strap down and kisses me where it was.

He pauses one more time. 'Are you really sure?'

I wrap my arms around his neck and kiss him to show him how sure I am. I know then his hesitation has faded for good. Our kiss has turned hungry and the excitement I felt earlier ignites again as his tongue flicks against mine. He lifts me up at the waist and carries me to the bed, climbing on there with me. Kneeling, I run my hand through his hair as his hands slide up my back. My body responds quickly, reacting instinctively. It remembers what this feels like.

Like he's a drug, I pull Robert closer, wanting to feel every part of him, willing him to kiss away any trace of my pain and take me far away from here. He lifts me again so that I'm straddling him and he kisses me down my throat, making me gasp a little. I didn't think I'd ever want anyone like this again, but something has taken over and I cling to him like he's the air I need to breathe.

'You're so beautiful,' Robert says, reaching behind me to take off my bra. 'So incredibly beautiful,' he says, moving his lips to where his eyes rest.

I'm just a woman again in this moment; nothing else defines me here, undressed in his arms, in his bed. This is what I wanted. This is what I needed.

As he leans over me, my body falling against the soft duvet, the world around us slips away, leaving just him and me.

Chapter Eighteen

I am curled up in bed with my hands on Robert's bare chest. The rise and fall of it under my skin as his breathing begins to slow down is comforting. We are both silent, lost in our own thoughts. I feel a tear roll down my cheek and I carefully brush it away before it lands on him. I'm not sure why my eyes are wet with tears. Maybe it's because this is the first time I've been with anyone other than Lucas and my heart feels heavy. It was lovely in the moment but now I'm unsure how to feel.

Do I feel guilty about being with someone other than Lucas? Robert starts to stroke my hair. Lucas used to do that too. I close my eyes, telling myself off for thinking about him whilst I'm in Robert's arms. But how can I help it? All those intimate moments spent with one man and now I'm not sure how to handle this intimate moment with another.

'Are you okay, Rose?' Robert whispers into my ear, taking hold of my hand gently. He tilts my face up so I'm looking at him. 'Are you crying?' He looks stricken and I hate to see the pain in his eyes. He brushes away one of my tears with his thumb and I shiver slightly at his touch. 'Rose?'

'I'm sorry,' I say, pulling my eyes from his. 'I just . . . this is . . . overwhelming.'

He's silent for a moment then he pulls me closer to him.

'It's okay to be confused. This is new for both of us. I've never felt this way before. And it's scary. I can't imagine what you're feeling right now but please don't shut me out of it. I'm here. I'll always be here. Whatever happens, okay? I promise.'

I pull myself up so I can lean my elbow on the pillow and look at him. All my conflicting feelings fade when I look into his eyes, and everything seems to make sense somehow. 'I never thought I could feel like this again.'

He reaches up and touches my cheek with his hand and then leans in to kiss me softly on the lips. 'That was amazing. You're amazing. You deserve to be happy. Let me make you happy?' His eyes search mine as he asks the question and I know that he means it.

I smile and feel my tears begin to melt away. I can't believe how well we fit together. I never imagined fitting with anyone other than Lucas. 'You're special, Rob,' I tell him, feeling a little shy, which is crazy considering what we just shared. But he is special. This feels special. I feel happiness surge up inside me. I was worried I wouldn't recognise it if I ever felt it again, but I do. It's reigniting me. Like I'm a burnt-out flame sparking back to life again.

Robert looks at me, his expression full of surprise and joy as if no one has ever called him that before. Maybe this is a first for him too. Maybe he's never had love in his life. He breaks into a smile that fills me with joy and he reaches for my lips, kissing me with such passion I fall back against the pillow. And I know in that moment that I could fall in love with him. I want to. I want to open up my broken heart to him. I want him to heal it.

To heal me.

My stomach rumbles mid-kiss and Robert pulls back to grin as I try to hide my face. 'So embarrassing,' I moan as he laughs.

He pulls my hands away from my face. 'I'll consider it a compliment that you've worked up an appetite.' He leans over me to look at his phone on the bedside table. 'It is well past lunchtime so I'll let you off.'

I smile and shake my head. 'Way to ruin a romantic moment.'

'Nothing's ruined. Let me jump in the shower then we can go and get some food. There's no room service here, unfortunately.' He gives me a quick kiss and gets out of bed. He walks into the bathroom naked and I watch him go, a blush appearing on my cheeks when I remember how he touched me and how good it felt to be touched again.

I climb out of bed and start to gather up my clothes. They haven't dried in the heap I left them in, so I hunt for a shirt I can borrow from Robert. I open up the wardrobe and pull out a crisp white shirt, one that's similar to what we both wore for our picnic on the beach. His musky aftershave lingers on the clothes and I drink his scent in as I hear the shower running in the bathroom. I put on the shirt and turn around to look at my reflection in the full-length mirror. I pull my tousled hair into a bun and smile at my flushed cheeks. I look different. My figure is starting to get back to its usual gentle curves and the circles under my eyes have gone after a series of good nights' sleep. My lips are full and red from Robert's kisses.

A slight frown creases my face. Is it okay that this has happened? I think I'll always wish that Lucas was my first and only. However, Robert took care of me and that was what I needed today. I didn't get forever with Lucas but I did get my first time, and that will always be special. I can't stop the pang of guilt inside my chest that another man held me, but I also can't stop the feelings I have for Robert.

I was forever changed losing Lucas. Everything is different now, including me. I can't alter that. I don't think it will ever be easy to know what is right now. I can't know if this was right or not. It felt right in the moment. I think back to Robert telling me that it's okay to be confused. I'm so relieved that he understands how complicated my feelings are about us.

I step away from the mirror to look for my phone. I need to text Emma; she will help me make sense of all this. I bend down to look on the floor but I can't find my bag. I stand up and look around and see it on the desk. The chair under it is piled with paperwork, with Robert's briefcase perched on top. As I reach over it to grab my bag, I knock it on the floor. It's unzipped so everything spills out.

'Crap,' I say, going over to pick it all up, hoping I haven't made a mess of his work. I shuffle all the papers together and pick up a folder. It's open and I see a newspaper article sticking out of it. I glance at the bathroom door, which is still closed. I pull out the cutting and see it's the article about my art sale. I smile. It's cute that he's kept it with him. The reason that brought him to Talting. And to me. I start to slide it back into the folder but then I pause, realising that the folder is full of cuttings. Intrigued as to what else he keeps in here, I start to flick through and then I understand what I'm looking at.

I pull one out and Lucas's face looks back at me. The gorgeous face that I loved for ten years. The article is about the car accident. The folder is full of newspaper cuttings about the crash and the trial afterwards. They are all about Lucas. I stare down at one heading: 'Not Guilty – case thrown out after police failings'. I gasp and let the paper drop on to the floor.

I feel sick. What does this mean?

The bathroom door opens then and Robert steps out. 'What are you doing?' he asks, looking surprised when he sees me kneeling on the floor surrounded by papers. Then his face drops. 'Is that . . .' He rushes forward but I hold up a hand to stop him. 'Rose, I can explain—'

I look up at him, confused, talking over him. 'I don't understand – why do you have all these cuttings?'

Robert looks terrified. He slowly sinks to the floor on his knees in front of me. 'Rose . . .'

'You have everything that was written about Lucas. Why?' I pick up the pen in front of me, needing something in my hands. Then I look down at the inscription: 'Green Associates'. 'Green?' I say, my heart beginning to pound inside my chest. I raise my eyes slowly to look at him. His eyes are full of pain. 'This is your law firm? Robert?' He nods once. 'Your surname is Green? Robert Green. But not the same Green as . . .' I trail off, unable to finish my sentence. It feels like I've been pulled into a nightmare.

He nods again. 'Jeremy Green is my brother,' he says slowly.

I drop the pen on to the floor. Jeremy Green. The drunk driver who ploughed his car into Lucas that night. Who was responsible for killing my husband. The Jeremy Green who was found not guilty and who walked free from court – no punishment, no justice for taking away the life of the man I loved. I shake my head, unable to take this in. My head spins.

'You're his brother?' I repeat, hoping desperately he'll tell me I misheard him. I will him to tell me it's not true, but somehow I know my hope is in vain. It's written all over his face. The silence drags on and all I can hear is my throbbing pulse.

Then, finally, Robert bows his head. 'Yes, I am. I'm so sorry, Rose.'

Chapter Nineteen

'Will you let me explain?' Robert asks, raising his head, his eyes catching mine.

My knees are aching. I shift position, bringing them up to my chest, hugging them tightly, my knuckles turning white. I look down at the pen I dropped, unable to hold Robert's gaze now that I know his eyes are full of lies. I don't understand. And I need to know it all because this makes no sense. I nod once to let him know he should speak. Right now, I can't.

'I think you've guessed that I don't have the best relationship with my family. I know I haven't said too much about it but I could see that you knew I wanted to get away from them this summer. Well, mostly my father.' He pauses, sucking in a breath. I feel him glance at me but look away again quickly. He's still on his knees in front of me.

'My father is a very tough man to please. All our life he has ruled the family with an iron fist, full of expectations for us all that are pretty impossible to meet. I handled this by doing everything he wanted me to. I became a lawyer and joined his company and basically tried to be the perfect son. My brother, however, handled it very differently. He hated the control my father exerted over us. He got thrown out of a succession of private schools and failed at everything my father tried to push him into. Eventually my father realised

Jeremy would never join the family business as I did and threw money at the problem; he was shipped off abroad, to New York, to a university that was paid to take him, and my mother and I barely saw him for years.

'When he finished college out there, my father brought him back here, hoping he would settle into a career of some sort. It turned out that Jeremy had developed a thirst for gambling out there and basically ran off to London at every opportunity to gamble and drink. They had a huge fight one night when my father found out how much Jeremy owed a casino. He told him he was cut off, that he wouldn't bail him out anymore and he was on his own. He thought it was the only way to get him to change. But my brother stormed out and drove straight to the nearest bar. I only found out about their argument when I came home from the office later that night and Jeremy wouldn't answer my calls. I had no idea where he was, otherwise I would have gone to get him.'

My hands fall in front of my face. I shake my head. 'Stop. Please stop,' I whisper desperately. I don't want any of this to be true. I need this not to be true. I look up then at Robert and see a tear falling down his cheek.

'I have to tell you,' he whispers back, his eyes pleading with me to listen.

I bury my head in my knees.

'We soon got a phone call, about eight o'clock. I remember feeling nervous as I went to answer it. My father was furious and I knew if Jeremy had stormed out in a similar mood, he could end up doing something reckless. I wasn't prepared though for what they told us. It was the police. I thought that was it, Jeremy had died, but no, he was alive but he had been in a crash. That's all we knew then. We went straight to the police station. He was fine, just a few cuts and bruises. I remember the feeling of relief when I saw him and he was okay. He was my brother and I loved him despite everything. I knew how hard our upbringing was, even though I couldn't condone how he handled it. And I felt guilty that I hadn't tried hard enough with him. I had put so much effort into pleasing our father that I had lost sight of my own brother. I hugged him. I hugged him.' He repeats the words like he still can't believe he did that.

It feels like I can't take a breath. I fight for air. The tears are falling fast on to my knees and I can't stop them. Like Robert's words, they keep pouring out and I have no control over them. I want this nightmare to be over.

'Then when I pulled back, I could smell the alcohol on his breath. He couldn't tell me, he avoided my eyes and shrank away, but the police told us. He wasn't hurt but he had killed someone driving on the other side of the road when he lost control of his car. He had left the bar to go to a party and he had killed someone. He had killed Lucas.'

I let out a gasp and I can't stand it. I jump up and start to pace around the room, everything blurry from my tears, my shoulders shaking with each tortured breath. 'Your brother,' I cry out, shaking my head. I am stunned. I am devastated. I am furious. I stop pacing and whirl around to face him. 'How could you have kept this from me?' I demand. 'Get up,' I snap, filled with bitter anger that he's still there kneeling as if begging for forgiveness. As if that's even an option.

Robert stands up slowly. He looks smaller somehow across the room, crying silent tears, ashamed as he looks back at me. 'There's more, Rose. My father went into lawyer mode instantly, taking control of the situation as usual. I just walked out. I couldn't bear to look at either of them. I wish I could turn the clock back – I should have stayed in there with them, then maybe I could have prevented what happened next. Maybe I could have persuaded them both to do the right thing.'

'But no one recognised you,' I say, confused how he could have been here all this time without anyone connecting him to Jeremy.

'I refused to go to court.'

It all comes flashing back like an avalanche. I didn't want to go to court. I couldn't. I was such a wreck. I hadn't slept or eaten; I could barely get out of bed. In the end, John went with Graham. Gloria didn't want to be there either. When it was the day of the verdict, she came to Emma's and the three of us sat there in silence with tea going cold in mugs in front of us, waiting for John to phone us. And that phone call. Emma answering her phone and her face crumbling in disbelief as she told us the case had been thrown out. 'He pleaded not guilty,' I choke the words out, still unable to believe that day.

Robert nods. 'Yes, he pleaded not guilty. The police officer on duty didn't administer the breathalyser correctly so the judge agreed that evidence was inadmissible. There was no proof he was over the limit. No witnesses. My father found an expert who agreed that with the tight corner, Jeremy could have lost control of the car without being drunk, that it was dark and a strange road and there had been accidents at the spot before. The judge threw the case against him out, saying there was no evidence for drunk or dangerous driving, that it was just a terrible accident.'

'We couldn't believe it. The police were so sure it was

drunk driving, we weren't prepared for Lucas not getting any justice,' I tell him. 'His parents lost their only child and the man who did it just walked away. And you knew he was guilty. And you didn't do anything.'

'My father told me he was going to plead not guilty. I spoke to Jeremy and tried to tell him to do the right thing. Admit he was over the limit and accept the consequences. I told him he would regret this, it would always hang over him, but my father scared him too much. He was so convincing. He told him this was his second chance, that he'd get him help for his addictions, that he'd be part of the family again if he went along with him. He told him his life would be over if he pleaded guilty. He was twenty-one and terrified. I'm not excusing Jeremy, or myself, but my father is a very hard man to go up against, he's impossible to beat.' Robert wipes a tear from his cheek. 'I should have done more. I have gone over it so many times but I didn't do more. I washed my hands of the both of them. I told them to keep my name out of everything. I stayed away from the trial. I buried my head in work and pretended it was nothing to do with me. I hate myself for that. I should have made Jeremy do the right thing.'

I feel myself waver slightly. It was Jeremy driving, not Robert, yet I can see he carries as much guilt himself. Then I push any empathetic thoughts aside. This man lied to me about who he was. He kept all of this from me. I have to ask the question that's been spinning around in my head since he told me who his brother was. 'Why did you come here?'

'I'd set up Google Alerts for anything to do with the accident so when the newspaper article about you appeared online, I got an email. I read your story, and I knew I had to come here. I was filled with shame that I hadn't given enough thought to Lucas's family and friends and what you all went through, especially not getting the justice you deserved. I felt sick that I had just carried on with my life without knowing how all of you had coped. Jeremy had gone to rehab and was making progress, but then he cut off all contact with us and we had to make do with updates from his therapist. When he was let out, he disappeared. I felt like I had completely failed my brother and I saw an opportunity to try to help you here, when I couldn't help him.'

I sink down on to the edge of the bed, exhausted by all his revelations. 'You thought buying my art would make up for what your brother did?'

'Not make up, of course not, but I thought if I came here and tried to help you then it might . . . make things easier, I don't know. I didn't really think it through. I just read about the sale happening, and I knew I had to come to the Fair. I wanted to do something, anything, and this seemed like the only way I could, I suppose.'

'But you didn't just buy my paintings, did you?' I look at the bed with its crumpled sheets and a wave of dizziness makes me jump up again, the room spinning around me. I stumble forwards to take hold of the chair to steady myself. Robert steps forward but the look I give him makes him step back again. 'Why did you stay?'

'At first I told myself it was because I could see how unhappy you were and how you wanted to paint but couldn't, and I told myself I could help you. And I liked it here. My family seemed so far away and I could just be myself here. And with you. God, I didn't even realise it was happening. I was lost in my feelings before I even recognised them. I knew

I should go, should stop this, but I couldn't. Rose, you changed me. I wanted to tell you the truth, I tried to tell you after the Fair but I just couldn't. There was suddenly this storm and I wondered if it was a sign . . . When I went home with your paintings, I wasn't going to come back. I wanted to ignore how beautiful and lovely you were, and the pull I felt towards you and this place. I knew I shouldn't come back. I was too scared to tell you who I was and, if I came back, if I stayed, I would be pretending to be someone else.' He sighs heavily. 'But I wanted to see you again. I wanted to be with you. I thought maybe if you got to know me, you might understand when I told you, so I came back . . .' He trails off.

'Everything we had was built on a lie. I don't know who you really are. You've lied to me for weeks. You saw how broken I was after Lucas and yet you still pursued me. You kissed me. You told me you liked me. You made me feel things that I haven't felt . . . God, you had sex with me, all the time lying to me about who you really were. Because what, you thought it would help me? To ease your guilt?'

He shakes his head. 'No, it started like that, but once I began to fall for you, it changed. I wanted to be with you. I thought I could make you happy. I don't know – I started to not want to tell you because I knew then it would be over. I didn't plan it, I swear.'

'I just can't believe this. I felt a glimmer of hope that I could start to move on, that I could be happy again, and now . . . this.' I start to grab my things from the floor. 'I need to get out of here.' I pull on my jeans and shoes and grab my bag. I don't want to be in the same room as him anymore.

'Don't go, Rose. Please. I know I should have told you. I

hate to see you hurting like this, tell me what I can do.' He walks over to me and reaches for my hand.

I snatch it away before he can touch me. I don't want to feel his touch now.

'How I feel about you is real,' he says pleadingly.

I back away from him towards the door. 'If what you felt was real, you would have told me sooner. You were the first man I've slept with other than Lucas, and you knew that. You knew what a big deal this was for me but you didn't care. You're not who I thought you were.'

He flinches as if I've struck him. 'I'm so sorry. Please . . .'

I wave my hand to cut him off. I don't want to hear any more excuses or lies from him now. 'It's best if you leave Talting. I don't want to have to see you here, and nor will anyone else when I tell them who you really are. It's best for everyone if you just go.'

'But . . .'

I open the door and glance back at him briefly. 'Goodbye, Robert,' I say, walking out and slamming the door on him and us all at once, regretting ever having opened it in the first place.

Chapter Twenty

I walk through the Inn as fast as I can without running. Keeping my head down to hide my tear-stained face, I cross the lobby aiming for the doors ahead when I hear my name called. I know that it's Mick but I can't bear for him to ask me what's wrong. I dive for the doors and rush outside before he can catch up with me. For once I'm grateful that it's still raining to prevent any chance of him trying to follow me. The rain immediately soaks through Robert's white shirt. I want to tear it off my burning skin but I can't. His words echo through my mind as I walk aimlessly for a minute, stumbling as I go. I fight to hold back the tears. And then I stumble again, my ankle twisting as I step off the kerb.

I stop in the middle of the road, unable to stop the tears now. I can't believe how I went from a moment of happiness to one of pain as quickly as I did. I feel so betrayed, so let down. I trusted him. I was falling for him. It felt like I had something special again at my fingertips and it's been snatched away. Why is the universe doing this to me again? The unfairness of it all stabs my heart like a knife. I just don't understand.

It's becoming hard to see through my tears mixed with rain pelting down on me. I need to get inside but I don't know where to go. I need to tell someone. I need to make sense of this. Even though it can never make sense.

I turn around and head for Emma and John's house. The place I always seem to run to. When Emma opens the door, her face is aghast. 'Rose, you're soaked,' she cries. 'Are you crying? Come in, Jesus, it's pouring.' She grabs my hand and pulls me inside. I catch sight of my reflection in her hall mirror – I look like a drowned rat. It would be comical at any other time. 'Rose, what's happened?' she asks me more gently.

I shiver. 'I have to get this shirt off – it's his. His shirt,' I tell her urgently.

'Okay, okay. Come upstairs.' She steers me up the stairs. 'Whose shirt is it? Robert's?'

I nod, walking into her bedroom. 'I don't want it on me.'

'Sit down.' She gestures for me to sit on their bed and I sink on to it, my legs shaking. She goes to her wardrobe and pulls out a big fluffy jumper. 'Here, you're freezing and you better get out of those jeans too.' As I get changed, she calls down to John to make tea. She takes the wet clothes from me as I pull on the ones she's found for me. 'Why were you out in the rain?'

'I had to get out of there. He's not who I thought he was. You won't believe it.' I pull the jumper over my head and look at my best friend, who's watching me carefully. 'I slept with him.'

I see her try to control her expression. 'Is that why you're upset?' she asks me gently, but she smiles as if it's good news.

I sink back down on her bed. I shiver again. It feels as though the cold is part of me, right down to my bones. 'No, I was happy, Em. He made me happy.'

She comes over to sit beside me. 'That's okay, Rose. You can be happy.'

I shake my head. 'No, you don't understand. He lied to me. I can't be happy. Not with him.'

'Why not?'

My head drops. I can't look at her when I say this. I can't bear to see the shock on her face mirroring mine when he told me. I don't want to see her anger when mine is pulsing through my veins. I don't want to cry again. 'He lied to us. He didn't come here because he liked my art, he came because he felt guilty and he thought he could ease his conscience by buying my paintings. None of what he said was true. He knew everything about me before he came here.'

'What do you mean, he knew you?'

I rub my thumb over my hand to try to numb some of my pain. 'His brother, Em. He did it. He was the driver that night.'

'His brother?'

I draw my eyes up to look at her. 'Robert's surname is Green. His brother is Jeremy Green. The man who killed Lucas.' My voice is shaking and it breaks when I say Lucas's name. I hope he's not looking down on me right now.

She gasps. 'No,' she breathes.

'I let him touch me. He kissed me. We . . . God, Emma, I liked him and all along he was hiding who he really was.'

'But why? Why did he come here? Why didn't he tell us who he was?'

'Us?' I snap. 'I'm the one he lied to. He didn't just buy my paintings, he slept with me! All because he felt guilty about what his brother did. He admitted it, you know, that Jeremy was drunk that night and that his father twisted the truth so the case would be thrown out. Lucas didn't get justice because of a technicality. Jeremy could have pleaded guilty, he knew he was over the limit, but no, he was a coward. No punishment for killing my husband.' I choke on the last words, letting out a sob, and burying my head in my hands.

She puts an arm around me and pulls me to her. 'But why didn't we know about Robert? I didn't even know Jeremy had a brother.'

'He said he hated what they did and wanted no part of it, so he told them to keep his name out of everything. He stayed away from court. His father is so powerful he probably twisted the news reporting too. No one mentioned Robert. And they don't look alike.' I remember staring at Jeremy's photograph in the newspaper. He looked so young. Robert looks so different. There was no way any of us could have made a connection between them. I wonder if he even used a different name to book into the Inn just in case. That wouldn't surprise me. Right now, nothing would. I've had enough shocks to last a whole lifetime. I can't take any more.

'So, he thought buying your art would help make amends or something?'

'Apparently. He wanted to help me, he said, but then he fell for me, and decided to stay and keep on lying to me.'

'I can't believe it. I thought he was so genuine. I thought you two had something, you know?'

I sniff and wipe away my tears. 'Maybe this is my fault. Maybe I let things happen too quickly. Maybe it was too soon after . . .' I look at my best friend. 'Am I being punished?'

'No,' she says firmly, taking my hand in hers. 'Don't even think that. You've done nothing wrong. He should have been honest with you.'

'I wouldn't have even looked in his direction,' I say quietly.

We are silent for a moment then Emma sighs. 'I'm so

sorry, Rose. I thought he was . . . I thought he was going to make you happy. I thought what you had was real.'

'None of it was real.'

'I don't know. I think the way he feels about you is real,' she says tentatively. 'I can't believe he would lie about that.'

'He's lied about everything else.'

John knocks softly on the door. 'Do you two want that tea?' he asks, holding two mugs. He looks at me. It's obvious I've been crying. 'You told her?' he asks Emma.

'Told me what?' I ask as Emma frantically shakes her head. 'Told me what?' I repeat, turning to her.

'It doesn't matter now.'

John steps back, seemingly realising there's more to our conversation than he first thought. 'I'll let you—'

'No,' I say. 'Tell me what's going on.'

Emma looks at me, her face full of empathy. 'I just did a test, before you got here. I'm pregnant.'

Everything stills. I see the way Emma looks at me, as if I might shatter into a hundred pieces. The worst part is – I'm worried that she's right. She didn't want to tell me after I burst into her house to cry on her shoulder again. This should be a happy moment for her, for John, for them both. I remember the painting I started of them on the beach and the light shining out of her. I know now where that radiance came from. It's bursting out of her. This is what she's always wanted. And I can't be happy for her. I feel terrible for thinking it, but I can't. I stand up. 'I need to go, I'm sorry. You two should be celebrating and I want to celebrate with you, but I can't. I just can't.' I push past John, who tries to grab my arm, but I shake him off. I hear Emma call my name and plead with me to come back but I'll just bring them both down. This is their moment and all I can think about is what's happened to me.

I break out of their house. The rain has slowed to a drizzle on the late afternoon breeze and I suck in the outside air, feeling lost and alone. The sky is as grey as my heart. I let down my best friend. I was betrayed by the man I was falling for. I miss my husband so much it hurts. I don't know what to do. I look around me, at the place I've lived in all my life, and I feel like I'm drowning in memories and pain. I need to get out of here. I need to be far away. I need to be able to breathe again. And I can't do that here, not right now.

As I walk back to my cottage, I can make out some lights ahead.

I frown and try to lean forward to see what it could be, but I can't make out what the light is until I get closer to my house and I stop. Hanging on the tree in front of my house are fairy lights, switched on and shining down on me. I stare at them, confused as to how they got there.

Then I remember Robert commenting how dark my road seemed at night and I wonder if he did this. He could have done it while I was at the beach this morning. I can see how brightly they will shine at night and I'm confused by this man. Why did he do this? It's like he cares about me. Like he does want me to be happy.

So why did he lie to me?

I wish these lights he left me could guide more than just the way home.

Then I look away. I can't bear to look at them any longer. I don't want to be reminded of him right now. I want to forget him and how he's made me feel. But it seems like an impossible task.

My phone beeps with a message. I pull it out of my bag nervously. Is it from Emma and John? Or could it be Robert? Taking a deep breath, I look and see it's from Amanda. My heart sinks. I'm not sure whether it's from relief or disappointment.

I got an A on my art project at school! Thank you for your advice! Xx

I feel a glimmer of pride in her and in myself.

I step up to my door and see my art supplies from the beach propped up under the porch. The start of my painting of Emma and John. Robert must have left it all here for me. I ran out of the Inn so quickly I forgot it all. I wonder if he's done what I asked and left it on his way out of Talting. I don't want to be around to find out, though.

A flash of inspiration strikes and I know how I can get away from all the pain here. I know exactly where I want to be right now.

I open the door and call out for Taylor, who lifts his head from his position curled up on the sofa. I go over and sit down next to him, clutching my phone and gathering my nerve to make the call. I scroll through to find Heather's name and hope that I'm not too late.

Chapter Twenty-One

Two days later, I'm on a train and heading to the art retreat in Scotland. The Cornish countryside blurs past my window and I lean back in the seat, relieved to be on my way.

Heather was surprised to get my call, having figured I had decided it wasn't for me, but agreed to talk to Daniel Smith and her persuasion worked; he agreed I could join them. I went round to see Amanda and Mrs Morris and asked them to look after Taylor for the four weeks I'll be away. It was quite a wrench saying goodbye to him, actually, but I know they'll spoil him rotten.

I stopped by the pub to talk to Joe, who told me not to worry about the bar and that he'd keep an eye on the cottage for me. He asked if I was planning to say goodbye to Emma – she had been pretty upset during her last shift and told him she'd left me messages, which I hadn't returned. I feel full of guilt at the fact that I am unable to be happy for her and John right now. It's just all too much to deal with. In the end, I just texted Emma to say I was going on the retreat. She still hasn't replied and I can't say I blame her. All she'd wanted was to tell her best friend her happy news, and I let her down.

There was one more thing I had to do before I made my flit from Talting. Robert had told Mick who he really was before he left the Inn – I knew that it would quickly be all over town and that Gloria and Graham should hear it from me. They deserved that at the very least.

It was so much easier when the drunk driver who crashed into Lucas was this abstract evil figure I could pour my hate on to. I didn't know anything about him and now I know everything. And I hate that. Now I know exactly who he is and where he came from. I know his brother. I know why he wasn't found guilty. I know why he's out there walking and living when Lucas isn't.

Graham opened the door to let me in, watching me as he led me into the living room where Gloria sat. I wondered what my face looked like to them. I couldn't sit down with them, I felt too restless, too pent up with all the emotions that I am still struggling to work my way through. I paced back and forth in front of them as I told them what Robert had told me. I could barely contain my tears as I watched them take in what I was saying. They held hands at one point and it almost broke me.

'I knew there was more going on than you wanted to tell us,' Gloria said, crying quietly.

'I'm sorry, I should have told you. But I didn't want to hurt our relationship. You both mean so much to me.'

'I can't imagine how it must have felt when he told you who he was,' Graham said.

'How it felt?' Gloria turned to her husband. 'He wouldn't have been here at all if it wasn't for . . .' She looked at me and I felt so ashamed. She blamed me for him being in Talting. And she was right to.

'Gloria, this wasn't Rose's fault. She was just trying to move on. You know how hard this has been for her too.'

Gloria let out a sob. 'I'm sorry, I can't . . .' She jumped up from the sofa and hurried out of the room. I heard her go upstairs and close a door behind her.

I looked at Graham, tears in my eyes. 'What do I do?'

'Nothing. You will go on your art retreat and we'll be fine. This isn't something for you to fix. You didn't know who he was any more than we did. It's taken us a long time to move past what happened, even with our faith. You never expect you're going to have to decide whether to forgive someone who took something so precious from you, when you've believed in forgiveness all your life. And it's something that we have to keep working on, keep trying. It's not a one-time thing.' He got up and came over to touch my shoulder. 'We'll be okay. Gloria will be, I promise. She knows, as I do, that Lucas would want you to be happy again. We all know that. We knew him. Just remember that.'

'But he wouldn't want me to be happy with Robert.'

'He would trust your judgement, he always did. And so do we.'

I left their house, my heart heavy. I still don't know if Gloria will be able to move past this. I don't want to lose her, or Graham, from my life. They are my family. And I know Lucas would have been gutted to see us fall apart without him like this. I'm hoping that my going away will give us all some much needed breathing space and we can work it all out when I get back to Talting.

My phone vibrates, signalling a new email. When I go to my inbox, my heart almost stops when Robert's name appears. He's sent me an email from his work address. I let out a shaky breath. I stare at my phone, deliberating as to what to do. Read it? Or just delete it?

The pull to know what he has to say is too strong to resist.

Dear Rose,

I am back in my flat in Plymouth and it has never felt less like my home. I didn't even spend two months in Talting but the place got under my skin. And into my heart. Mostly because of you.

I know that you will find it hard to believe how much I care about you now. But I swear that I never wanted to hurt you. I came to Talting with only good intentions and I never expected to feel the way I do about you. I know that doesn't justify me not being honest with you all about who I was. But maybe one day you can understand why I found it so hard to tell you when I knew it would be the end of everything between us. I wish more than anything that we met as strangers. I wish for so many things.

Mostly I suppose I wish that it wasn't the end for us. That one day I could be in your life again. I know we had something special. And maybe I have no right to be emailing you or hoping that there is some place in the future for you and me. But I'd always regret it if I didn't reach out to you.

I love you, Rose. It's something I didn't plan and I know it's something you don't want to hear right now. But you need to know how special you are to me.

I don't want to say goodbye to you but I'll respect your wishes if you ask me to. I wish for you the life you want. I wish you all the love in the world. And I wish one day I can hold you in my arms again.

Yours always,
Rob

I put my phone down and wipe away the tear that has fallen down my cheek. I lean my head against the window and turn away so no one can see I'm crying. He loves me. There was a time when I didn't think I would ever have love in my life again. And here it is being offered to me by someone who will forever be linked to the person that cost me the love of my life. Why did it have to be him? Why did he have to come into my life and cause such chaos?

I miss the one person I shouldn't miss. My heart is full of those three words 'I love you' and I hate myself for it. Everything is a complicated mess. All I know after reading his email is that I can't bear to reply and tell him that I want this to be goodbye for good. That would be a lie.

But I don't understand why I can't say goodbye to him now that I know who he is, and that he's been lying to me all this time.

Chapter Twenty-Two

Sunlight streams through the window, waking me up. I open my eyes, disoriented, and it takes a moment to realise that I've arrived at the retreat, and this is my bed for the next few weeks.

After taking the train to London, I flew to Edinburgh and then got on to another train to take me beyond the city, into a regional park. At the local station, I was met by a teenage boy in a four-by-four, waiting to drive me to the sheep farm where the retreat is being held.

We bounced along the twisting lanes in semi-darkness, and then across a field to the row of cottages on the edge of the farm where everyone would be staying for the retreat. The other cottages appeared to be empty, and after my long journey I was too exhausted to explore any further, so I collapsed straight into bed.

I yawn and check the time, and see it's later than I'd planned and the breakfast introduction meeting must have long passed. I jump out of bed and hurry into the bathroom to shower and dress. The cottages were perhaps once two barns that have been converted into small and cosy places to stay in. Mine has two floors and two bedrooms – although I'm not sharing it with anyone as far as I can tell – and is decorated in chintzy florals. The smell of fresh lavender wafts through from the table by the door. I pull on warm clothes as despite June having arrived, the air is chilly here. Then I head outside to try to find everyone.

Even though I'm still tired, the peacefulness of the place settles over me as I walk and I experience that rare feeling that I'm exactly where I'm supposed to be.

As I approach a woodland area just outside the cottage, I see five people are sitting in a circle on the grass and they all turn to look at my approach. The guy at the head of the circle stands up and offers his hand to me. 'You must be Rose. I'm Dan,' he says, tipping his head so his sunglasses slip down a little. Daniel Smith was a big deal in the seventies and is still considered one of our modern art greats. I shake his hand and tell him I'm grateful he fitted me in here. 'You can thank me by being great. Now, come and join us. We're just getting started.' He speaks with a heavy Yorkshire accent and is wearing skinny jeans, even though he must be in his sixties by now. His T-shirt shows off the tattoos that cover most of his arms. He kind of looks like an ageing rock star and is exactly how I'd pictured him.

I'm introduced to the other four artists and realise I'm the youngest here by ten years. I sit down on the grass with them and cross my legs like they have. I'm a bit worried how William, the guy to my right, is going to get back up again as he looks about seventy.

Dan clears his throat. 'Now we're all here, I want to say welcome. Thank you for coming. The main reason I run a retreat each year is to help artists feel inspired again. I lost my way once. I was a struggling young artist and I fell in love with a girl who shattered my heart. How could I paint then? How could I connect with my talent again when nothing inspired me?' He seems to look directly at me then and I shift uneasily. 'The answer was to look into that shattered heart of mine and paint how I felt about her.' He picks up a sketch pad and opens it to a page where he has drawn several pictures of a woman. I lean forward and recognise the woman from the print I have hanging in my cottage back home. 'My pain inspired me. It was hard to paint her after she broke my heart but it was the best way to deal with all the hurt, and in the end helped me to move on. The reason my painting of her became my most sought-after work was people felt something when they looked at it. They understood what I was feeling. They had felt that way too. It was a shared moment between us.' He sighs wistfully as if remembering that time. I lean forward, fascinated. I knew I could learn from this man but this is so close to what I'm going through. 'You're all here because you've become too scared to paint. You don't feel inspired because you're not looking in the right place. I see fear on your faces but you will only be free if you face that fear. Art is fear. Art is pain. And art is beautiful because of that.'

I hadn't thought of it like that before. I have always played it safe with my art. And I have always been a good, but not great, artist. I want to try it this way. I want to face my fears. I just hope I'm able to take this leap.

A woman to my left who introduced herself as Pam nods in agreement. She has a blue stripe in her grey hair. 'I've never had any confidence with my painting. My family always said I didn't have any talent so I turned my back on it all, but I'm retired now and, well . . . I want to be free of this fear I have that I'm no good.'

'You should only listen to yourself, Pam. No one gets

anywhere by doing what other people tell them to do,' Dan tells her.

Pam's admission seems to inspire William, as he clears his throat and we all turn to look at him. 'I'm an alcoholic. I used to think that drinking made my art better but it stopped me feeling all the difficult things that could have inspired me. I realised it was all rubbish. I wanted to have something to say again. I have been sober for two years now.' He looks a little embarrassed but Dan starts clapping and we all join in.

Julia speaks then. She's the closest in age to me, with lovely auburn hair and a smile that could light up the whole room – if we were indoors, of course. 'I had a child when I was a teenager. I gave her up for adoption. My family put so much pressure on me and the father disappeared. I have always painted but I've never painted what I really wanted to; that's why I wanted to come here and open up that part of my heart I've locked up for so many years. I have a husband now, and a family, but it still haunts me, I suppose. I've never been able to find her.' She touches her heart. 'She's in here, though.' She brushes at her eyes and I do the same.

Peter gives her hand a squeeze. He's in long shorts even though it's freezing out here, and I have to kind of admire his spirit. 'My wife left me last year and I thought she was my muse. She has always inspired my work and I felt so . . . depleted when she left. It felt like I'd never be able to paint again, but then I got angry and I felt more inspired than I had in years. I want to feel that pain, I want to harness it and use it wisely. I need to make something good out of all this hurt, I suppose.' He looks a little embarrassed by the venom in his voice. 'I want to be able to forgive us both.'

I'm struck by their bravery and honesty. If nothing else,

they have inspired me. So then the girl who hated reading aloud in English so much that she used to fake being sick to her mum instead of risk being called on, tells these people she's never met before just why she's here. 'Someone I trusted hurt me and I feel . . . betrayed. I don't know how to get past his lies, but I want to. I feel as if there's so much inside of me that I want to get out, you know. But I've never really painted how I feel before. I'm scared that I'll find out how I feel, and not like it.' I realise how raw my pain over what happened with Robert is but that I also want to find a way to move past it.

'This has been brilliant,' Dan says, smiling at us all. 'You've decided what you want to do, and during these four weeks we will make it happen.'

We all start walking back to the farm and I hang back from the others, wondering whether I can really do this.

Dan touches my arm. 'Just put it all down on paper, darling.'

'Darling?'

He grins. 'You're going to be trouble, I can see that. Come on, I think we could all do with a pub lunch, don't you?'

The pub lunch turns into a session that stretches well into the evening. Dan persuades me to have two tequila shots and suddenly I feel like I'm on top of the world. I'm very aware that I don't want to sink into drink as a way to numb everything that's happened, though; I want to do what Dan led us all here to do – paint it all out. And I don't want to wait. As we walk back to the cottages, midnight approaching, I announce loudly, and most likely slurring my words, that I'm going to start right now. Sleeping is for wimps. I stagger into my cottage and try to grab what I need, giggling as I knock my knee on the coffee table.

When I go back outside, I realise I probably should have brought a coat, but then I remember coats are for wimps too. I find a good spot on top of the hill and look out at the farm and the parkland beyond, lit only by the stars and moon above me. It's so strange – almost eerie – not to see any artificial lights. Grass on rolling hills stretches out as far as I can see until the woods appear with their tall trees that may have stood on this spot for hundreds of years. The whole landscape is rugged and untouched. So different to Talting, but beautiful in its own way.

Ten minutes after sitting down on the dewy grass, sketch pad open on my lap and pencil in my hand, even though it's too dark to really see anything, Dan comes and sits down beside me. And one by one the other artists join us, no one wanting to sleep right now.

'Usually, I'd just paint the landscape,' I say, speaking in a whisper as it's so quiet out here. I'm sure I hear an owl hoot in the distance.

Dan leans back on his hands. 'Instead of painting what you're looking at, think about what it makes you remember, what it says to your heart,' he says, so softly I think I'm the only one who can hear him. 'If you were trying to tell someone what this place makes you feel, what would you say? Just don't say it, paint it. A painting is a visual story. You're trying to make the person looking at it feel how you felt painting it.'

'What if you don't know how you feel, though?'

'That's still a feeling, honey. Confusion. Indecision. Conflict. It can all be shown on that white page in front of you. Tell it what's in your heart.'

I nod. I know he's right. This is what I've been scared to do since I first held a pencil in my hand. Bare my soul on the page. 'What if I don't like what's in my heart, though? What if I don't like how I feel?'

Dan thinks for a moment, and lifts his face to look up at the twinkling stars above us. My heart thuds painfully in my chest as I think about painting what I feel. It would be so easy to go back to painting landscapes and hiding from all the emotions circling like birds inside the deepest corner of my heart. But do I really want to keep taking the easy way out? After losing Lucas, I couldn't paint because it all seemed so pointless when I was dealing with something so devastating. And I don't think I can go back now. I don't want to go back either. I want to keep moving forward. And dealing with everything I'm feeling seems like the only way I can do that.

Dan answers my question finally. 'That's how you know you're feeling something worthwhile.'

Chapter Twenty-Three

The following morning, I feel more hungover than I ever have in my life. Including the morning after my twenty-first when Lucas and I did shots on the beach and were woken up by the sea lapping over our feet after passing out on the sand. I groan as I stagger out of the cottage.

Bloody tequila shots.

I walk into the main farmhouse where the others are seated at a long pine table filled with an array of breakfast foods and jugs of juice. Dan follows close behind me and we sit down. I pour myself a black coffee and put bacon, eggs and toast on my plate, needing something to bring me back into the land of the living.

'Now I've checked the weather, which is something I never thought I'd do, and it's going to be dry, so I thought we'd start our first proper day of work outside,' Dan says, pouring himself a coffee and not touching any food. 'I don't do any bullshit exercises like they make you do in art school, like painting yourself as a tree or anything.'

'Is that why you were asked to leave art school?' Blue-streak-in-her-hair Pam asks with a smile before realising what she just said and opening her mouth in horror. Despite saying she lacks confidence in her art, she doesn't seem to lack it in expressing her opinions, which I must say I admire. We fall into an uneasy silence, looking at Dan to see how he might react. We've all heard stories about some artists and their diva-like behaviour.

Dan roars with laughter, making us all instantly relax and smile. 'Actually, yes. Art school can teach techniques but not how to be an artist. You are either born to be one or not. It's all about your passion for the subject.'

I sip my coffee, letting his words sink in. I think back to my art teacher telling me I wasn't putting any of myself into my work. Was I born to be an artist? Can I actually be a great one like Dan is? I'm in the best place to find out. But that doesn't stop the butterflies begin to circle inside my stomach when I think about painting how I feel. Because to paint it, I need to examine it. I need to relive it. I need to wallow in it. And I've spent every single day since that terrible night desperately trying to avoid doing just that.

After breakfast, we all troop behind Dan across fields to a patch of woodland. All we have with us is our notebooks and pens. He said we need to do some planning before we can get started. He was right about the weather – it's clear, dry and sunny, but there's still a chilly breeze so we're all wearing jackets.

'I've never been the outdoorsy type,' Julia confides to me as we walk into the patch of trees. Her auburn hair waves around her shoulders in the breeze. 'My husband is always trying to get me to take the kids camping but I don't know how I would survive,' she says, looking nervously at the dark canopy of leaves above us.

'I grew up in a coastal town so I've spent a lot of my life outdoors. Don't you ever paint outside, then?'

She shakes her head with a shudder. 'What about bugs?'

she asks, making me laugh.

'Being outside always makes me feel hopeful,' Peter says, turning around. He's left the shorts behind today and is wearing chinos instead. 'Whatever happens in my life, nature is always there. The seasons always come around, there is always sunshine and rain, and always things dying and being reborn. Is that corny?'

'I like that idea,' I tell him. 'I've always been inspired by nature. Not so much lately, though.'

'Maybe you haven't been looking in the right place,' he suggests.

I wonder if I'll find the right place here.

Dan finds a clearing for us to stop in. Twigs and leaves crunch underfoot as we follow him. He lays out a blanket for us to sit on in a circle. 'So, I always aim to have a goal on a retreat. I think creating one great piece whilst you're here would mean this has all been worthwhile – what do you think?' We all nod and murmur our agreement. 'So, what will you do? I want you to paint the subject that scares you the most. This is what this retreat is about, after all – what do we fear the most? You've told us why you're here but I want you to write down what you've been avoiding painting and how whatever it is makes you feel. Words like "angry", "rage", "raw", "pain" are all excellent mood words that could spark off an idea for a painting.' He winks at us. 'They have done many times for me in the past.'

We lapse into silence once he's finished speaking, each of us trying to decide what to write down. I stare down at the blank page. There is always something slightly terrifying and yet exciting about looking at a blank page. The potential for many possibilities, but also the worrying prospect of not being able to come up with anything at all at the same time.

I'm scared of so much. Of exploring that black space I lived in after Lucas died. There was so much sadness then, and anger too at him being snatched away from me like that. I lost myself at the same time as losing him.

I fear retreating back into that darkness.

Finding out who Robert was has filled me with anger again. I have been betrayed. I feel bitter at having more pain to deal with, having dealt with so much already. I opened my broken heart to him. I let him start to heal some of my pain. There was a spark of hope that I could fall in love again.

That hope seems very far away right now.

But it had been there.

I have moved away from that dark time and I don't ever want to go back to it. I write down the mood words as Dan suggested. He walks around the group watching us as we write but I block him out. I block the world out and examine what's inside my heart.

Fear, anger, loneliness, betrayal, uncertainty, sadness, grief.

But I force myself to also write down how I felt before Robert confessed everything and we both left Talting.

Passion. Spark. Warmth. Hope. Happiness. Light.

Two extremes. Robert and Lucas. Two sides of my heart.

An idea forms in my mind about what a painting of my heart might look like. I can't just paint landscapes anymore. I have to paint something meaningful, something real.

I look at the light slipping through the trees and send up a message of hope, willing that everything will be okay.

Chapter Twenty-Four

Listening to LeAnn Rimes turned up loud in my cottage, I watch the rain dance against the window behind me. Curled up on the sofa with a blanket draped over me, I hold a sketch pad and pencil in my hand. Dan getting me to think about what I fear to draw was helpful. Putting all my feelings down on paper in black and white was emotional in itself. It made me acknowledge that I've been through life-changing pain, and I can't hide from that anymore.

Which sounds scary as hell.

As is art.

But I want to inspire people. I feel as if I was born to be an artist, and now I need to become one.

I need to decide how to share this on canvas. I liked the abstract drawing that came out of watching Emma and John on the beach together. I bite my lip; I don't like how I left things with them. It's weird not being in constant contact with Emma. I want to tell her how things are going here but I'm scared she won't want to speak to me after I walked out on her. Until I'm sure I can be the friend she needs, it's best to stay quiet. Maybe it'll be good for us to have this break. I wonder sometimes if I've been a burden on them both.

Absentmindedly, I sketch out an outline of a large heart on the sketch pad. I look at it, tapping my pencil on my knee

186

in time with the music streaming into my ears.

I look at the outline of the heart and think about how I could convey the darkness I felt within my own. It was as if I lived in summer with Lucas and when he was taken from me, a group of trees had their leaves stripped from them by a sudden wind rushing in and ripping them away. Like summer turned to winter in an instant.

Then sunshine had begun to thaw the winter. The darkness was starting to become light. Robert came into my life when spring was arriving, and he continued to brighten the path I was walking along, making it feel as if summer might soon fill my heart again.

I start to sketch as my thoughts move from my brain and flow down into my hand. On one side of the heart, I draw a bare tree with winter surrounding it. Some of the branches are Lucas, some are Robert and some are the love I've yet to find or lose. Snowflakes and icicles touch the branches and each one represents some of the pain, some of the loneliness, some of the emptiness I've felt in my heart. I start to notice my tears falling on the paper. Even though this part is almost unbearably sad, I feel some of my strength returning as I pour it all out on paper. I am healing my soul somehow with every stroke of my pencil. And I know this is what I need to paint. This is what I need to say. A flash of lightning lifts my eyes from the paper. The storm moves overhead, enveloping the cottage in darkness.

It continues to rain for three days – summer avoiding this part of Scotland. We retreat to the dining room of the farmhouse, sitting around the long pine table, a log fire crackling behind us.

I finish sketching out the left side of the heart. Dan comes over to look at it, and I wait to hear what he thinks. 'I like it. You've kept everything within the heart, though – what about having some of the branches coming out of it? Like this.' He grabs a pencil and sketches his suggestion. 'Otherwise it will all be locked within your heart, but you want to let it out, don't you?'

Looking at the page, I nod, a lump in my throat making it impossible to speak. I do want to let it all out. Pushing the boundaries of the heart makes everything stand out and it looks like the emotions are so powerful that the heart can't keep them within it. Which is exactly what happened. Dan pats my shoulder as he moves on to help William with his drawing. I feel more excited about this piece than anything I've done before. I need to move on to canvas whilst I'm feeling so inspired.

The following day, the sun finally breaks through and we all meet on top of the hill overlooking the acres of land around the farm with our canvases propped up on stands to begin our paintings. I look down at the farm buildings, which are a hive of activity, far removed from the still and quiet up here. We sit in a row, each on small stool, the sun beating down on our necks, as we try to set our fears free.

I paint my canvas in a light grey colour. The winter side of the heart will be in a darker grey, and the other side I paint in a light blue. I still need to sketch out exactly what I want in the opposite side but this colour works well against the grey.

The heart looks incredibly emotive when I've drawn it on the canvas in charcoal and I start drawing in the branches and add the snowflakes and icicles in softer pencil draped over the branches.

I start to paint the bare branches on a gorgeous June day on the hill. We've all been out here all day, lost in our pieces, barely acknowledging Dan when he comes to have a look at our work. The sun starts to set behind us and Dan tells us to get ready to pack up for the day so we can all go out for dinner. He walks in front of us and looks behind us at the setting sun. I hear him tell us to look at him and as we do he takes a picture of us.

When Dan sends it to my phone, I am impressed with his eye. We are all in a row with streaks of orange and pinks behind us, the sun just visible before it slips behind the hill. More than that is our expressions – we are lost in the moment, looking up at him with joy and passion all over our faces. I look wild somehow with my messy hair, paintbrush in hand, an old shirt on, hanging off my shoulder slightly, but I look happy.

'Glad you came?' Julia asks, bringing me a glass of wine in the pub that evening.

'I am. Are you?'

'I feel like I'm finally laying some of my ghosts to rest, you know?'

I nod, understanding completely. Robert comes to my mind as I look back at the picture of us on the hill. Despite my trust in him being so betrayed, I can't deny the fact that the reason I'm here right now in this place is down to him. He believed in me before we even met. He believed in my art before I did. He knew I could do this when I wasn't sure. Even though part of the reason I took the plunge in accepting my place here was to get away from everything back home, it was also because I knew I had to paint again, and he made me see that. I feel alive right now because of him.

And that's scary and so confusing after everything that happened between us. I think about the email he sent me, which I still don't know how to reply to. I think about him wondering if I want to say goodbye to him for good, and I still don't know my answer. My head says yes. My heart says no.

Impulsively, I forward the picture of us to his email with just one sentence with it:

I need time.

Chapter Twenty-Five

As the second week of the retreat progresses, I'm ready to start tackling the other side of my heart painting. This painting is my most abstract. Abstract in the sense that I know what feelings have gone into it, what I'm trying to say with it, but no one else will. Everyone will have their own interpretation; it will make everyone looking at it feel differently, because that's what any kind of creative project does.

The left side of the heart has had a wintery spell cast over it, capturing my coldest and darkest moments. And it's been hard to face that time, but in a way I fear thinking about the happy times even more because it's painful to know the times with Lucas can't be repeated, while the moments with Robert come loaded with guilt now. Accepting that there will be summer for me after this long period of winter isn't easy because it means accepting that I'll be having it without Lucas. And accepting that I can be happy again.

I shall always mourn the fact that we didn't get our forever. But two years ago the idea of building a life that didn't include Lucas was unthinkable and now, slowly, I'm starting to feel it is possible. A different future to the one I had planned with him. One that is just about me and the things that I want.

And I've realised that it's okay. It's okay to want to try to move on. It's okay to try to find out what I want from my life now. I'll never not be sad that I've had to do this. But death parted us and I have to live without him.

That's why putting my heart and soul into this painting has helped me so much. It's part of my new future. I didn't know I could become this artist, but I'm so excited about this project.

I sit with my sketchbook on the grass in front of my canvas and Dan comes over to see my work. 'Why do you run these retreats?' I ask him as he looks at my painting. Dan is an open person and I feel myself becoming more open with him in return as the days move on.

He thinks for a moment. 'I suppose I felt I had been pretty selfish through my career. I focused on my art to the detriment of relationships, friendships and family, and when I started to feel like maybe I was getting past it when it came to shaking up the art world, I wondered if I could help other artists to do it instead.'

'It's a wonderful idea.'

'A simpler answer to your original question would have been, to discover talent. You have it, Rose. You should be really proud of this painting. I think this is already your best work. You have the most potential here,' Dan tells me.

'I am proud of it so far. I feel like I've lived with so much pain. Seeing it in front of me makes me wonder how I made it through, you know?'

'You've had to deal with more pain than a lot of people your age have to. And that's what is going to make you into a brilliant artist.'

I mull that over. 'Why do you think that so many artists,

and not just painters, but writers and musicians too, struggle so much before success?'

'Nothing worth having ever comes easy, kid, and the reason they have success is *because* they struggled. They turned their pain into something we could all relate to. We relate to pain, it's the human way. You need drive to succeed, and nothing drives you more than years of struggling. They never gave up. The ones who gave up just didn't have it in them, so those who are successful are the real deal most of the time, you know?'

'I think that's kind of a beautiful way of looking at it,' I tell him, moved by his words. I begin to hope that I can create something beautiful out of my sadness. I suppose that's the whole point of this heart painting. A heart doesn't just hold sadness, it holds happiness too. Winter doesn't last forever. Spring arrives every year. The trees don't stay bare. Your heart doesn't stay empty even though there are moments when you think it will. I think about how Robert was able to find a way into my heart despite the cloud of grief that I was under. It showed me – well, he showed me – that I can still love, that I will be able to love again. And there were moments when I never thought I would.

I start sketching out what the rest of the heart will look like, working until the sun sets again. As I walk back to my cottage to change for dinner, I pause to look up at the inky blue sky. Stars are starting to appear there. I love how you can see the sky so clearly here.

What was that quote that my mum kept on our fridge when I was growing up? *When it's dark, look for stars.* I used to think it was a corny sentiment, but it's clear that in moments of darkness, pockets of joy are more noticeable. My sky became so dark but then stars began to light it up again.

The emotions that will form the right side of the heart painting are those stars.

Love, passion, joy, hope.

I felt it all in the moments I had with Robert. I didn't think I'd feel any of it again after Lucas was taken from me, but I did. I also know that having felt them once, I will feel them again. Being here and reconnecting with my love for painting has lifted my heart once again. I suppose this is what I'm trying to say with my heart painting. Your heart is never a fixed point. It evolves with you and the people in your life. I think through this painting I'm learning not to be scared of my heart anymore.

Whether it's full of love or pain, I don't ever want to close it down again. People say that you should follow your heart and it's not easy to do, especially if it's been broken before, but I think all it really means is you should try to open your heart to everything you want to be open to. Don't ever be afraid of letting things you love in. Whether it's people or your passions.

And that's what I'm determined to never be afraid of doing, despite all that's happened.

I spend the next few days painting the rest of my heart. On the right side I draw another tree, but this one is full of leaves reaching up to a clear blue sky, the summer sun shining down upon it and birds circling in the distance. One of the branches lifts up to the sun and I have drawn a fire starting on the tips of it, the flames flickering against the edges of the heart. This branch came out of nowhere. I started painting the fire without really understanding why.

It kind of doesn't fit with the rest of the painting, but that's why it had to be there. Most of this side is about all the happy moments I had with Lucas but it felt right to also paint how I feel now. To represent this summer when my heart is coming alive again.

The others on the retreat compliment me on how the painting is coming together. I am the least experienced of the group but I am focusing on my emotions and not my technique, so I'm actually feeling more confident about my work than I ever have. It feels as if I've broken through a barrier and now I can paint what I have always been destined to paint.

Spending each day outside on the hill surrounded by like-minded people and their talent seems to have made us all productive. You can't fail to be inspired in these surroundings and with these people. I feel nervous that we're in the third week of the retreat. Four weeks away seemed like forever when I left Talting, but it is moving at a rapid pace. I'm not sure I'm ready to face everything back there yet.

We all go for a walk one morning after breakfast before we start work for the day. It's cloudy today with a gentle breeze. Everything is so green here. I'm used to being surrounded by the sea but it is more tranquil here. I look over at the farmer opening a gate into the field of sheep that live to the side of the farm. I gaze up to the hill where we have painted so often. It's such a remote spot. It's impossible not to find some kind of peace here. We all seem to have done so.

'I wish we could just stay here,' Julia says, seeming to read my thoughts as we stroll through the woods side by side.

'I'm scared to go back into the real world.'

'Do you ever think about moving somewhere new?' Julia

asks. She lives on the outskirts of London and says she's learned to appreciate the country air for the first time here.

'I never have before. I don't know. It would probably be easier if I went somewhere new. There are a lot of things I don't want to face at home.'

'I think we all feel that way. But you still called it "home". You can't choose where your home is, you can only feel it's your home.'

'This place has made me feel braver about going home,' Peter says. 'It'll be hard still without my wife, but I have my children and they need me.'

William nods. 'Walking past some of the places I used to drink in was the hardest part of recovering.'

'It's true,' Pam chips in. 'It's braver to go home and face everything; it would be easy to just run away. And let's face it, we're artists – we never choose the easy path, right?'

We chuckle in agreement with that. I don't think anyone chooses to be an artist because it's easy. But nothing worth having in life comes easy. And being here has been incredibly worthwhile.

I don't know if I would describe myself as brave, though. I didn't choose to experience these things. Life just threw them at me. All I can do is choose where I go from here, and that is a decision I'm not ready to make yet.

I'm scared to go back to Talting and face everything there, but if I don't go back, will all the pain just come with me anyway? I could find a new place to call home and try to move on from the past, or I could return to the people I've shared it all with. I do miss Talting and the people there, especially Emma. It feels like part of me is missing not being with her. And things were left in such a bad place with Gloria.

I would regret not mending the damage there. I couldn't bear Lucas seeing us estranged.

It doesn't matter how far away I am from Talting, it is part of me.

I know then I have my answer. I will be going back home when this retreat is over.

My future is there.

Chapter Twenty-Six

There are just a few days left of the retreat now. Dan decides that we need to do something as a group to commemorate our time together. We agreed to his proposal at the pub last night. William doesn't even have drink as his excuse for going along with Dan's mad plan. Perhaps it's the air out here making us delirious.

We all pile into the minivan and the farmer's son who brought me here drives us into the nearest town. I've never done anything remotely crazy before. I actually get an image of Mrs Morris shaking her head at me and I chuckle to myself at how she'll probably spread the news around town. She would be shocked. I'm a little shocked at myself for contemplating this. But I want to remember these weeks. I want to acknowledge this as the moment I became the artist I've always wanted to be, and I can just blame it all on Dan.

I look out of the window nervously as the tattoo parlour comes into view.

'No going back now,' Pam says, clapping her hands together. If she can do this, if William can do this, I'm bloody going to do it too. I slide open the door and look down at my wrist and try to imagine what Lucas would say to me if he were here. 'My parents will probably freak the hell out, you know. I'll get one too,' I imagine him saying with that mischievous grin of his, high-fiving me like we were still kids doing something our parents wouldn't approve of. Just thinking about him encouraging me makes me bolder and I throw my shoulders back and follow Dan inside.

I have always seen tattoos as an art form but never really thought about having one done myself. I learned last night that Dan's tattoos don't just cover his arms but his back and chest too, and he has one on each foot. Peter has a cartoon from his rebellious youth but this is the first time for the rest of us. I volunteer to go first as I think watching the others might put me off. I'm wary of the whole needle thing, but luckily my design is really small so I'm not in the chair long. The noise is a little off-putting, like being at the dentist, and the needle feels like a hot scratch marking my skin, but Dan tells jokes to keep my mind off it. His jokes are appallingly sexist so I spend the time telling him off and don't notice any pain.

Once it's done, I look down at the heart that now adorns the underside of my right wrist – the outline looks like pencil lines, as if I have drawn it there myself. I smile, instantly pleased that I did this. I wanted something to represent the painting I have done here and also to remind myself of the love I've had in my life – and that I will always have love in my life.

Love doesn't end, even if the person can't physically be part of your life anymore.

As I stand up to give the chair to someone else, I look at my rings, the only other adornment to my hands. I have got so used to them being there, I haven't thought about a time when they won't be.

'When did you take off your wedding ring?' I ask Dan as we watch William get his tattoo.

'Which time? I've been divorced twice.' He grins then catches my serious expression. 'There is no right time, you know.'

I told Dan the whole story of Lucas and Robert one night. It was a relief to tell someone who didn't know either of them, only me. To be honest, I hoped he'd have a nugget of wisdom for me, but he just shrugged and said, 'Life's a bitch.' Maybe I should have had that tattooed.

'There's only a right time for you,' Dan adds now, walking away to help Julia choose her design. I look at my right wrist, which is now covered so my new tattoo will be protected, and my left hand, which is covered in a different way with the symbol of my love for and commitment to Lucas. I understand that both covers have to stay until what they are covering has properly healed. I just hope I recognise the moment when that has happened.

My phone rings then, playing my favourite Miranda Lambert song. I am surprised to see John's name light up the display. I slip outside, my heartbeat speeding up as I wonder what he's going to say. I wince at the memory of walking out on him and Emma as they shared their good news with me. He has every right to yell down the phone.

'Hi, John,' I say tentatively, pacing back and forth in front of the parlour, taking my anxiety out on the pavement.

'Rose, thank you for picking up,' he says, his voice quiet and strained. 'I wouldn't call unless it was a real . . . I know you're in Scotland, but is there any way you could come back early? Please, I don't know what to do.'

My blood runs cold. 'What's happened?'

He takes a deep breath, then tells me in a whisper, 'We lost the baby.'

'Oh no, John,' I gasp, stopping my pacing in shock. 'I'm so sorry.'

'I know she was only six weeks, but she's not taking it well. It's a lot to ask but I don't know what to do. I think she wants to see you; I don't think I'm helping like you could,' he says, his voice breaking at the end.

It sounds as though he might cry. I have never seen or heard him cry. I lean against the wall feeling incredibly far away and helpless. 'Are you sure? The way I left? I haven't heard from her since . . .'

'You're best friends,' John replies simply.

I nod, even though he can't see me. Of course he's right. I push aside my fear of going home because Emma needs me. There is no decision to make. She's been there for me through the hardest times of my life. Her family took me in when I didn't have anywhere to go. She has never let me down and I'm not about to let her down now. 'I'll be there as soon as I can,' I promise and hang up, taking a deep breath to prepare myself for going home.

When everyone has got their tattoos, we drive back to the farm and Dan comes into my cottage with me. He stands in front of my heart painting and whistles. 'It's stunning, darling. I knew you had potential, but . . . Heather is going to want to see this.'

I pause in my packing to smile at him. 'Really?'

'Absolutely. You are going to be a big deal, kid. You promise you'll tell everyone it was down to me, right?'

I chuckle and shake my head. 'You're crazy, I'm not going to be a big deal.' I glance at the painting. 'But I'm proud of it. This place really was inspiring.' I bite my lip. 'Do you think I can do it again? I mean, back at home, on my own . . .'

It's his turn to shake his head. 'After this, you can't have any self-doubt about your talent, Rose. You've got this.'

'You called me Rose,' I say in disbelief after all the terms of endearment he's come out with here.

'You're a bad influence on me,' he says, but he steps forward and holds his palm up. 'To the art world's next big thing.'

I high-five him, laughing. I'm not sure I've ever met anyone quite like Dan before.

When I'm finished packing, I wrap up my canvas in brown paper and string and order a taxi to take me to the station. Looking around the cottage as I pull on a jacket, I feel like these almost four weeks have helped to heal me more than I thought possible. I'm excited about painting again and have turned a corner in expressing my feelings on canvas. I feel able to go back home because Emma needs me and I will put things right with Gloria and Graham. I'm still angry with Robert and hurt that he lied to me, but I have also recognised how much I opened up my heart to him before I found out the truth. It's impossible to forget that he's the reason I came here.

Dan is outside smoking when I come out with my things. 'Are you going to be okay, Rose?'

'I hope so.' I smile. 'I think I will.'

'Just don't let your pain take over every part of your life. You lost love once, you don't want to lose it again if it comes back your way, okay?'

I look into his eyes and see how serious he is about this. They are tinged with sadness and I feel as if I'm looking at someone with a bag of regrets weighing him down, despite all he's achieved in his life. There's wisdom in his words. 'I won't, I promise.'

He winks at me and the sadness melts away behind a grin as the others join us. I hug each of them in turn, sad that we're parting, but I'm sure we'll all keep in touch.

It's time I went home.

I don't think there was ever really a choice for me. It won't always be easy living in Talting surrounded by so many memories and the people who know my past as well as I do, but it holds such a significant place in my heart that I can't let go of it. I don't want to let it go. I want to try to build a future for myself there. I belong there, I suppose.

I climb into the taxi and wave to everyone as it pulls away from the farm, then I glance down at my fresh tattoo and know that I'll always have a piece of them and this place with me now. I turn around and look ahead to returning home, certain that I'm stronger from the time I've spent here.

Chapter Twenty-Seven

Darkness envelops Talting as my taxi pulls up outside Emma and John's house but the warm sea air is welcoming. The front door opens before I even get out of the car and John appears and rushes out to grab my bags. When I look at his eyes, I can see the life has been sucked out of them. I pull him silently into a hug and we stand like that for a few moments as the taxi leaves us alone in the silent night.

'Don't worry about me,' he says finally, pulling away and adjusting my bags in his hands. 'She's in bed but I don't think she's asleep.'

'I'll go up and see her.' I pause. 'I'm not sure what to say.'

He rubs his chin. 'Nor am I.'

I head upstairs as John takes my bags into the hall. I feel his eyes on me as I go up. I sense he feels helpless right now. I knock softly on the door but there's no response, so I peek around it and see Emma lying on the bed, staring up at the ceiling. She looks small to me for the first time since I've known her.

'Can I?' I ask. I walk tentatively over to the bed and perch on the edge of it. She avoids catching my eyes. 'I came straight home as soon as I heard,' I say finally. 'I'm so sorry, Em.'

She sighs. 'You didn't have to come home.'

'I hate that you think that.' I slip my shoes off and lie down next to her on my side so we're facing each other. 'I wanted to be here with you. I've missed you. You're my best friend. I hate that I ran out on you like I did. I've been a shitty friend back to you, after all you've done for me.'

'You had a lot to deal with.'

'I should still have been there for you.'

She shakes her head. 'It's okay.'

I brush back her hair from her face and look into her glistening eyes. 'How are you doing?'

'I know it's crazy but I just feel so guilty.'

'Why on earth would you feel guilty?'

'Because I must have done something wrong. I've failed at being a mother before I've even started,' she says, brushing away a tear.

'What did the doctor say?'

'Just that sometimes it happens before three months and it doesn't mean there's anything wrong. I could still have a baby, but how does he know? It has to be my fault.'

'Come here.' I pull her towards me and wrap my arms around her. 'I know now that people say things to you and they can sound reasonable and make all kinds of sense, but if you don't believe, if you don't accept it in your own heart, then it doesn't make any difference to how you feel. I need to tell you that this is not your fault, that you haven't failed, that unfortunately this is common and you will be an incredible mum one day, but I completely understand you feeling that way.'

Emma leans on my shoulder and I can feel her tears wetting my top. I wish I could take her pain away but I know she just has to feel it. It's the only way to make it out the other side. 'Everything will be okay,' I say softly, stroking back her hair. 'I promise,' I say, a tear of my own falling on to my shoulder. I feel as if it's taken me two years to feel that way. But I know that even if you are filled with pain, love will find a way to heal your heart in the end. Emma squeezes my hand once, so I know she's heard me. We lapse into silence, and somewhere between our tears we fall asleep, still leaning on one another.

'You got a tattoo?'

I open my eyes as Emma grabs my wrist to look at it. I blink at the light, then study her face. She looks a little more like herself, so hopefully that means she slept through the night like I did.

'Peer pressure,' I reply with a wry smile.

She shakes her head. 'I let you out of my sight for five minutes . . .' then her smile abruptly stops and she looks down at the bed, her hands fiddling with a loose thread of her duvet. 'I forgot I shouldn't be smiling,' she whispers.

I know that feeling. I remember wondering if I'd ever smile again – maybe you could forget how to smile – but then it just happened, when I least expected it, when I wasn't thinking about it, and then I felt guilty for doing it.

'Tell me how to make this better for you.'

'You can't, but I'm glad you came back. I'm grateful. I thought maybe you . . . well, that you wouldn't.'

That stings my heart. 'I wish I'd never made you feel that way. I felt like the universe was punishing me by taking away that brief moment of happiness I'd had, but that doesn't excuse me not being able to be happy for you. I want us to share everything. I want you to be able to tell me everything.'

'Me too. You're my sister; it doesn't matter if we argue because we'll always be sisters.'

I kiss the top of her head. 'Now I'm going to make you and John breakfast, okay?'

'I'm not hungry,' she protests weakly.

'It's my turn to look after you,' I tell her, clambering off the bed. I go downstairs and find John getting up from the sofa where he slept last night. 'I'm sorry . . .'

He holds up his hand. 'She slept, that's what matters.'

'I'm going to get us some breakfast. Try to get her to have a shower, maybe. I'll call Joe too and explain she won't be at work for a couple of days. I'm back now, so I can cover her anyway.'

'Thank you, Rose.'

'It's the least I can do. I should have called her.'

'You needed the break. Emma told me what happened with Robert. I understand why you needed space; it was a shock. I'm pissed at him. Mind you, I'm pissed at the world right now. Go, I'll see you in a bit.'

I return with croissants and make them both coffees. Emma doesn't want to come downstairs, so I eat on the bed with her. She barely touches it but drinks her coffee. I run her a bath despite her protest that she just wants to go back to sleep. I know that there is nothing I can do for Emma but to be there for her. I understand how helpless she must have felt watching me feeling pain. I need to be strong for her now. I don't want her to fall into the same darkness that I fell into.

John keeps an eye on her when she goes into the bathroom, and I head off to the cottage to leave my bags and painting, then go to Mrs Morris's house to reclaim Taylor. Amanda lets me in as her grandmother is at the café, and Taylor runs up to me when I walk in. I scoop him up and bury my head in his fur for a moment, letting his purr soothe me. 'I missed you,' I tell him and he looks at me solemnly as if he understands.

'He missed you too. A few times he seemed to be wandering around looking for you,' Amanda says, collecting his bits. 'He's a real sweetie.'

'Thank you so much for looking after him.'

'It's fine, I enjoyed it.' She gives him a stroke before I put him in his carrier. 'Did you always want to be an artist?' she asks me shyly.

'I'm not sure you can want to be an artist – you either are or you're not. I feel like I have always been an artist, but I'm only just discovering exactly what kind I want to be.'

I feel like I'm now discovering the kind of woman I want to be too.

Chapter Twenty-Eight

Being back in my cottage with Taylor is better than I could have imagined. I finally feel as if the place is my own. I stare up at the heart painting in the living room as I sit cross-legged in front of it on the sofa, finishing off a yoghurt. Taylor is perched on my lap, purring and staring at me, so when I've finished I offer him the tub to lick, which he does with enthusiasm.

I promised Heather that she could see what I produced at the retreat in return for her getting me there at such short notice, and I don't want to chicken out of it, but pressing Send on the photo I've taken of it is proving difficult. It feels as if I'm sending off a piece of myself to be judged. But then I've never felt like this about any of the work I've done before.

Away from the protected, bubble-like world of the retreat, I was worried I would lose some of my excitement about the piece, but if anything, it stirs up more here. I was so lost for so long; I feel found looking at it. It just remains to be seen what other people feel when they look at it. Taking a deep breath, I hit Send on the email.

Then the doorbell rings, startling me out of my thoughts. Taylor jumps off my lap and runs towards the door, looking at me as if to ask who is out there. I shake my head at him, having no idea. I put the empty yoghurt pot down and join him by the door. I'm unprepared for visitors – unwashed, and wearing the vest and shorts that I slept in last night, with my hair piled on my head – so I open the door reluctantly. I am surprised and immediately nervous to see Gloria out there, but I swing the door open to her.

'I'm sorry to come by so early, but I've just dropped off some flowers at the church and this was on my way home. Mrs Morris said you were back . . .' She trails off, seemingly as nervous as I am. She looks around the room and I realise that this is the first time she's ever come around here. Taylor approaches her, sniffing her shoes, and she laughs as I shoo him away.

'Tea?' I ask, leading her through to the kitchen. 'Apologies for my state of undress. I slept for hours last night, must have still been shattered from the journey,' I babble as I put the kettle on.

She sits down at the kitchen table. 'I should be apologising. I should have called you first.'

'You never have to call first.' I lean against the counter as I wait for it to boil. 'What do you think of the cottage?' I ask, trying to work out if she's still angry with me. I desperately want her to forgive me. I have been part of Gloria and Graham's family for so long – I always felt like they thought of me as a daughter, not just a daughter-in-law. And if Gloria thought of me as a daughter, then how must she have felt to know I had let another man into my heart?

'It's lovely, Rose. I can see why you fell in love with it,' she says, giving me a tentative smile.

I understood why she'd never come round after I moved in. Seeing me in a house without Lucas would have been too hard. Taylor brushes against my legs, so I reach down to stroke him. 'Gloria, I'm sorry about what happened before I left,' I begin, as the kettle whistles behind me.

'No,' she says quickly. 'It's me who needs to apologise. 'I'll be honest, I haven't thought about much else apart from our conversation since you left. I knew I had to see you as soon as I could when you got back. I need to explain why I reacted the way I did . . .'

I bring over two mugs of tea and sit down opposite her. 'I understand, Gloria, I—'

She holds up her hand to stop me speaking. 'Please, let me get this out, Rose.'

Reluctantly, I gesture for her to continue and take a sip of my tea.

'I have always thought of you as the daughter I never had,' she tells me, her voice shaking a little. 'You and Lucas were together for so long, you were part of our family too. Your wedding was one of the happiest days for us. We were so excited for you to build a life together, and maybe have children one day . . .' She takes a deep breath to compose herself. I reach across the table and squeeze her hand. She nods. 'I know how much we all lost when Lucas died. We lost a future. I didn't think our relationship would change, but I realised after you left that it has to change, and I've been fighting against that. I wanted to keep you as Lucas's wife because then it would feel like he was still with us. I hated the thought of you moving on, and when I heard things around town about you and Robert, I wanted to stop it. I wanted to make sure you knew that I wasn't happy about it; I wanted to make sure your heart stayed with my son, that you kept his rings on, kept coming for Sunday lunch . . . that you would stay his wife, because I knew if those things changed, I'd really have to accept that life was moving on without my son.' She brushes away a tear that has fallen down her cheek.

I never knew that crying could be as infectious as yawning, but seeing Gloria cry makes me succumb to it too. It's as though I've found a shortcut to my tear ducts these past two years. I never thought of myself as someone who cries a lot, but I dread to think how many tears I've shed since I lost Lucas. 'It's okay. But I want you to know that it's not the ring around my finger that makes you my family. I love you and Graham, you will always be my family,' I choke out. 'I never want to lose you guys from my life.'

'We don't want to lose you either. I know that Lucas would have been so disappointed to see us argue . . .' She tries to compose herself to continue. 'If we had talked about all this more, you would have felt comfortable to tell us about Robert. I should have been more supportive. The last thing I want to do is push you away.'

I shake my head. 'It isn't your fault. I should have been honest with you, but I was worried about what you would think, and I was scared of hurting our relationship. I didn't want to push you away. And then I found out who he was . . .' I break off with a sob. 'How can I expect you to forgive me?'

It's her turn to squeeze my hand then. 'There is nothing for me to forgive. You opened your heart again, and I know it's something you need to do. I never met Robert, but it's clear he had feelings for you and chose to lie to you about his connection to . . . us. That isn't your fault.'

'I feel so confused about it all. I hate that he lied to me. I don't want to have connection to the person that . . . to his brother, but he inspired me to start painting again and I can't deny that he was making me happy. It's been a long time since I felt like that. He said he loves me and . . . I . . . I can't seem to forget him.'

Gloria is silent for a moment and I worry that I've been too honest with her about my feelings for Robert. 'No one can tell you what to do,' she says eventually. 'He's made a lot of mistakes and only you can decide what you can forgive. I think we all have more questions for him. But there's no time limit. If he really loves you then he'll wait for you. And I'll be here to help you if you need me to.'

'I'll always need you.'

Walking to Emma's in the afternoon, I answer a phone call from Heather, who in a businesslike manner books an appointment with me so she can see the heart painting in the flesh. 'You can't gain any sort of perspective through a camera, I find. What is it called?'

I can't gather any thoughts she has about it yet. I look down at my healing tattoo and tell her the name I've chosen for the painting: '*Without winter, there would be no spring*'.

She's silent for a moment. 'It's perfect,' she says before hanging up.

Emma is sitting on their patio when I arrive, the sun pouring into the small garden, promising a hot July on the horizon. I take out two glasses of ice-cold Coke for us and join her at the table. 'Too early for alcohol then?' she asks, taking the glass I offer her.

'I'm working at the bar tonight.'

'I don't want too much time off. All I do is think about it. I want to think about something else.'

'Give it time.'

She looks at me. 'Talk to me about something else. Tell me about the retreat.' I fill her in on my four weeks away and then I tell her about the email Robert sent me, finishing with my conversation with Gloria earlier. She sighs. 'I wish Robert had just been honest from the start, but at the same time I can't blame him for falling in love with you and being too scared to come clean.'

'I understand why he did it, but does that mean I can forgive him?'

'And he hasn't seen his brother since it happened?'

'He said that he went to rehab and then disappeared. I know that it wasn't Robert driving that night, but he admits he didn't help his brother or stop their father from covering it all up. I feel like maybe I don't respect him now, you know? He acted very cowardly, I think.'

Emma nods. 'He did. And it sounds like he knows it and is trying to turn things around. I can't believe how happy we were just a few weeks ago and now . . .'

'You will be happy again,' I say firmly.

She looks off into the distance. 'It feels very far away right now.'

When it's nearly dinner time I get up to leave so I can eat before my shift, giving her a warm hug as I go. John is coming through the front door when I reach it.

'How is she?' he asks me quietly so she can't hear us.

'Sad, mostly.'

'She doesn't want to talk to me about it. I can't seem to get through to her at all. It's horrible to see her this heartbroken and not be able to help her.'

'I'm not sure either of us can help her, she just needs time.

214

She knows we're here for her,' I say, reaching out to touch his shoulder. 'How are you doing?'

'It was always going to be tougher for her, I know that. But it's still hard, thinking about how excited we were and then nothing, you know? She said earlier she doesn't want to ever try again. I don't know if she means that or not.'

'It's so hard to even think about the future when you're in pain like she is,' I tell him, remembering how difficult it's been for me to think of having one without Lucas. 'You guys will be okay, I know it.'

'Thanks, Rose.' He forces out a smile and gives me a kiss on the cheek.

I don't know a stronger couple than them. They will get each other through this tough time, I'm certain of it. I think about the drawing I did of them on the beach and know instantly that will be my next painting. After all they've done for me, I need to do something to help them. Hopefully it will remind them how strong they are together.

I can't believe they've had to go through this. I hope better things are around the corner. We've all experienced enough pain to last a lifetime.

Chapter Twenty-Nine

I'm in my painting room where the heart painting stands proudly on its easel and I set up a blank canvas next to it. Finally, this room doesn't scare me like it used to. I turn on my iPod speakers so Little Big Town are blasting out and pull my hair into a messy bun. Taylor has followed me up here and is curled up on the floor in a patch of sunlight, looking up at me and wondering what I'm doing. I prop up the drawing of Emma and John at the beach and start to copy it on to the larger canvas.

I feel it again. That buzz I always got from painting. I tap my feet to the music and lose myself in the picture I'm creating. I don't have to worry that the retreat was a fluke as the brushstrokes come as easily as breathing, and I'm even more excited by my work now that I'm able to paint exactly what I want to say.

I am pulled back from my painting haze by the shrill doorbell that Joe installed buzzing downstairs. I sigh as I step back, looking at what I've done so far and pleased it's coming along how I want it to. Taylor follows me downstairs and I open the door to a petite woman who I'd guess is in her early forties who is wearing a dark blue suit, with her light brown hair cut in a chic bob. She holds out her hand. 'It's lovely to meet you at last.' I look at her stupidly, pencil still in hand, then she smiles. 'Heather Jones.'

Realisation dawns. 'Oh my God, I'm so sorry,' I say, hurriedly shaking her hand and stepping aside. 'Please, come in.' I'd been so caught up in my work I didn't realise morning had faded into afternoon and our appointment time had arrived. I instantly feel a mess compared to her smart appearance but reason she must know a lot of artists so is hopefully used to it.

'I've spoken to Dan, who I've never heard enthuse so much about an artist on one of his retreats before,' Heather tells me as I lead her upstairs.

'I hope he hasn't oversold it,' I say, trying to be funny but suddenly feeling very nervous. I know that Dan was very excited about this piece, but it's one thing to hear the opinion of another artist who knows how much you're plagued by self-doubt, and quite another to hear from a critic who isn't bothered about hurting your feelings. And this piece is part of me. I feel like she'll be judging my heart and soul.

I stop and let Heather walk forward into the room. I scoop Taylor up into my arms and sit down in the chair in the corner to wait for her thoughts.

She stands a couple of feet away from the painting and stares at it. Then she starts walking back and forth in front of it, looking at it from different angles. I watch her, growing more and more nervous as she stays silent, her brow furrowed in concentration. The silence feels deafening. I absentmindedly stroke Taylor as I watch her stop again and tilt her head. Then she lets out a long breath and I can't take it any longer.

'Um . . . I'm dying here.'

She spins around and laughs. 'I'm sorry, I forgot you were here.'

'Is that . . . is that a good thing?'

'It's a very good thing. This painting makes me think about the people I have loved and lost. I didn't study art, you know, I grew up surrounded by it, and what I learned at an early age is that technical ability is all well and good, but a true artist, someone who can paint something that people will want to buy and keep forever, is based on how they make you feel when you look at their work. You made me feel something with this, Rose. You are a true artist and this is a great painting.' She takes my hand in hers. 'Damn it, I hate it when Dan is right.'

I burst out laughing and she joins in again. When she laughs she looks ten years younger. It makes me wonder if she laughs enough. 'Thank you, that means so much to me.'

'You never need to thank me. I need to thank you. How about a cup of tea and I'll tell you what I'm thinking we should do?'

I lift Taylor off me and he curls up in the chair, ready for a nap, so I leave him there and take Heather into the kitchen. I make us both a cup of tea and bring the mugs over to the table and sit down opposite her.

'You were right before I'd even met you, that I needed to tap into how I felt to paint,' I tell her. 'I'd been scared for years to do it, to be honest, but I feel so much better now I have.'

'As I said before, you have always been technically great, but I saw that you were missing a connection to what you were painting. I honestly didn't expect quite such a turn-around. It's really wonderful to see. And very exciting. You have such potential, I think the art community are going to want to snap your work up.' Heather takes a sip of her sugary tea. 'I have a proposal. Based on that painting, I'd like to show your work in my gallery. But I always think it works better to exhibit several paintings so people can get a real feel of your work. Do you think you can produce something else for me? Ideally, a concept that links all the pieces together would be what I'd be looking for.'

'An exhibition?' I repeat, unsure that I heard her correctly.

She smiles. 'I want to show your work, Rose. I'm wondering if you could produce three other pieces and I'll exhibit them at my gallery. I take a fifteen percent commission on what you sell at the exhibition, and I have no doubt you will sell out.' She says this in a brisk, matter-of-fact way. 'Don't look quite so dumbfounded – you're the one doing me the favour if you agree. You could go to a gallery in London but I'm hoping I can tap into your local loyalties; I know you've lived here all your life. I think it would be lovely if you had your first exhibition in Plymouth.'

First? As in there may be many more in the future? 'I just sell pictures to tourists.'

'Not anymore, if I have anything to do with it. I'd like to show your work before Christmas, maybe in November? But only if you feel you could produce the work by then. It will be great to build on the buzz from the retreat. Based on the time it took to produce this piece . . . and I noticed you've already started another one.'

'That's of my friends . . . I planned to give it to them.'

'You still can if you want to. It feels as if it could work with your heart painting. A series about love, perhaps?'

I can't seem to take this in. 'Can I think about it?'

She looks a little disappointed but readily agrees. 'This is your time, Rose,' she says as she's leaving.

I watch her go, thinking that just three months ago I was worried I'd never paint again and now I have a piece that a gallery wants to show, something that has never happened before. I have always been content with the artist I was and now I'm on the cusp of something completely different.

Am I ready for that?

Chapter Thirty

July is flying by at a rapid pace and I wake up at dawn on what would have been my fourth wedding anniversary with Lucas. I know there's no point in trying to go back to sleep, so I get up and look out of the window. The sun is starting to rise and the sky is streaked with pink and orange. It's a clear morning and promises to be a warm, bright day. I wonder how we would have spent today if he were still here with me. I think we would have gone to the beach for surfing, maybe taking breakfast to eat there afterwards. I haven't been in the sea since he died and I suddenly am gripped by a need to be out there once again.

I go to my shed in the garden and pull out a wetsuit and surfboard, glad I didn't throw them away. I walk to the beach in the wetsuit, carrying the board at my waist. It's still early for tourists and I have it almost to myself save for a couple of dog walkers and a windsurfer in the distance. I have never surfed without Lucas. I sit for a moment on the sand, lifting my face up to the rising sun, and wish I could talk to him about everything. I know he would have been so excited that a gallery wants to show my work, and I wouldn't have felt nervous about it because he always made me feel as if we could get through anything together.

But I'm on my own now.

I stand up and carry the board with me into the water. It's cool and the temperature shocks me for a moment before I get used to it. I wait for a good wave, feeling my pulse start to quicken. I remember what Lucas taught me. I suppose like riding a bike I feel the wave approaching and my body automatically reacts to it. I paddle on the board towards the shore until the wave moves under me and I start to move forward on it, then I stand up and, hitting the right point, I am able to ride the wave. The adrenaline is there instantly and I laugh as the saltwater sprays over me when the wave carries me along with it. I don't need to imagine Lucas here with me: it feels as if he is. I ride the wave as he taught me and I know he would be proud of me.

Afterwards, I lean on the board and float in the sea, watching the beach start to fill up now the sun is fully in the sky and the warmth is slipping through my wetsuit to my skin. That moment riding the wave made me feel fearless – which is exactly what Lucas loved about surfing. He won't get the chance to feel that way again, so I should feel it for him. I don't want to spend my life being scared of new things. It feels wrong somehow when he doesn't have the opportunity. I know he would want me to live life for the both of us.

And that's exactly what I'm going to do.

After I tell Heather I want to do the exhibition, I throw myself into finishing the painting of Emma and John. I think it will complement the heart painting, and the series can be about love as Heather suggested. *Without winter, there would be no spring* now stands next to the canvas with their picture on. Emma and John, linked by their eyes and hearts. A link that cannot be broken by anything that gets thrown at them. *Without darkness, there would be no stars to shine.*

Emma comes to the cottage at my request. Her eyes still lack their usual sparkle. I hate to see her in this much pain. 'I've finished my second painting for the exhibition,' I tell her, leading her upstairs. 'And I want to show it to you.'

Curious, she follows me into the room and lets out a gasp when she recognises herself and John in the picture. I watch her as she looks at it. 'I saw the two of you on the beach that day, and I saw so much happiness and love between the two of you. Most of all, though, I saw a strong and confident and beautiful women inside and out. You lit up with life; you always have done. I've always envied how it radiates from you. I had to capture you both that day, because I realised whatever life might throw at you, you have this strong link between the two of you that can't be broken. No matter what you two go through, your love will get you through it. In the end, that's all that really counts. Looking at this, I know that whatever happens, you will get through it, because the girl in that painting can make it through anything.'

Emma lets out a small sob. 'Do you really think so?'

'Of course I do. I would never have got through this time without you. You must know that. You've been so strong for me. You made me believe that I would make it through all the pain. I almost gave up, but you didn't let me. I don't say it enough, but I love you and I don't know what I would have done without you in my life. You're the sister I never had and it kills me not to be able to take away your pain, because you've taken away so much of mine.' I let out my own sob then.

'Oh, love.' She wraps her arms around me and I give her a

tight hug back. She pulls back to look at it again. 'It's such a beautiful painting. I've never seen you do one like it before.' She looks at the heart painting then. 'They're both amazing; no wonder she wants to do an exhibition. This is the start of something wonderful, I can feel it.'

I wrap my arm around her waist and pull her closer. 'I want you and John to have this after the exhibition. So you never forget how strong you are together.'

'I can't accept this. It will be worth a lot of money; you should sell it with the others.'

I shake my head. 'It belongs with you two. Let me do this to thank you for being there for me. Please, Emma.'

She sighs. 'If you're sure . . . but you don't need to thank us. You would have done the same if it had been—' She breaks off with another sob then we hug each other tightly.

'Did John tell you I don't want us to try again? It feels like something I've dreamt of for so long came true then it was snatched away. I'm scared it will happen again. And that maybe I didn't deserve my dream to come true.'

'You deserve all of your dreams to come true,' I tell her fiercely. 'This is a shit time, but we've made it through worse, okay? You were my star and I will try to be yours. You and John love each other so much, and I know you guys will be okay.'

She looks at the painting again. 'I was pregnant there. I look so happy. All lit up inside.'

'You will find that light again, I promise.'

She smiles at me. 'So will you.'

I think about the star that shone through my darkness, but I don't know if I'm meant to find that light again.

Chapter Thirty-One

Everyone in Talting seems to retreat in August. It's peak tourist time as all the families arrive for the obligatory summer holiday, more now than ever thanks to the supposed glamour of a 'staycation'. The serious surfers make way for people trying it out. If you run a business you work your socks off and bring in as much money as you can; if you don't, then you avoid the town centre as much as you possibly can if you want to stay sane.

So I retreat into the garden of my cottage to work on my third painting. I realise I've painted significant people in my life so far but there are more who I'd like to represent. This exhibition is already incredibly personal, and it feels right that it should continue to be.

I'm painting the pieces of my heart.

I didn't only lose Lucas but my mum too. I wish she could be part of this with me. She would have been a perfect sounding board for all of my ideas, she was so creative herself. But I know that I'm lucky still to have mother figures in my life without her. Gloria and Sue are Lucas's and Emma's mothers, but they have always been there for me too.

Three strong women in their own different ways. All three have shaped the woman I am and the woman I want to be.

Without struggle, there is no strength.

I draw three lines and start to shade them in. I realise they look a bit like feathers and with a rush of excitement, I add in more lines and curve the tips so they are wrapped around each other. I want to symbolise my mother no longer being here. It's difficult when you're not sure if you have faith to know where someone has gone after they die, as I know Gloria does. Part of me would love to think my mum is with Lucas in a lovely place of peace, watching over me and the people they loved in life, but I just don't know if I believe that or not. But my mother was such a free spirit; I'd love to think of her in the sky somewhere. That's when inspiration strikes and I sketch one of the feathers turning into a bird. One doesn't seem enough, though, so I imagine the feather blowing in the wind and turn the bits floating outwards into birds flying. I stop and look at the quick sketch. I can picture a burst of birds that will fill up the top of the painting, flying across a startling sunset.

Once again I'm not sure how thinking about my mum, Gloria and Sue has transformed into this picture, but I can envisage what it will look like, and excitement flows through me as I think about how stunning this will be on canvas.

When the painting is finished, I want to show it to Gloria. It's her and Graham's wedding anniversary tomorrow, and I found a lovely distressed-looking photo frame online for their present. I dig out my photographs and find one of them with Lucas and me. I think we're at the Fair based on the background, and we look like a family. I look at our smiling faces and I smile. It still hurts to see Lucas and myself like this, but I want to cherish our memories, and I know that Gloria and Graham do too. Graham is playing golf, so Gloria comes round for lunch on her own.

'Thirty years,' she marvels as we finish up our lasagne, salad and garlic bread.

'You should be so proud; it's pretty rare nowadays,' I say, raising my wine glass. 'To you guys.' We both take a sip. 'You two inspire me,' I tell her, almost shyly. 'I wanted Lucas and I to last as long.'

'You would have. You were best friends, and that's what matters.'

I nod, swallowing the small lump that has appeared in my throat. She's right, and God, I miss my best friend. 'I wanted to give you both this,' I say, handing over the frame wrapped in tissue paper.

She unwraps it and breaks into a smile when she sees the picture. 'We all look so young.' She runs her fingers over the photo. 'You two were so young, though, I always forget somehow.'

'I forget sometimes that I'm still young,' I say softly. 'I feel kind of middle-aged.'

'You were too young to have to . . .' She reaches for my hand. 'We are all so proud of how you've moved on, Rose. This cottage and your painting – you've dealt with everything amazingly. It makes us all forget how young you are. Lucas would be so proud of your exhibition, you know.'

I take Gloria into the living room to show her the latest painting, which I finished in the garden earlier. 'You helped to inspire this. The three feathers are you, Mum and Sue. It's called *Without struggle, there is no strength.*'

Gloria sinks on to the sofa. 'It's beautiful. I helped inspire it?'

I sit down next to her. 'You've been like a mother to me, you know that. I admire how strong you've been these past two years. I can't imagine what it was like losing a child.'

'It was so hard, but I still feel as if I have a daughter.' She pats my hand, her eyes filling up. 'You've given me something beautiful. I was going to give you this before your exhibition, but I think perhaps it would be better now.' She goes to her handbag and pulls out a small velvet box, which she places in my lap. 'I didn't actually get it for you; this was mine and my mother's before. It's been passed down to me and I wanted to pass it on to you now.' She bites her lip and watches me anxiously.

I stare at the box, the enormity of it hitting me. She's passing it on to me like her mother passed it down to her, as though I really am her daughter. I take a deep breath and open it up to reveal a delicate silver chain.

'It's really beautiful,' I say, remembering seeing her wear it before. I lean over and kiss her on the cheek 'Thank you so much.'

'Actually, there's a reason I thought you should have it,' she says, lifting the chain out of the box for me. I look at her and see tears forming in her eyes. 'I was going to get you a pendant to hang on it, but then I thought . . .' She pauses to clear her throat. 'You already have something that would be perfect for it.' She taps the rings on my finger.

I look down at my hand in surprise. 'My rings?'

She takes my hand in hers. 'I remember when I first wore my wedding ring. It felt so strange to have something there all the time, but soon it became an extension of my hand, I couldn't imagine not having it there. It starts out as a symbol of your love but it quickly becomes a habit.' She wipes away a tear that has rolled down her cheek and I try to remember to keep breathing; my throat feels like it may close up completely. 'Why do you still wear your rings?' she asks me gently.

I know what she's saying. Yes, it is a habit to keep wearing the rings that have been part of me for so long, but it's more than that. 'Because if I take them off it means I have to let him go,' I whisper, a tear escaping my eye now as I look down to my hand entwined with hers, and the diamond and white gold band Lucas gave me, promising a future that he can't give me now.

'Darling, you never have to let him go. None of us do. He will always be with us, but sometimes you have to let go of things that are stopping you from moving on.' She reaches up and wipes a tear from my cheek. 'There will never be a right or a good time to do it, but this way you won't have to put it away in a drawer like it never happened. Lucas will always be part of you, and the life you had with him will always be part of the life you're going to have. We're all scared of moving on, and you know how scared I've been of watching you do it, but I've realised it's a lot less scary when we do it together. Shall we try it?'

I nod, furiously wiping away the tears and trying to pull myself together for her. Her tears have stopped and her voice is no longer shaking. She's being so strong, and I have to be strong like her. She's had to say goodbye to a son and I know she's doing this for me so she never has to say goodbye to a daughter. She is the bravest woman I know.

She slides the rings off my finger and threads the chain through them. I turn so she can hang them around my neck, lifting my hair out of the way. She helps me up from the sofa and leads me to the large mirror hanging in the hall. I touch the chain and the diamond glistening next to the plain band on my neck, looking beautiful hanging from the simple chain. Somehow they look even more stunning there than they did on my finger.

'I love it,' I whisper.

Gloria touches my shoulder with her hand, smiling into the mirror at me. I smile back, so touched that she did this for me. I know it has helped us both. Never letting go, but hopefully moving on.

'He'll always be with us,' she says again. I turn around and fling my arms around her, pulling her close to me. She squeezes me back silently and we take strength from one another. Which I know is exactly what Lucas would have wanted us to do.

When we pull away, Gloria goes to the bathroom and I touch my heart where Lucas's rings hang and I know he will always have a place in it. I think that's what I was so worried about – that somehow he wouldn't be part of my life anymore, that taking off his rings was so final – but our love will never be final, it will carry on with me.

I'll carry it, and him, with me. Always.

Chapter Thirty-Two

Summer reaches its peak and then starts to fade. Emma comes back to the bar and we're working with Joe and Adam on one of the last nights of the season. I go outside to clear some of the outside tables and Adam follows me. I look out on to the dark beach, hearing the waves gently rolling on to the sand. It feels as if this summer has gone by in the blink of an eye and yet it feels as if nothing is the same.

'Can I talk to you?' Adam asks from behind me.

'Okay,' I agree wearily. We step off the terrace and on to the sand, out of earshot of the patrons.

'I'm leaving tomorrow to get ready for university, and I didn't want to leave without saying I'm sorry. I was upset that you didn't like me the way I wanted you to,' he says quickly and carries on before I can say anything. 'I didn't understand why you chose him over me, but when I saw you together, I got it. He inspired you. I'm sorry if I made you feel bad when you shouldn't have, it was all my fault.'

'But you know what happened with Robert.'

He nods. Everyone here does. 'I still think if he made you happy, you should be with him. When you find someone who's right for you, logic goes out the window.' He gives me a wry smile.

Is he right? 'I don't know. Even if I forget who he is, I

don't know if I could forgive him lying to me about it.'

'I think when the moment comes then you'll know.' He smiles. 'You deserve to be happy.' He leans in to give me a quick kiss on the cheek, before hurrying back inside the bar. I watch him go, hoping that any pain he feels about me will be over soon. I know what it's like to like someone you shouldn't. I look out to the dark sea and wonder how love can be so complicated. I'm not used to it. I was so lucky with how easy it was with Lucas and now I just feel adrift. I wonder where Robert is and what he's doing, and then I feel guilty for thinking about him. His brother took Lucas from me, how I can move past that? And yet I miss him. I want to know what's happening in his life. Is he missing me? Does he think about me? Does he still love me? I send these questions out into the dark void, hoping that one day it will carry the answers to me somehow.

I walk home after my shift, turning down offers of a lift as I want to breathe in the fresh sea breeze. I put in my earbuds and play Kacey Musgraves softly as I walk slowly back to my cottage with just street lights and the stars in the sky to guide my path. I walk past all the familiar sights, feeling blessed that I live somewhere that feels so comforting. I can feel annoyed sometimes at how closely knit this town is, but I am grateful at how everyone has looked out for me these past two years. I know then that I'd like to pay homage to the town in my final painting.

I've painted landscapes of the area so often, but I've never painted how I feel about this place. The way it gets under your skin but also fixes itself in your heart. No matter what I've been through, I am still happy to call this town my home, and its people, my people. I've lost family and my husband, but in a way Talting is my family and it's still looking after me, and I hope it always will. It seems as though I make it through anything because I am part of this community. And not everyone has such a place to call home.

I think about Robert again as my cottage comes into view and the fairy lights he left me light up my way with a warm glow. He fell in love with this place. I saw it. He has never had a place that's felt like home. His family life has always been difficult and I imagine their mansion as being cold and empty. Perhaps if they had had a home like I have, things would have turned out very differently. I don't want to make any excuses for his brother, or for him lying to me, but I suppose I have a flash of empathy for the boys they were growing up in their world.

So very far removed from mine.

I let myself into the cottage and scoop up Taylor, who has rushed to greet me. I carry him on to the sofa and turn on a lamp so I can start sketching ideas for the final painting of my exhibition. Taylor promptly curls up on my lap and falls asleep. We stay like this for most of the night as I work on my drawing.

I draw a figure standing at a crossroads with two signs – one pointing left says 'lost', and beyond it are the bright lights and skyscrapers of a city, and the sign pointing right says 'found', and behind it you can see Talting with its golden beach and crashing waves, the colourful beach huts, and behind them on the hill the church looking down on everything. I finally fall asleep in the early hours, exhausted but happy with what I'm creating and the title of it coming to me as my eyelids close.

Without being lost, you won't find your way home.

*

I keep the final painting under wraps. I don't want anyone from the town to see it before the exhibition. I want it to be a surprise and so I hide it up in my painting room and refuse to let anyone up there. As I finish it, hints of autumn start to appear around me. The foliage around the cottage starts to change into oranges and reds and I need to wear a cardigan when I leave the house. I see the tourists packing up their cases and heading back to where they come from. The evenings draw in earlier as summer starts to become a memory.

I have to make my first visit to Heather's gallery in Plymouth to show her my pieces. John borrows a van and he and Emma drive me there with my paintings. Heather and a colleague come out to help me carry the paintings inside. Emma and John go for a coffee whilst we prop the paintings against the wall and uncover them.

Heather walks up and down the long, narrow room, her heels clicking on the polished wooden floors in time with my rapid heartbeat. She has an infuriatingly serene expression that makes it impossible to guess her thoughts. I look around to try to take my mind off her pacing. Above us are steel stems with exposed light bulbs hanging down, giving the space a modern, almost industrial edge. At the front is a smaller room with the reception desk and paintings for sale. I imagine this place on the night of my exhibition. The space will be blank save for my work, and I'm nervous and excited to see how the pieces will look hanging here.

Heather clears her throat. I turn around slowly and fearfully to meet her unwavering gaze. She is dressed in another power suit today, not one strand of hair out of place, and I completely admire her look, but to be honest the thought of having to wear tights is enough to make me feel happy to stay in my jeans and T-shirt, my hair hanging loose, wavy from the drizzle outside. She bursts into a wide smile.

'They are completely perfect. When I first saw your work I could never have imagined how much you would blossom. They are full of light and life and love. They are thought-provoking and inspiring, and they work perfectly together. "Pieces Of My Heart" is going to be one of the most talked about exhibitions this year, I can feel it.' She holds out her hand for me to shake but I can't be satisfied with that and grab her shoulders and pull her in for a hug.

'Thank you so much,' I say, hoping I don't cry. She doesn't seem like she could deal too well with crying.

She laughs and pulls back, a bit embarrassed. 'The show is going to be a huge success, trust me.'

'Really?' I feel a strange mixture of bewilderment, happiness, hope and fear, but above all I'm so pleased I took a leap of faith with my work, because I have never been so proud of something I've created before.

'Yes, really. This room will be packed and everyone will be fighting over these pieces. I just know it.'

'Just don't sell the one of Emma and John; I've told them it's theirs.'

She shakes her head. 'Far too generous of you, in my opinion, but I promise. Now, if we hold it in the first week of November then we need to get the invitations out in a couple of weeks. I will start publicising it online, as should you on your social media. I'll need a list of everyone you'd like invited and I'll draw up one of critics, industry people and buyers, the people you want creating a buzz about your work.

Let's sit down with a coffee,' she says, sensing I'm a little taken aback by her brisk words.

Sitting on the small sofa with a strong black coffee, I feel better, ready to discuss the evening with her. Heather gets out a notebook and starts jotting down everything we need to arrange. She asks me to think about some quotes I could give her to use on her website about the 'Pieces Of My Heart' exhibition. 'I think people would like to know how the collection was conceived and your inspirations for the pieces. It would be interesting to focus on this being your most personal work to date – what do you think?'

I nod. 'That's a good idea. And it really is my most personal work. Thanks to you and Daniel.'

'And Robert? Can I ask about him? When he came in to tell me about your art, I thought he was your boyfriend, but then I got a sense it was more complicated than that, and I haven't seen him since. But you mentioned to me that he helped to inspire one of the pieces.'

'I don't really know what he is right now. He encouraged me to paint again, and he's part of the reason that my art has become more personal, I suppose,' I reply slowly. I don't know how much I want to share about what happened with Robert.

'Relationships are complicated beasts,' she says, sensing my hesitation. 'I think that's why people are going to relate to your paintings: you show, especially with the heart piece, the light and shade that colours our lives.'

I nod. 'I think that's why my work has become more personal; there were so many feelings that I needed to sort through.'

Heather jots some notes down then leans back against the

sofa and sighs. 'I wish I had an outlet like that. It's been a long time since I've been close with anyone. I'm not sure that I'm good with relationships, full stop, really. Sometimes I think about my last boyfriend and wonder if things could have turned out differently.'

'What happened, if you don't mind me asking?' I'm intrigued, as Heather seems so together that it comes as a surprise that she's not as successful in her personal life as she is in her professional one.

She takes a sip of coffee. The soft acoustic music playing in the background is the only sound for a couple of minutes until she speaks again. 'We'd been together for four years and lived together. I wanted us to get married but there was always an excuse why it wasn't the right time. I worked for a gallery in London but had always dreamt of opening my own place. Someone I knew contacted me to say this gallery was up for sale. It seemed perfect – I could finally have my own place and it wouldn't cost nearly as much as a place in London would, plus it had a good reputation with art collectors looking for local works and I felt like I could build on that and just make it my own, really.' She sighs. 'But Gary didn't want to leave his life in London, even for me. I realised he didn't love me enough to put my dreams first for once. So I left him and chased my dream. I haven't regretted it, either. We just weren't meant to be.'

'That's so inspiring. I think it's great you went after your dream like that.'

'It's not easy to follow your heart, is it?'

I look down at my mug of coffee. 'No, it really isn't.'

'Your husband, can I ask, were you happy?'

I smile. 'Very. We were childhood sweethearts and I was

devastated after the accident. I didn't know how to be without him. It's been a long, hard road to build a life on my own. I felt so uninspired without him. Robert was the first man since . . .' I trail off, the pain of it all still so raw.

'I'm sorry, Rose. To lose the love of your life like that . . . Do you think it's over for good with Robert? It's pretty special to meet someone who can inspire you after the loss you had. I haven't found anyone to inspire me, I suppose.'

I look at her in surprise. I haven't thought about it like that. All I could think about was how guilty I felt about getting close to Robert when he was so tangled up in why I lost the love of my life. But I know that Heather is right about how hard it is in life to find someone you connect with, who can love you no matter what and be by your side through all the good and bad stuff and who can inspire you to be the best version of yourself. Sitting across from Heather, my exhibition imminent, I know that Robert inspired me to be the best artist I could be and he doesn't even know it. I just wish I could have inspired him in turn. The thought of him living here, working for his father, being stuck in that family and being unhappy, makes my heart ache for him despite his lies.

'It will all work out, you know, I do believe that,' Heather adds, giving my hand a pat.

I send out a little piece of hope into the universe that she is right. I get the sense that this woman in front of me isn't often wrong.

Chapter Thirty-Three

Heather sends me the e-invite she's created for the exhibition to make sure I'm happy with it and asks for my guest list. I have it all ready to go, except for one name that I keep adding and deleting from the list.

Robert Green.

I don't know what I will say to him if he comes, but I feel as if none of this would be happening without him. I can't believe it's possible to be this confused about one person.

I give Heather all my names save his and decide to ask Emma's opinion as we walk into Hampton to hit Julie's boutique and find something to wear for the exhibition. I have no idea what I should wear, and Emma, my usual style adviser, is just as lost as I am – neither of us has even been to one before. It's a cold, grey day and I wrap my red scarf tightly around my neck. I can't put off wearing my winter coat any longer. 'It depends whether you want to see him or not.'

'It's not just that. I feel as if he kick-started everything, and I should acknowledge that. I don't know how I'll feel about seeing him, though.'

'Well, there will be lots of people there, so you wouldn't have to talk about anything to do with the two of you.'

'Maybe he won't want to come,' I say, wondering if that would upset me.

She snorts. 'You know how much he loves your art. Add to that seeing you again and, well, the combination will be irresistible for him.' She sees my face and slips her arm through mine. 'It's okay to want to see him. That's all I'm saying. I think you should send him an invite. Let him decide.' I nod, deciding that she's right. 'Are you excited about it? The exhibition?'

'Yes, but I'm nervous about talking to all these art people that Heather says will be there. What if I don't fit into their world?'

'You're an artist, so of course you will,' Emma says. 'It's your world too. Don't have a panic attack; it's going to be great. We'll all be there to support you,' she tells me firmly. 'And we will stomp on anyone who is snippy with you, which they won't be because everyone will rave about your work and you. Got it?'

'I haven't needed a pep talk from you in a while.'

'I was worried you didn't need me anymore.' She gives me a smile and I see my Emma coming back to me. 'You've got this, hon, I promise.'

I kick a pile of fallen leaves with my boots. 'It's starting to feel far too real.' I start torturing myself with nightmarish scenarios like the paintings falling off the wall or me passing out in the middle of the room and needing to be carried out on a stretcher. Ugh! I need to stamp out my imagination, and fast. My phone rings then and I answer it dully. 'Hello?'

'Rose, it's Mick. About your show. Now, what time should I set off in the minibus?'

My eyes widen. 'Minibus?'

'Well, so many of the town want to come, I thought I might as well use the Inn bus to ship everyone over and back.'

'How many?' I stutter, clutching the phone in a death-like grip.

'About twenty so far.'

Oh, God. 'Um, be there for eight o'clock,' I say, wondering if anyone will notice if I don't turn up.

'Lovely, looking forward to it,' he says, hanging up.

'Seriously, Em, I can't do this. There's going to be a minibus.'

'Well, I know they're not the sexiest vehicles, but—'

I give her my most withering look. 'Mick's taking a busload of people to the gallery. The whole bloody town will be there.'

'Oh, right. Yeah, he did mention that. They just want to support you.' She pats my hand. 'At least you don't have to worry about no one showing up. That would be far worse.'

'Not right now, it wouldn't.' I had an email from Dan last night, cheerfully telling me that he and everyone from the retreat would be there as well. Maybe Emma's right and at least I'll have a lot of support, which is great. I just wish I could calm my nerves down a little. I don't want everyone I know to witness some kind of meltdown from me.

When we reach Hampton, it's almost empty but so pretty with all the trees along the pavement in full autumn colours. We head straight for Julie's shop and she is waiting by the door to pounce on us.

'Girls, it's been too long,' she cries disapprovingly. Julie is just three years older than us but always calls us girls and acts like she's our big sister. The shop has been in her family forever, but since she took it over she's transformed it into a trendier boutique, which caused some grumbles from the older residents of Hampton but doubled their turnover.

'I've been racking my brains since you called. I've pulled these out for you.' She drags us into the back where there are two metal rails full of clothes. 'I even Googled it and the consensus for an art exhibition is smart casual.'

'Ugh, everything is smart casual nowadays,' Emma moans, as if she used to live in a time where everyone wore bonnets and gowns.

'Well, don't worry, my smart casual will top all the other smart casuals,' Julie says confidently. She holds up a black dress. 'Rose, try this one on.'

'That looks more black tie than smart casual,' I complain, but they protest so loudly I snatch it and go into the fitting room begrudgingly. I guess I can't just wear jeans really, but right now I wish I could.

I take off my clothes, ruining my hair in the process, and slip on the knee-length black dress. The sleeves are long but made of lace and there's a pretty scoop neckline. It actually makes it seem like I have some curves and when I look in the mirror I can't help but smile. It's chic but also a bit different, just right for an artist doing smart casual. Maybe Julie is actually a smart casual genius. I pull back the curtain and step out into the shop.

'Rose, you look amazing,' Emma cries in delight, looking me up and down like she's never seen me before.

'Gorgeous,' Julie agrees. She hands me a pair of suede ankle boots with a chunky heel. 'These will edge it up.'

'Is it really okay?' I ask, not used to feeling kind of glam. I look at myself in the dress and shoes and a sliver of nerves evaporate. If all else fails, at least I will look great.

'It's perfect,' Emma says, looking at me. 'And your hair should be messy. Also black eyeliner – lots of it.'

'You, try this,' Julie says, sweeping her gaze from me to Emma, who grins at me but dutifully takes the clothes from her and changes. I get changed back, not wanting to somehow ruin the dress.

'What do you think?' Emma asks, stepping out in a pencil skirt and polka dot top.

'Too waitressy,' Julie declares and throws something else at her. 'Try this.'

When Emma comes back out she's wearing a red blouse with the skirt and looks great. 'I have a lipstick to match this,' she says excitedly.

'It's perfect, you two will be the centre of attention,' Julie says decisively, thrusting a pair of red shoes at Emma. Emma lets out a yelp of excitement and I chuckle. I've never met anyone so thrilled by shoes. It's great to see her excited. I'm so glad we came.

'I'm coming with Marie,' Julie says of the bookshop owner, taking my dress and shoes over to the till and wrapping them in tissue paper. I bite my nail.

'Rose is scared about everyone being there,' Emma says in a mock whisper as though I can't hear her.

'Don't be silly, it will be a great night. All your friends will be there, so there's nothing to worry about, right?'

It all sounds so straightforward coming out of her mouth but I can't shake the churning in the pit of my stomach. I force a smile and hand over my credit card, crossing my fingers that I can blag my way through this. I focus on the fact that this is about my work and not about me, and that helps a little. Although if everyone hates my work then I'm in trouble.

'Get out of your head,' Emma orders. She knows me far too well. 'Come on, we need a drink.'

She hooks her arm through mine again after we kiss Julie goodbye and we carry our bags out and walk to the village pub opposite. It's a tiny place with a genuine thatched roof, and at this early hour, we are the only customers. We take a seat near the open fire with two beers.

'Maybe I can turn up drunk?' I suggest, taking a long sip of the warming amber liquid.

'Maybe not the best plan. So, I've been thinking . . .' she says, looking down at her drink. 'I think I want to try again.'

'Oh, Em, that's really great.'

'I'm really scared but this is something I – well, we – really want, and I feel strong enough now.'

I touch her hand. 'You are strong, Em, I'm so proud of you.'

She smiles. 'Your painting helped – John and I can make it through anything together, and even if it doesn't work out, we'll be okay.'

'Of course you will. I've got everything crossed for you.' I raise my glass and she clinks it. I really want this to happen for them both. I see the fear in her eyes but it's matched with determination, and I resolve to let her strength inspire me with my exhibition. This is something I thought I would only dream about happening. And I'm scared but I want my dream to come true, just as Emma does.

If your dreams don't scare you, they aren't big enough.

Chapter Thirty-Four

Heather surprises me with a phone call a couple of days before the exhibition. 'I have an offer for you,' she says, not bothering with pleasantries. 'As expected, I've already had enquiries about purchasing your three paintings available for sale. As a result the guide prices we talked about need to be far higher. I know how much *Without winter, there would be no spring* means to you, though, and I wondered how you'd feel about me purchasing it for the gallery? That way it will stay in the area and people will be able to view it.'

'You want to buy it?'

'It's the centrepiece of the collection and I feel it's perfect for the gallery. What do you think?'

The painting feels as if it's part of me and the idea of it going to a stranger has been making me feel a little uneasy, but to know that Heather would look after it, and people would be able to see it, means I'd be able to part with it but still have it close by. I know I need to let it go. I painted what I felt I needed to and now it's for others to enjoy, hopefully. 'I'd love it to go to you,' I tell her.

The offer feels too high to me, but then Heather advises me to accept two offers on the other pieces that are as high, so I have to concede this must be what my work is currently worth. I feel as if I'm being accepted by a world that I thought would never open its doors to me since I wasn't good enough. I'm not sure if I'll ever feel good enough exactly, but I feel as if I'm doing what I'm meant to be doing.

When the night of the exhibition arrives, I pull on my new dress and stand in front of my full-length mirror trying to recognise the woman staring back at me. It's not just the fact I'm dressed up, which has always been a rare occurrence, but I no longer look tired, weary, too thin, sad – I look . . . well. My hair is shiny and hangs with bounce past my shoulders, my skin is glowing even with minimal make-up, the dark circles under my eyes have disappeared and the weight I lost has returned. So, added with this dress, my figure looks as good as it ever will.

I look down at my hand empty of rings. It still feels strange not to have them there. Sometimes I go to touch them and then remember that they are gone. I look at them hanging around my neck. I love that I never have to stop wearing them.

Then I realise what the biggest difference is with my reflection. My smile. I'm smiling and I can't stop. My reflection beams back at me. I've missed smiling. I lift the rings from my chest and kiss them. I hope you're with me tonight, Lucas. I need you. I always will. 'Go get 'em, babe,' I imagine him saying and I silently promise him that I will.

The doorbell rings and I turn from the mirror to open the front door. Emma stands on the doorstep looking lovely and John waves to me from the car. He's actually wearing a suit.

'Rose, wow,' Emma says, whistling in appreciation.

I laugh, annoyed as ever that I can't whistle. 'Let's get our gorgeous butts to this thing.'

'Yes, boss.' She leads the way to the car and I glance back

at the cottage, the fairy lights glowing against the dark sky, and excitement finally takes over my nerves. I'm ready for this.

I climb into the back and John pulls away. I laugh when I realise they're listening to Take That – the early years. Emma and I were obsessed with them at school.

'You can't be nervous listening to them,' Emma explains loudly over the music and then starts singing along.

The car ride goes really quickly with us singing and laughing at our old love for the boys and then suddenly we've arrived in Plymouth and John is parking near the gallery. I take a few deep breaths before I get out of the car. My heart is pounding in my chest and my hands are clammy and slipping on my clutch bag. But I feel more confident than I have in weeks. This is my night. There might even be a little swagger to my walk.

Or it could just be that I'm in heels.

We walk up to the open door together. I'm so glad I didn't have to turn up on my own. I look around, my mouth dropping open in wonder. The gallery is lit with a dreamy orange glow and soft music streams out from the speakers. The room is almost full of people talking and laughing.

A sign in the gallery window says 'Rose Walker – Pieces Of My Heart' in big, bold red letters against a white background accompanied by the small painted heart I drew for Heather when I popped in, which matches the now healed tattoo on my wrist. The three of us stop to stare at it. Somehow seeing it in black and white, well, red and white, makes it all real. Goosebumps prick my arms under my jacket. I can't believe I really did this.

'Oh my God,' Emma cries, pulling out her camera and

taking a picture of it. She makes me stand in front of it for another picture and then we walk inside.

'Rose,' Heather greets me, appearing from nowhere and kissing me on both cheeks. 'You look beautiful. It's really early but there are already lots of people here and they all love your work,' she hisses at breakneck speed into my ear. She greets Emma and John with efficient handshakes, recognising them from their painting and yanking them over to it so people can see them and the likeness I captured.

'Your paintings are wonderful,' Gloria says, taking Heather's place and giving me a hug. I look over to the group she came from – the Talting contingent was early as expected and are all standing together in front of my painting that pays homage to our hometown. They turn to wave and smile at me. I might actually cry. Oh God, my eyeliner.

'I think you're wanted,' she says, nodding at Heather, who is beckoning me over. I thank Gloria for coming and she waves me off.

I walk through the gallery looking at the walls, which now display my paintings. Hung up they look different, bigger and bolder somehow, the white walls making them stand out. A small card next to each reads 'sold'. A table at the side is filled with drinks and snacks, and more people start coming through as I stand there trying not to pinch myself because I can't actually take it all in. I watch as someone takes a photo of Emma and John beneath their painting, beaming proudly, and then I have to discreetly wipe a tear from my cheek.

'Rose, let me introduce you to Peter Wells,' Heather says, bringing over a man in his fifties wearing a dark suit. He looks vaguely familiar.

'It's a pleasure to meet you,' he says, shaking my hand briskly. 'I am a big fan, Miss Walker.'

'Thank you so much.'

'Peter runs a gallery in London,' Heather says smoothly.

'Oh, really?'

Peter smiles. 'That's right, and I have already told Heather I'd like to display one of these in the British painter collection I'm showing next year, if one of the buyers will lend it to me.' He gives Heather a significant look.

'I'll think about it, Peter. Come and meet your buyers,' Heather says to me. We say goodbye to Peter and she introduces me to the two people who have bought the other pieces, both of them art collectors who describe me as 'up and coming', which I quite like. It's hard to believe this is all for me. I keep hearing praise and enthusiasm and find myself waiting for someone to shout, 'Get out of here, you're a fraud.'

But thankfully no one does.

'Hello, trouble,' a voice in my ear wakes me from my disbelieving haze.

'Dan,' I squeal, hugging him happily. 'You actually came.'

'Of course I did. I had to take credit for it, didn't I? The whole gang is here too.'

I go over and give everyone who was with me on the retreat a hug, pretty overwhelmed that they came from all over the country to support me. Heather comes over then and Dan kisses her on both cheeks and she rolls her eyes at him. I watch him look at her greeting the rest of our group and he catches me.

'What?'

'Do I need to warn Heather about you?'

He sighs. 'She already knows, she's been dodging me for years. I must be losing my charm.' I see a hint of real sadness in his eyes despite his jokey response.

'She's been hurt before,' I say in a low voice. 'You have to show her she can trust you.' I wink. 'And you better listen to me, I have an exhibition all about the heart, you know.'

He smiles and kisses me on the cheek. 'I'm proud of you, kid.'

Halfway through the evening, Heather drags me to the middle of the room and clinks her glass for silence. All eyes turn to us to listen. I've never been so on show before and it's totally alien but actually not unpleasant. Everyone is smiling at me and I feel much more relaxed now I know my work has gone down so well. I never thought I'd enjoy being the centre of attention but I'm having a great time.

'First of all, thank you all for coming. This is probably the best attended exhibition I've had at the gallery, which is down to the talent of this young lady next to me but also the part she plays in her community.' She nods to the Talting gang who all murmur in agreement. 'I haven't been this excited about an artist for a long time. She has grown so much in the short time I've known her, so I can only imagine what work she will produce in years to come. I'm sure her future will be extremely bright and I'm so grateful and proud that she is having her first exhibition here. So, ladies and gentlemen, please raise your glasses to the talented and lovely Rose Walker,' Heather says, raising her own champagne glass and then clinking it against mine.

There's a crashing sound behind us and everyone spins around to see Robert scrabbling about, trying to save two trays of canapés he's just knocked out of a waiter's hands. He stands up, face red, and his eyes meet mine. I bite my lip to keep from laughing. Just like that, the four months since I've seen him fade away and our eyes connect like it's just the two of us here. He grins sheepishly at me then hurries to help the waiter pick things up, apologising profusely.

'Rose,' Heather says then, clearing her throat to bring back our attention. 'Did you want to say anything?' she asks quietly.

I nod and step forward and take a steadying breath.

'I've never been very good at making speeches. I suppose I'm better at putting how I feel down on paper rather than saying it all out loud, but I just wanted to say thank you so much for coming tonight. I used to think my painting was really just for fun and I was never confident about what I created, but being here tonight, I finally realise that this is what I always wanted – people to see my work and enjoy it.' I cast my eyes over the room. 'There are three people that made tonight possible. Robert, who forced Heather to look at my work and let me believe I could do this; Dan for inspiring me to be the artist I always wanted to be, and Heather for being the best cheerleader of my work that I could have asked for.' I glance at Robert, whose head is bent so I can't see his eyes. A few of the Talting gang glance at Robert too, unsure if they should be speaking to him or not. Whatever he's done, though, I would never have met Heather without him and I had to thank him for that. I see Dan raise his glass of champagne to me then I turn to Heather. 'I might wake up and discover tonight is still just a dream, but in case it isn't, thank you for making my dream come true.'

Heather gives me a big hug as the room starts clapping, then Emma rushes forward to hug me next. The next few minutes are a blur of hugging and kissing and congratulations and liberal toppings up of my champagne glass.

Finally, I manage to extract myself and search the room for Robert, who I haven't seen since the toast. Whatever our personal relationship is at the moment, I'm glad he accepted my invitation tonight. If the only role he's meant to play in my life is helping me grow as an artist then it's a bloody brilliant one.

I glance outside and see him leaning against the wall outside the gallery.

'Is that Robert?' Dan asks, coming to stand beside me. I nod. He takes my champagne glass off me. 'Go and talk to him, kid. Don't regret anything, right?'

'Thanks, Dan,' I say, giving him a smile. I grab my coat and nod towards the side of the room. 'No regrets, right?' He follows my gaze to where Heather is and gives me a wink.

I don't know if I'm doing the right thing, but I can't let Robert go without speaking to him.

Chapter Thirty-Five

'Hey,' I say, stepping down on to the pavement outside. I walk over and perch next to him on the wall, putting my hands in my pockets to keep the cold night air out.

'Hey,' he replies, glancing across at me. He's wearing dark trousers, a grey shirt and skinny black tie and has that line of two-day stubble outlining his chin that suits him so well. 'Thanks for mentioning me in the speech,' he adds lightly.

'I was pretty annoyed when you first went to Heather, wasn't I?' I remember with a wry smile. 'I meant it when I thanked you in there; you really gave me the push I didn't know I needed.'

'You would have got here eventually, you're too talented not to be successful.'

His praise feels good and that confuses me.

'Maybe. Maybe not.' I swing my legs gently. I look down at the ground; it kind of hurts to look at him. 'So, how have you been?'

Robert clears his throat nervously. 'Actually, I quit my job.'

My head lifts sharply in his direction. 'You did?'

'I did. I told my dad I needed to do something else with my life. I don't want to be my father's pawn anymore.'

I try to absorb his words but my head suddenly feels all foggy. 'That was brave,' I tell him. My heart has inexplicably lifted at the thought of him leaving his old life. I wish it hadn't. It's too confusing. 'How did he take it?'

Robert grimaces. 'Not well. There was a huge row and he told me I'm not welcome at home anymore and he's planning to disown me, but I stood my ground. I actually think in a weird way he respects me for it, not that he'll ever admit it – he's far too angry with me right now – but that doesn't matter, I have to do this. I put my flat up for sale too. I never liked that place, it never felt like home to me.'

I let this news sink in. I'm amazed and impressed by what he's done. 'What will you do now, though?'

He shrugs. 'I really don't know but I feel relieved. I wasn't happy.' He turns to me. 'You knew that before I did. I hadn't wanted to face up to it, but I knew you were right.'

Hearing that my opinion had an effect on him gives my heart another lift. He played such a large part in making my dreams come true, and I wanted to do the same for him too. Knowing he's broken free of his old world, one that destroyed so much, gives me some hope for us.

'I suppose you made me see that every second in this life counts. Thank you.' He reaches out and touches my hand and I'm shocked by the heat he can still send through my body. 'I want to start making mine count.'

I let myself touch his hand back and his skin feels like an extension of mine. I wonder what it is about touch that can evoke so much. I remember his lips on mine, his arms around me, and his smile when he was above me. I swallow hard and look away from his eyes before I sink right into them and never come up for air again.

'I might not get another chance to say this,' he says then, his voice low and urgent. My breath catches. 'I miss you, Rose. I think about you every day. I know that you need time, but I wanted to ask you something.' He takes a deep breath and lets go of my hand like it hurts to keep touching it. My hand instantly feels the loss of his. 'I want to get away and think about what I want to do, and to be honest Talting is the only place I've come close to being happy in for too many years. Would you mind if I booked into the Inn for Christmas? I can't be with my family, I just can't.' He ends in a volume barely above a whisper. 'I won't, though, if it will make you unhappy. That's the last thing that I want.'

I think about seeing him in town again over Christmas. I would like to see him there again. I don't know if I'm ready to forgive him but I don't want him to be alone over Christmas. 'If you come, would you consider something?'

'Anything.'

'Would you consider meeting with Gloria and Graham, Lucas's parents? I feel as if they deserve to hear everything from you.'

'You're right. Rose, I want to make things right between us. I am so sorry that I wasn't honest with you about who I really was. And if I can help them in any way, then I want to try.'

'Thank you.'

'I should have left my father a hell of a long time ago. Maybe things could have been different now . . . but all I can do is make things different from now on.'

'I'm proud of you.'

'I'm proud of you.' He nods towards the gallery. 'Your paintings are so beautiful.'

'I've painted out everything that was in my heart. I think it's helped me to know how I feel and what I want to feel. And also who I want to be. Does that make any sense?'

He nods. 'It does. I'm trying to find out who I want to be, and to become that man. I wish I could change everything that happened, go back and start again with it all.' He looks out into the darkness, sadness in his eyes.

'You can't go back, none of us can, all we can do is keep moving forward. I'm glad you came tonight.'

He looks at me. 'I'm glad you invited me.'

'The painting of the heart with winter and summer, you inspired some of it,' I tell him, wanting everything to be honest between us now.

Robert shakes his head. 'I don't think I deserve to have inspired that; it took my breath away.' He touches my hand. 'But I'm glad that I was in your heart, Rose. You haven't left mine since I met you.' He touches my hand again and then frowns, looking at it. I follow his gaze and realise he's noticing my hand is empty of my rings. I lift up my necklace to show him where they now hang.

'He'll always be in your heart,' he says softly, like he understands.

I nod. 'Yes,' I whisper, my throat constricting suddenly.

'You are a beautiful person,' he says. He lets go and steps off the wall. 'I should let you get back inside, this is your night.'

'You're leaving?' I realise I don't want him to go. I think back to when our eyes met during my speech. I knew in that moment that I still had feelings for him.

'Will you let me know when Gloria and Graham can see me? Will you be there too?' I nod my answer. 'Thank you for giving me this chance, Rose.' He leans down and brushes my cheek with his lips. 'Enjoy tonight, you really deserve it.' He turns away and walks into the darkness. I stay there for a few minutes alone and look up at the clear dark sky shining with stars and I wonder how and why the universe chose to pull the two of us together. I don't know what will happen at Christmas but I feel as if things aren't finished between us. So much remains uncertain but I want to figure it out with him. That scares me but it also feels right. I can't say goodbye to him. He hasn't left my heart since we met.

I rise off the wall and slip back into the gallery. Emma is waiting for me by the door and passes me a glass of champagne.

'Everything okay?' She obviously saw us out there.

'Yes. He wants to come to Talting for Christmas. He's left his job, his flat, his family . . . He wants to make things right, I suppose. I don't know. I told him he needs to speak to Gloria and Graham. I can't lose them, Emma. If he's going to stay, the town needs to accept him too, you know?'

'I know. If you two are meant to be, it will work out. He came into your life for a reason.' She smiles at me. 'You seem happy and I've waited for a long time to see that in your eyes again.'

'You too,' I tell her. I look at my heart painting hanging above us. Robert helped to bring me back to life after losing Lucas. If I had a choice I would have chosen someone not connected to why I lost Lucas, but that's the whole point of love, isn't it? You don't choose it. It chooses you.

Gloria and Graham come over then to say goodnight and all thoughts of Robert fade as the room empties and I say goodbyes to everyone who came to support me and watch the new owners of my paintings organise their deliveries with Heather. My heart swells with pride and as I walk out of the empty gallery with Emma and John, I feel on top of the world.

The excitement doesn't fade when I climb into my bed in the early hours. Taylor curls up beside me and his purring is the only sound in the silence. I stroke him as I lie awake processing all that's happened. I almost feel like a different person now. I think about what I want for the future and I know it's changed. It's different to the future I had mapped out before, but I was forced to change it, and I'm going to embrace it because I can't do anything else. Maybe life doesn't always work out how you've planned, but you can turn it into something beautiful regardless.

I want someone who opens my heart. I want someone to push me to be the best that I can be. I want someone to bring out my passion. I want someone to inspire me.

But the same man would also be capable of ripping my heart in two. Before I was happy with a safe love. I knew that Lucas would never break my heart intentionally. And he never did. But my heart got broken regardless. Playing it safe just didn't work. Life isn't safe. Love isn't safe, but that's okay.

I know now that I can make it through pain to feel happiness again.

So even though I'm terrified about Robert coming back and how it might make me feel, and I'm worried about my heart breaking in the future and it being worse than the first time, I know that I want to have love in my life. I don't know yet if it will be Robert, but I know that I want to follow my heart from now on, wherever it may lead me.

Chapter Thirty-Six

By the time Robert returns to town, winter has coated Talting with its silvery touch.

I let him in to the cottage and lead him through to the living room where Gloria and Graham are already seated, untouched cups of tea in front of them. I know we all need to do this if Robert will be staying here for Christmas, but it doesn't make it any easier. It feels both awkward and tense as we sit opposite them. Even Taylor seems to feel it and heads upstairs to sleep away from us.

'Thank you for meeting with me today,' Robert begins, clearing his throat and running a hand through his hair. He leans forward on his knees then leans back again as if he doesn't know quite where to put himself.

Graham shifts in his seat. 'We are willing to hear what you have to say.'

I smile at him gratefully.

Robert clears his throat again. 'I wanted to apologise, even though the word "sorry" feels too small to use. I didn't mean to cause anyone any pain by coming here. I know now that I should have been honest with you all about who I was, and why I really came here, but I really did have the best intentions, however misguided they turned out to be.' He sucks in a breath. 'I wish I could go back and make different choices.

I should have stood up to my father and persuaded my brother to tell the truth. I can't imagine what you all had to go through with the case being thrown out. Your son deserved justice.'

'Rose tells us you're not in touch with your brother?' Gloria asks after a short silence.

'No. When he left rehab, he had a friend collect him and we haven't heard from him since. The facility said he was doing well. I understand why he didn't come back to us. My father is a formidable man. I'm not making excuses, though, I should have been stronger. Rose – she opened my eyes to how I let him dictate my life. I'm trying to change that now. But I realise that it's far too little, too late.'

'I think you should have been honest, especially with Rose, about your connection to your brother, but I think you're blaming yourself for an awful lot,' Graham says. Gloria shoots him a questioning look. 'I don't know if you're aware that Gloria and I belong to the church here,' Graham continues. 'We consider ourselves Christians and we have faith, but last year tested us like no other time in our lives. The vicar here talked to us a lot about forgiveness, but how do you forgive someone who is responsible for taking your son away?'

Robert looks at him and nods. 'I don't know that I have the kind of faith that you do. I find it hard to even have faith in people, to be honest. I'm not sure I can forgive Jeremy, and he's my own brother. And I don't know if I deserve forgiveness for lying to you all.'

'Everyone deserves it if they ask for it. You're trying to make things better, and I commend you for that,' Graham tells him kindly. 'As I said, I don't think I will ever be fully able to forgive your brother for taking our son away from us. Lucas lit up our lives.' His voice catches and I feel my own breath catch too. 'But I am glad to know that both your brother and you are trying to be better men than perhaps you have been taught to be. I remember your father in court – he was indeed a formidable man, and I can . . . understand.'

'Thank you,' Robert says simply. His eyes move to Gloria. As do mine.

'Part of the reason we wanted justice for Lucas was to make sure that your brother didn't get into a car in that state again. We couldn't bear it if anyone else had to suffer as we have.' Gloria wipes a tear that has rolled down her cheek. I make to get up to comfort her but she shakes her head to say it's okay. 'It seems as though he's trying to make different choices for himself, and I hope he has learned from what happened. I can see that you have. I can't hold you responsible for what your brother, and your father, did. As difficult as it is to have a connection to the man who took away my wonderful Lucas, I know that it wasn't your fault. You shouldn't take all their blame on to yourself.'

'I just wish I could have done more.'

Gloria sighs. 'I think everyone wishes that. I wish I could have stopped Lucas getting into his car that night. I wish I could have warned him . . . but we could never have known what was about to happen. I don't think it's healthy to dwell on regrets. You can only change the future.'

I let her words sink in. A tear of my own escapes. I feel as if so much of the past few months have been about learning to look forward instead of back. I glance at Robert, whose head is bent low. He nods in agreement.

Graham takes hold of his wife's hand. 'What is it that you wanted from us today, Robert?'

He thinks for a moment before lifting his head up again. 'I think I wanted your blessing to stay here. I don't want to cause any more pain.'

Gloria looks at me. 'I think that's up to Rose to decide. I understand why you want to spend Christmas here. I would never wish for someone to be alone at this time of year.'

Robert looks at me. It feels as if his eyes pierce through my skin, stripping it layer by layer until my soul is laid bare.

'I don't want you to be alone,' I say, my voice barely above a whisper. I don't add my own wish not to be alone. I know I'm never really alone in Talting, but I wonder if I would feel lonely without Robert being here. I think I might. I don't understand how I can think about spending more time with him after everything, but I see next to me a man who wants me to be happy. This led him to lie to me, but I know how much he regrets that. I see a man who wants to live his own life and be who he wants to be now, and I admire him for it.

He has made mistakes. But who hasn't? The point is to try to do better. I can't fault him for what he's trying to do. Coming here to face Gloria and Graham took so much courage. He is brave. And I can't deny the love in his eyes when he looks at me. So much of what happened was because of how he felt about me. And I wonder how I would have acted had I been in his shoes. There is something between us. It fizzes and bubbles in the air around us.

It is both thrilling and terrifying.

I can't define or explain it. But I feel it. And I don't want to regret letting him go. More than that, I want him to stay. I want to know what this could be.

The Second Love of My Life

After Robert leaves, I hug Gloria and Graham in turn. 'I wish I was as brave as you,' I tell them.

'You are braver than you know,' Gloria says. 'Loving someone is the bravest thing you can do. I know that you will love again.' She searches my eyes with hers. I know she's wondering if I am already in love.

I am wondering the same thing myself.

Chapter Thirty-Seven

The street that winds along the seafront is draped with fairy lights, and small Christmas trees are attached to the walls above all the shops. Christmas in Talting is always celebrated in this way but the main event of the season is the tree-lighting ceremony held at the Talting Inn. It happens on the weekend two weeks before Christmas every year and we all turn out for carols and mulled wine. The tree stands in the middle of the driveway and is massive. It takes three people on large ladders to decorate it with tinsel and lights and a star is always perched on the top. I think that star is older than me.

The temperature has cooled further but there's no sign of snow, just a chilly breeze and a layer of frost on the ground in the mornings. I bake a batch of Christmas cookies to take along tonight and decorate them with white icing and silver balls. It's something my mum and I used to do every Christmas and I carried the tradition on after she died. I guess my love of baking came from her. She used to sometimes talk about opening up a cupcake shop in town but never ended up leaving her teaching job. I guess sometimes dreams are just kept as dreams. I'm sorry she never got to have hers come true. It makes me more determined to continue to challenge myself with my art. I feel as if losing her and Lucas has made it important for me to try to make my dreams come true. Not just for me, but for them too. I want to live life three times as fearlessly.

Heather called me to see if I was working on something new. She said I should build on the momentum from the exhibition as soon as possible and think about new paintings but also prints that I could sell on my own website. I've decided to tackle it all in the New Year. I want to wait until I have something to say again. I don't want my art to ever become complacent again. I don't ever want to be complacent again.

Taylor comes over to sniff the box that holds the cakes. He really has a sweet tooth. 'Not for you,' I tell him, smiling at how I've got into the habit of chatting to him. Hopefully it's not considered a sign of going crazy.

I check the time and go upstairs to get changed. It will be freezing out there tonight so I pull on jeans, a thick red jumper, my parka, a red woolly hat and matching scarf and gloves. I add black knee-high boots and a thick layer of lip balm to ward off the wind.

The breeze whips around my face instantly as I step out of the cottage and the sharp chill compared to the warmth inside takes my breath away. I decorated the cottage last week and I somehow feel my old festive spirit returning this year. I've always loved this time. To match the fairy lights on the tree outside, I looped a set over the door, and in the lounge the artificial tree I've had since I was little stands proudly decorated in red and gold with as much sparkle as I could fit on it. In my bedroom, I have a small tree on the windowsill, which you can see from the road. Taylor had a ball watching me decorate, running off with baubles and getting tangled in the lights, and I laughed all day with him. It feels so good to laugh. I'm glad I made the effort. The cottage is bright and welcoming and I love coming home now.

As I walk towards town, coloured lights light up my path. Everyone has got into the spirit and decorated their house. It all feels magical as I stroll towards the Inn. A huge, lit-up inflatable Santa on the roof of the Gilberts' house makes me giggle. I can just hear Mrs Morris tutting about it lowering the tone of the place.

As I approach the Inn, I can see a crowd of people already gathering around the unlit tree outside the entrance. The Inn has lights draped all over the wide frontage and warmth seems to flow from it out to us. My eyes graze over everybody here and I find Robert instantly. He's moved into the Inn and, like all the guests, is out here tonight with most of the town. He's standing near the table chatting to a couple I don't recognise, so guess they're guests at the Inn too. He's wearing a long dark wool coat and the breeze ruffles his dark hair. He looks over, maybe sensing my gaze, and gives me a small wave before turning back to the couple. I wonder what it is about just seeing him that makes me smile instantly.

'Rose,' Emma calls to me and I go over to where she and John are standing chatting to Mick and his wife Joan. I give Joan my cookies and she takes them over to the table, distributing cups of steaming mulled wine.

'It's time,' Mick says, walking towards the tree, ready for the annual lighting ceremony. Emma links arms with me and we follow with John. I take a cup of mulled wine and everyone forms a circle around the tree. Robert stands opposite me and I try to focus on what Mick is saying and not on him watching me. I'm glad to see that I make him smile too.

'Welcome, everyone. As always, thank you for coming to mark the start of the festive season with us,' Mick says loudly so everyone can hear him. 'I just wanted to say we wish you a very merry Christmas and a happy New Year. So without further ado . . .' He lifts his hand up dramatically and starts the countdown. 'Ten . . . nine . . . eight . . . seven . . . six . . . five . . . four . . . three . . . two . . . one.' He pushes the button and the tree lights up in sparkling gold. We ooh and ahhh on cue and there's a round of applause as we gaze up at the bright lights.

The Inn's chef Dean starts strumming on his guitar and song sheets are hastily passed around so that we can all join in with Slade. I see Robert look at the lyrics in surprise and then glance around, a grin forming on his face at the people of Talting singing the hilarious Christmas song, especially the elder residents, who really get into it as if they're singing hymns at church. It is pretty funny and to a newcomer this town must often seem quite weird, but I love it. No boring carols here – just lots of fun. I watch Robert join in and wonder how Christmas in Talting will compare to the ones he used to have with his family. I can't help hoping he loves it here at this time of year as much as I do.

'He can't stop looking at you,' Emma hisses into my ear, glancing across at Robert.

'You're crazy,' I hiss back but I look at him again and he meets my eyes, smiling as he sings. I can't deny there is electricity crackling in the air between us. I hide my grin by looking down at the lyrics as Emma snorts beside me.

Then the festive atmosphere is shattered by a loud groan.

'Mick, are you okay?' A loud cry sounds out, lifting above our singing.

267

I look over to Mick, whose face has turned red and who is wincing in pain. I stop singing instantly and around me everyone does the same as Joan rushes over to her husband. We look on in horror as his knees buckle and he hits the floor. Everyone rushes around him then as he cries out in pain.

'Call an ambulance,' Joan cries, trying to hold on to him.

'It's done,' Robert says, suddenly standing beside me and putting his phone in his pocket. 'Can you lie him down? Everyone step back and give him some air.'

'It's a heart attack,' I hear John say quietly to Robert, who nods.

The sudden hush that has come over the group feels eerie after the festivities just minutes ago. We all wait in anxious silence, Joan's sobs and Mick's groans the only noises until the sound of sirens finally breaks through.

'The guests,' Joan says suddenly, looking around at everyone in panic.

Robert lays a hand on her shoulder. 'I'll look after everything here, don't worry.'

'I'll help,' I add, keen to do something. She gives us a grateful nod but doesn't take her eyes off her husband.

The ambulance pulls into the Inn and we all move back to let them through. I look at Joan's stricken face and know exactly how she feels. Mick is put on a stretcher and Joan scrambles up after him inside the ambulance, which disappears in a blaze of blue lights.

'Their children,' Mrs Morris cries out then.

'I have their numbers,' John says, whipping out his phone.

We all look at each other in shock. The wind picks up and I'm suddenly cold to the bone.

'We should all go inside,' I say, the only thing I can think of to say right now.

'I'll make hot drinks,' Dean replies with a nod, ushering the Inn staff in ahead of us.

'Right, come on, everyone indoors,' Robert calls out with authority. We all troop in after him, passing the glowing Christmas tree.

Chapter Thirty-Eight

The next hour passes by in a blur. Robert takes charge, giving people things to do; Dean and the kitchen staff hand out hot chocolate and brandy; and I help John and Emma to build up the open fire in the living room where everyone congregates. The Inn always has a cosy feel with its beams criss-crossing the ceiling, dark wood furniture and comfy sofas with piles of cushions, but it's hard to feel warm as we stand around anxiously waiting for news.

No one wants to go home without finding out what's going on and finally we get a call from a nurse saying Mick is stable now. Robert hangs up the Inn phone and calls out the news to everyone. 'Joan is staying with him tonight but he's going to be okay. It was a relatively small heart attack so they expect him to make a full recovery, but he needs a lot of rest.'

Everyone claps in relief that he's going to be okay. Mick is seventy and was born in Talting and seemed indestructible, so this has shocked us all.

'If anyone wants any more food or drink, let us know,' Robert adds.

'I guess we better head home,' Emma says to me.

'I'll stay in case Robert needs any help.'

She nods. 'Call me in the morning?'

'I will.' I give her and John a hug. They walk out with Mrs

Morris and a few others, and the room feels emptier. A couple of the guests go up to bed.

'Is there anything I can do?' I ask Robert.

'Some of the staff are heading home. I'm going to the kitchen to make some bacon sandwiches for the guests who want them, if you wouldn't mind helping me?'

'Of course.' I follow him through into the kitchen and we set up a conveyor belt where I butter the bread and he fries the bacon. It's weird how you can still be hungry after a shock, but my stomach rumbles anyway and Robert hands me a sandwich and takes the rest out on a tray. I lean against the counter to eat, relief washing over me that Mick's going to be okay.

'It's just the guests left now,' Robert says, coming back in with an empty tray. 'And I sent them off to bed.' He tells Dean and the remaining staff to go home too. 'Shall I drive you home?' he asks, grabbing a sandwich for himself. 'Or there's a spare room if you want to stay?'

'Maybe I should, in case Joan needs any help in the morning. You were great tonight; you knew exactly what to do.'

'Well, my uncle had a heart attack last year at work. I stayed with him. My dad just kept on working.' He makes a face and puts his half-eaten sandwich down. 'Mick's a good guy, I hope he'll be okay. Joan looked devastated.'

'They've been married for something like fifty years.'

'I can't imagine that,' he replies. He grabs two glasses and fills them with brandy. 'Sit and talk for a bit?'

'Okay.' I follow him out and we sit down on the sofa. I swirl the dark liquid around in my glass, watching the flames flicker in the fireplace, starting to die down. I feel Robert's gaze on me and finally he speaks.

'Do you . . . do you think you and Lucas would have been together as long as Mick and Joan have?'

I rest my head against the sofa and think about it. 'I suppose you never know whether you'll end up growing apart, but I always thought we would stay together. I think that's been the hardest thing to accept – that we won't be together. Having to build a future for myself without him, you know? Learning to live without him after ten years together. And not just ten years, but ten years of growing up together. We were so young. But I know Lucas would want me to build a life without him; he'd want me to live for the both of us.'

'What did you love about him?'

'His zest for life. His easy-going, kind, carefree way. How much he loved people, and this town. How I could talk to him about anything. We were best friends. A team. He was funny. Goofy sometimes. Everyone loved Lucas, it was impossible not to.'

'I really am so sorry,' he says softly.

I look across at him. 'I know you are. I am happy that I knew Lucas and got to love him and be loved by him for ten years. It was special. And I was so lucky. Losing him was the hardest thing I've ever gone through, and I'll always miss him. But for the first time I'm looking forward to Christmas and New Year. I'm looking forwards instead of backwards.'

'I want to do that too.'

'You are doing it. You're changing things. You're moving forward. When you told me who your brother is, all I could feel was guilt that someone who made me happy was connected to why Lucas was taken from me.'

'I should have told you as soon as we met. It got harder

every day. I will never forgive myself for not being honest with you.'

I shake my head. 'It's been hard for me to work through, but I understand why you didn't tell me at first, and then when things started to happen . . . you were just scared. I have forgiven you, Rob. Life's too short to hang on to negative feelings, to let the past hold us back. Especially when you've brought so much happiness back into my life.'

Robert wipes away the tear that has rolled down his cheek. He takes my drink from me and sits it down on the table next to his. He takes one of my hands in his. 'You've changed my life and you've changed me. Even if that's all there will ever be, that's something so special. You know that I love you, Rose. I want us to try again; I want to show you that I'm the man you thought I was, but I understand if you can't do that. I have never felt this way before and it scares me, but it's so beautiful. I'm so grateful to know you.' He reaches towards me and strokes my hair back from my face. 'Thank you for showing me what love is.'

I feel my own eyes well up. The love I can see in his eyes does feel life-changing. I have so much more I want to say to him, but I just don't know how yet. It's been a long night and I feel exhausted. All I want is to lie in his arms and fall asleep.

'Can we go to bed?'

'Together?'

'I just . . . can you hold me?'

'Of course I can.' He kisses my forehead and helps me up. I take his hand and we go up to his room.

We lie down on his bed in our clothes and he pulls the cover over us and holds his arm out to me. I lie against his chest and love the warmth of him holding me. I close my eyes. It feels like home somehow.

'Everything's going to be okay,' Robert whispers to me.

'Can you promise me that?'

'I promise.'

I know then that I've moved past his lie. Somehow I fit with him. I want to be with him. I open my mouth to tell him but he speaks first.

'Go to sleep, Rose,' he whispers, pulling me tightly. 'I'll be here all night.'

My eyelids droop and I think I can tell him in the morning. Right now, this moment is perfect the way it is.

I lift my head and search for his lips in the dark. He works out what I want and brushes his against mine. A shiver runs down my spine. I lay my head back down and hear his heartbeat speed up, my ear pressed to his chest. He sucks in a breath and holds me tightly. I listen to the sound of us breathing together.

When it's right, love should be like breathing – something you don't need to think about, you just do, and something that you need to live.

Could I really find a love like that twice? And if I have, do I get to keep it this time?

I'm asleep before an answer can find me.

Chapter Thirty-Nine

Crisp winter sunlight streams in through a gap in the heavy drapes, creating a pool of light on the carpet. I watch it for a minute, my brain catching up to my senses. The soft pillows under my head are the Inn pillows and the strong arms wrapped around me are Robert's. Last night comes back to me slowly as the fog in my brain clears. It's as if I'm hung over, but I didn't even finish that glass of brandy so I can't be. Perhaps it's just the stress of all that happened. Delayed shock or something.

I need to focus on something. I concentrate on the sound of gentle, steady breathing in my ear, slightly tickling my neck. It calms me. Even though last night was a nightmare, I know Robert and I made a good team, and after it all, I just wanted to be with him. I didn't want to go home alone. I needed his touch. His comfort. It wasn't just the pull of someone lonely, but of something deeper.

I lift my head and turn a little so I can watch Robert sleeping. He looks peaceful and annoyingly gorgeous considering we slept in our clothes. His hair is messy and I reach out to touch it. He feels me move and turns his head to face me. Opening his eyes, he meets mine and we look at each other for a moment. Warmth runs through me.

Without thinking, I follow my instinct and lean towards

him. I kiss him softly and feel that familiar spark between us. Robert murmurs and pulls me closer. Our lips move together and I pull him closer still, deepening the kiss. Robert's breath hitches and he shifts me so I move on top of him, his tongue searching mine, his hand moving down to my back. I find it so easy to lose myself in his kiss. I always have. It's like his lips were formed to be a perfect fit for mine, as if they were half of a puzzle piece.

'I have something to show you,' he whispers, his lips touching my cheek as he speaks.

I look at him questioningly, trying to catch my breath. He gently lifts me off him and I sit on the edge of the bed as he steps over to the wardrobe and pulls out something wrapped in brown paper. He unties the paper and it slips away to reveal a canvas. He props it up against the wardrobe door and I let out a small gasp as my heart painting is revealed.

'How do you have it?' I ask him.

'I was always the buyer, not Heather. When you sent me the invitation to your exhibition, I looked at the pieces on the gallery website, and I'm not ashamed to admit it, when I saw this one I cried.'

'You cried?'

'To me, it showed perfectly how my life was before and after I met you.' Robert comes back over and kneels on the floor looking up at me. 'It was like I was living in winter – it was cold and lonely, but then I met you, and it felt as if everything would be okay. It was like summer again. I felt happy for the first time in too long. When I saw this piece, I knew that no matter what happened between us, I wanted it to remember you, and everything you did for me. I would never have left my job and stood up to my father if it wasn't for you. Your love made me brave. I feel stronger for knowing you. And if what we had is over, then it's okay, because I am a better man for knowing you.'

I shake my head, a lump lodging itself in my throat. 'I can't believe you were the one who bought this painting, Rob. So much of the summer in it is down to you. It wouldn't exist without you.' I look into his eyes gazing up at me and I know that I want to be with him. I want to take a leap of faith. I want the risk that comes with loving him. Even though it still scares me, I have to. It just feels right between us now.

It hits me then – the only way I can move on and accept that I won't spend my life with Lucas is to spend it with someone completely different to him. Someone who makes me feel completely different and whose love is completely different.

I can't compare them because they don't compare.

Robert isn't second best. He's a second chance.

I think about all the things Robert has done for me since we met. He went to the gallery and made sure my art would be recognised; he gave me the push to be the artist I always wanted, but was too scared, to be; he brought me to Taylor because he knew how much I'd always wanted to have a cat; he didn't want me to feel alone in my cottage and he put lights on my tree so I'd have something to guide me home at night; and he came to talk to Graham and Gloria because he knew I'd never be able to forgive him or move past his lies without them accepting his being here. He knew that I couldn't accept his love while he was still tied to his father and everything that his father stood for. But mostly he knew I could never be happy with him until he was happy with himself.

Ever since I met him, he's done things for me, things I

didn't have to ask him to do because he knew I needed them. He's shown how much he cares for me instead of just telling me. And he's waited for me even though he didn't know if I'd ever be able to move on from the past. He's loved me even though he couldn't be sure that I could ever love anyone else after Lucas.

He has my heart. He has since we met.

The heart that he holds is now racing like crazy. I climb down from the bed and kneel in front of him so that our eyes are level. 'Life has felt impossible since Lucas died, but you've made me happy again. It hasn't been easy for us, but I don't know, I can't help thinking that we were meant to find each other. And I know you're unsure about how I feel but . . .' I stop to take another breath and try to hold back the tears. 'I love you. And it's no less than I've loved before. And if I hadn't had that other love, we would never have met. Sometimes I wonder if Lucas brought us together somehow. It feels as if we're meant to be. That we have his blessing.' The tears really start flowing then and Robert is crying too.

'You love me?' he asks so softly, I barely hear him.

I smile through my tears. 'Yes, I love you.'

His eyes light up and he pulls me to him, wrapping his arms tightly around me. I lean into him, glad that we had time apart because I think we both needed it to decide who we wanted to be, and to be sure we wanted to be those people together. 'You have my heart, Rose,' he says then.

'And you have mine.'

When he leans back, he wipes away a tear and then smiles at me. 'You scare me, Rose.'

'Why?' I ask him nervously.

'I've wanted so much for my life that I've never thought I

could have. I've spent so much time wishing I could tell my father to back off, to go after what I want, but I've never had the guts to do it – but you make me feel like I can do anything. That's scary, Rose. Really scary, but also kind of wonderful.'

'It's the same for me,' I tell him, reaching out to trace the stubble on his face with my fingertips, causing him to take a sharp intake of breath. I smile up at him. 'I don't know how long you're going to be here.' Now it's my turn to look uncertain.

He leans in to whisper in my ear. 'You've got me for as long as you want me.'

'Well, that's good, because I think I'm going to want you for a long time.' Desperate to feel his lips on mine, I clutch his shirt with my fist and pull him towards me. Then I pause before our lips meet and search his eyes. 'But you don't know what you're going to do, do you?' He's left his job and home and I don't want him to decide what he wants to do is far away from me here.

'I will,' he promises and closes the gap, crushing my lips with his. I wonder if I'll ever not feel the heat that pulsates through my body as we kiss, pressing our bodies together as we frantically try to be as close as possible.

We stay on the floor as we shed our clothes. Our time apart has made us so much stronger, and every time he touches me my body lights up like it's on fire and Robert relishes making me burn.

279

Chapter Forty

Robert and I meet Emma and John for breakfast at Mrs Morris's café the following morning. We sit at a corner table huddled over steaming cups of tea to fight off the bitter frost of the morning, and then Mrs Morris brings over a plate of bacon and egg sandwiches.

'So, we have a big birthday coming up . . .' Emma says, grabbing a sandwich and taking an enormous bite, ketchup spilling out of the corner of her mouth. John hands her a napkin.

I groan. 'I can't believe I'm going to be twenty-seven.'

'Wait until you're almost thirty-one before you complain,' Robert replies, giving me a nudge to remind me he's older than the rest of us.

'We have already made plans,' Emma continues with a mischievous grin playing on her lips.

'What plans?' I ask, instantly curious.

'We have to tell her,' John says to Emma. 'Remember the twenty-two incident?'

Robert looks at me questioningly, so I explain what happened for my twenty-second birthday. 'Well, Lucas decided to have a surprise party for me at Joe's. He didn't know that I'd asked Joe for the night off weeks before, so he left work early and met everyone on the beach. Then they came to the bar ready for a big surprise, but there was just Joe there looking confused,' I tell him with a laugh. 'Lucas had to call to tell me to come to the bar.'

Robert chuckles. 'Surprise parties always seem to go wrong.'

'Okay, you didn't hear it from us then, but there is a surprise party planned,' Emma says. 'I want to make sure you turn up to this one.'

'How will I look surprised now?'

'You'll have to practise. It's at the Inn – Mick and Joan wanted to thank everyone, I think, so this was the perfect opportunity.'

Robert's phone rings. 'Unknown – probably a cold call,' he says, looking at the screen. He answers it. 'Hello? Yes, speaking. Who? What? Oh . . .' He stands up hurriedly and gives us an apologetic look before walking outside to continue with the call.

'I hate having my birthday at Christmas time,' I say, glancing through the window to see Robert pacing outside the café as he talks on the phone.

'We promise not to give you a joint present,' John says. Emma elbows him. 'What was that for?'

'I've already got her present.'

I lose track of their bickering as I watch Robert put his phone in his pocket and run a hand through his hair before kicking the kerb with his foot.

'Something's going on,' I say to Emma and John, standing up and going outside to him, feeling their eyes on me. 'What is it?' I ask, going over and putting a hand on his shoulder.

He turns to me and I see tears in his eyes. 'It's Jeremy.'

I take an involuntary step back.

'What's happened? I ask, fearing the worst. My pulse starts to speed up and I can feel it throbbing in my neck.

'He's in hospital. A suspected overdose. The hospital had no one else to contact. He's unconscious. In intensive care.'

'Oh, Rob, I'm sorry.'

He looks at me and I see the fear in his eyes. 'I have to go to him. Now.'

I don't miss the implied words 'before it's too late'. 'Of course.' I watch helplessly as he moves to his car parked a few feet away and then I step forward. 'I'll come with you.'

He looks up as he pulls open the car door.

'No, Rose.'

'You might need me.'

'But it's . . . Jeremy.'

I take a deep breath. 'You might need me,' I repeat. The man I love needs my help and I'm not going to let the past hold me back from being there for him. 'Let me help you.'

He hesitates and I take that as agreement, jumping into the car before he can stop me. He climbs in beside me.

'Are you really sure?'

'Just drive, we're wasting time.' Robert starts the car up and I grab my phone to hastily text Emma to explain our sudden departure from the café.

I watch Talting roll past us silently. I take Robert's hand in mine and he squeezes it gratefully. I know that if a member of my family were in hospital, I'd want him with me. I try not to think about it being Jeremy, about seeing the man who destroyed everything; I just focus on being here for Robert. But in the background my mind buzzes with the word 'overdose'. Could he have done this because of the accident? Tried to take his own life because of his guilt?

We drive out to the hospital just a couple of hours away, and find the intensive care unit. We walk hand in hand in nervous silence through the corridors to get there.

We find Jeremy's doctor in the unit. 'Jeremy took an overdose of sleeping pills. The friend he was staying with found him and called an ambulance. He was conscious for a few moments when he arrived but hasn't woken up since. We are getting the pills out of his system and then it's a waiting game to see if there will be any . . . lasting damage.'

'He took sleeping pills?' Robert repeats, looking dazed. His face has no colour.

The doctor nods gravely. 'I need to do my rounds now, but you can go in and see him. And do you have a contact for his parents?'

'I'll call them,' he says quickly.

The doctor nods. 'Any questions, just ask,' he says before walking away briskly.

Robert steps forward to look through the glass. I join him and we see Jeremy on the bed full of tubes, the steady beeping of a heart monitor next to him. 'I can't believe this. I thought he stayed away because he was okay, you know? But . . .'

I take hold of his hand again and squeeze it. There are no words to say right now. 'What about your parents?'

He shakes his head. 'My mum would be hysterical and my dad would immediately start worrying what people will think. Jeremy can decide when to tell them.' He looks at me. 'He will be okay, won't he?'

I pull him to me and wrap my arms around him. It kills me to see Robert in pain. I look at Jeremy again, trying to reconcile this weak and defenceless man with the monster

I've long believed him to be. Robert loves him in spite of everything; he's his brother, and for that reason I will him to be okay. And then I feel guilty all over again, even though this is all beyond my control, because he has the opportunity to be okay whereas Lucas doesn't. I look away and go to sit on one of the plastic chairs in the corridor. If he isn't okay then two lives will have been wiped out because of one night. Can I ever wish that?

We stay in the hospital most of the day and I buy us coffee and sandwiches that we barely touch. The doctor and nurses are in and out and pronounce him to be stable, but still he lies in that bed unconscious. When there is no sign he'll wake up as night draws in, I persuade Robert to come to a hotel nearby with me to get some rest.

Here Robert paces the room, unsure if he should be calling his parents now. Because what if the worst does happen?

'If they lose out on the chance to say goodbye . . .' I say finally, unable to watch his agitation silently any longer. I lie on the bed as he paces in front of me. I don't want his parents involved any more than he does, but I think about Gloria and Graham and how they would have done anything to have been with Lucas during his last moments.

He stops and nods. 'I can't believe he did this. I never thought for one moment . . . I'm sorry, you're right, they should know,' he says, taking his phone out of his pocket and looking at it as if it might explode in his hands. Then he looks at me. 'Are you sure you're okay with this?'

I think about it for a moment. How will we get through this and any other emergency that may affect his family? 'He's your brother. He's important, I get that. Look, if we are going to be together . . .'

He sits on the bed by me and smiles a little. 'If? I thought this was a done deal. It is for me.'

I smile too. 'And for me. Okay, so we are going to be together, well then . . . What do we do about your family in our lives?'

His phone rings in his hands, making us both jump. He answers it quickly and lets out a long breath. He looks at me and smiles.

'He's awake,' he mouths. 'Thank you, we will.' He hangs up. 'They want him to rest tonight but we can see him in the morning. I better call my parents now. He's going to be okay.' He climbs off the bed then looks back at me. 'Thank you, Rose. You amaze me.'

I shake my head. 'I just love you.' I realise that it's enough for me. We can get through anything because we have each other now.

He looks at me as if he feels exactly the same. 'I love you too.'

He calls his parents and I lean back against the pillow thinking about the strange turn of events. How could I have imagined that I would end up being so closely linked to the man who drove into Lucas that night? And yet here I am supporting Robert, his brother, and feeling relief that he'll be okay for Robert's sake. And I suppose part of my anger was always about Jeremy being able to carry on with his life when Lucas's ended, but it's clear now that he has been struggling enough to ingest a bottle of sleeping pills. I can't feel any sense of satisfaction, though. Instead I just feel more heartbreak that another person has had their life ruined by that night, and that someone Robert loves was so close to being gone too.

For Robert's sake, I need to find some kind of closure. I can't spend my life confused as to whether I want Jeremy to be miserable or happy, and terrified before any family event in case he's there. I want Robert and I to build a life together – so does that mean accepting his family like he would accept mine?

I think about how great he's been about me being so close with Lucas's parents. He's never stopped me remembering or talking about Lucas; every day we're surrounded by memories of my life with him; and yet he wants to be with me, wants to be in Talting and has always been respectful of my marriage and the life I shared with Lucas.

Can I do the same for him? I close my eyes, wishing for a sign to show me what to do. I wish I knew what Lucas would want me to do. I feel the familiar ache of missing him that I think I always will.

Robert hangs up the phone and comes to lie beside me. He wraps his arm around me and I lean into him, taking my usual comfort from his proximity. He kisses me gently on top of my head and I feel myself slide into sleep, exhausted by the day and nervous about what awaits us tomorrow.

Chapter Forty-One

Robert admits to not sleeping much when we get up the next morning and picks at the room service breakfast we order. He is obviously anxious to see his brother and offers to order a taxi for me back to Talting but I tell him I'm coming with him. I know that if I don't see Jeremy now then it will weigh on my mind, possibly even for years, and if Robert and I stand a chance of making it as a couple, I need to face this sooner rather than later.

The hospital is eerily quiet when we arrive, dawn having just broken. We go back to the ICU and through the glass I can see Jeremy looking up at the ceiling. He looks so small. His hair is scruffy and fair. I can see why no one from Talting linked the two of them. They couldn't look more different.

I watch Robert staring at his brother as if he's looking at a ghost. He hasn't seen him for two years, so the description isn't far off. He looks at me. 'Will you . . .' I take hold of his hand and we step inside the room, drawing slowly closer to the bed.

'Robert?' Jeremy says, his voice just a croak. Robert walks up to him and sinks into the chair by the bed, taking his brother's hand in his. Jeremy's eyes drift to me. I hover behind Robert, looking into the eyes of the man who took Lucas from me, and almost extinguished himself too.

'This is Rose,' Robert says softly. Jeremy looks confused and Robert nods. 'Rose Walker.'

'Rose?' Jeremy looks at me, frowning as he tries to place me. I wonder if he recognises me from the newspaper reports at the time.

'She was Lucas's wife,' Robert confirms, his voice soft. 'We are . . . together.'

'Together?'

I sink down into the chair at the edge of the room, no idea what to do with my hands. I shift uncomfortably under Jeremy's piercing gaze.

'How are you doing?' Robert asks then, drawing Jeremy's attention from me.

'I've been better,' Jeremy answers with a wry smile. Then he coughs, wincing at the pain that follows. He shifts himself in the bed.

'Why did you do it?' Robert asks with urgency. 'Why didn't you call me? All this time I haven't heard from you, I didn't know where you were, or anything . . .'

Jeremy sighs. 'I had to get away from . . .' His eyes find mine again. 'Him,' he finishes, his voice cracking.

I stand up. I feel as if the room is closing in. 'Coffee,' I blurt out. 'I'll get . . .' I hurry out of the room and around the corner where I lean against the wall and suck in two deep breaths. I am filled with pity for him and that is a hard feeling to bear. I walk off in search of coffee and sit alone outside to drink it, giving them time to be alone. I saw the questions in Jeremy's eyes – how could Robert be with me? I don't know how Robert will answer that. It makes no logical sense and yet here we are.

After I've sat with an empty plastic cup in hand for half an hour I know I should go back in. I have things I need to say to him. When I walk back into his room, the brothers are talking quietly and both look at me when I enter. Robert smiles, his eyes lighting up, as I know mine do when I see him. Jeremy looks cautious, nervous, scared . . . small.

Jeremy looks at me and then his brother and then me again. Then he picks up their conversation. 'I just thought it would be easier for everyone if I . . .' He trails off and an uneasy silence follows his sentence.

Finally, Robert clears his throat. 'You made a mistake.'

'It was more than that,' Jeremy snaps.

'I know that,' I say before Robert can respond. 'Your mistake cost me my husband.'

He flinches as if I've slapped him. 'You don't know how sorry I am, how I wish I could go back in time. I thought I was okay to drive . . .' He coughs and his eyes drift to the ceiling again. 'Mark should have just left me . . . let me . . .' He trails off and I walk right up to the bed so he has to look at me.

'Do you know how selfish that sounds?' I say, my anger rising. 'Lucas didn't have a choice that night. Do you think if he had he would have chosen to die? You got a second chance and this is what you choose to do with it? You could have died too that night.'

'I should have done,' he says quietly.

'I'm not going to lie to you, if I had the option, then yes, I would want Lucas to have lived over you. Of course I would. But I've fallen in love with your brother and for his sake I hope that you'll be okay. He doesn't deserve to be put through any more pain because of you. You owe it to him, to me, to yourself, but most of all you owe it to Lucas to do something with your life. To make something of your life.' I am breathless by the end of my rapid speech. My hands are shaking afterwards and Robert stands up and wraps an arm around my waist to hold me steady.

Jeremy's eyes glisten with tears. 'How do I do that?' he whispers.

Robert looks down at him. 'You turn things around. You find something positive to do. You rebuild yourself and your life. You don't let the past ruin your future.'

Jeremy coughs and wipes his eyes. 'It's that easy?'

'Of course it's not easy,' Roberts says. 'You think these past years have been easy on any of us? No. It's been hard as hell and it will keep being hard. But what's the alternative? We all just give up? No. We can't. We all owe it to Lucas to live our lives to the full.'

Jeremy chokes back a sob and I look away, my own eyes filled with tears. There's a long silence. I sink into a chair again and Robert returns to his brother's side. Jeremy quietly cries. I see someone broken on the bed. I think we all broke that night. Now we need to put the pieces of ourselves back together again. Finally, Jeremy looks at me. 'I am so sorry about what happened,' he whispers, his voice so fragile, I have to lean forward to hear him. 'I know that can't mean much to you.'

I wipe my own eyes. 'It does mean something, I can see you are sincere. And I wouldn't want anyone to feel so desperate they do what you tried to do.' I lean my head against the wall behind me, feeling exhausted. 'I know that you didn't set out that night planning to get into an accident, but the fact is, it happened and you shouldn't have been driving. And then you avoided any consequences for it. We didn't get any justice for Lucas and I'm never going to be okay with that. You should have gone to prison and if I could make it happen even now, I probably would still want you sent there.' I pause to take in a long, shaky breath. 'But I can't change the past; all I can do is try to move on and think about the future. I don't know what twisted bit of fate thought I should fall in love with your brother, but it's happened, and I've had to come to terms with the guilt I felt about that and hope that Lucas would understand and want me to be happy.

'Being with Robert means you'll always be in my life, however dimly, and I know he wants to see you happy as well. I can't ever forgive you for what happened. I lost my husband and he was the best man, better than you'll ever be however hard you try, and I'll never forget him or how he was taken from me. What I'd like, though, is not to see you waste your life. I know that Lucas wouldn't want that either. He loved life and he'd want to still be here if he could, so you need to respect your life, and make something positive happen out of all this devastation.' I lift my head up. 'You need to promise us you will,' I add, meaning us in this room and Lucas wherever he is. I can feel him somehow giving me the strength I need for this. I hope he'll always be there to bring me strength. I think he will.

Robert's phone beeps with a text – his parents are on their way.

'I don't think I can . . .' I start to say, trying to stop the tears from flowing. I can't deal with meeting them too today. I need more time for that.

'I'm taking you home,' he says firmly, understanding instantly. 'Jeremy?'

Jeremy holds out a hand to me. 'Rose?'

Hesitantly, I get up, walking slowly towards the bed. I touch his hand, which feels cold against mine, and he curls his fingers around mine. Jeremy's eyes meet mine. 'I promise,' he says.

I nod, having to trust his word for now. I can see someone who's fallen so far and I hope that he will lift himself back up. I let go of Jeremy's hand and have to admit I feel a sense of peace in letting go of some of my anger towards him. I needed to do this. I hope he lives up to his promise. Robert takes my empty hand and leads me out of the room, enveloping me in a tight hug once we're outside. I sob in his arms, releasing everything I've been holding on to.

It's time to let it all go.

It's time for us to be free.

Chapter Forty-Two

Snow arrives on Christmas Eve, an event I haven't ever seen in Talting before. The white flakes flow in thick sideways sheets, covering the roofs and pavements like a cake being dusted with icing sugar. The town looks like a Christmas card picture.

I fiddle with my outfit, hoping this evening goes well. I chose a red velvet dress for tonight and have covered it with my thick black wool coat to ward off the weather as I wait for Robert to pick me up, listening to Christmas music.

It's been a couple of weeks since Robert and I visited the hospital and Jeremy has been allowed home. He has chosen to stay with their aunt, and his mother is going to stay there too. I think Robert is pleased they will all be taking some time away from his father. He's going to see them on Boxing Day. I think he's determined to help Jeremy now to make sure the past doesn't repeat itself. And I'll give him the support that he needs.

There's a soft knock at the door and I open it up, smiling immediately when I see Robert. He looks good in a white shirt, skinny tie and dark trousers topped off with a dark wool coat. I prefer him in his casual Talting look, but he looks sexy tonight. He kisses me on the cheek, handing me a single red rose.

'You look stunning,' he says, giving me an appreciative look up and down.

'So do you.' I lay the rose down on the table and pick up my bag. 'Ready for our dinner?'

He winks. 'Definitely.' He takes my hand and we step outside, hurrying to the car but instantly getting covered by a layer of white.

'It hasn't snowed at this time of year before,' I say, shutting the car door quickly.

'Emma is pretty stressed about it, worrying about the caterers—'

'Caterers? How big is this thing?'

Robert grins as he switches on the engine and a welcome blast of warm air hits us.

'I don't think Emma does anything by halves, right?'

I lean back in the seat. 'Oh, God.'

Robert pulls away and drives towards the Inn.

'I thought my time of being the centre of attention was over after my exhibition.'

'No way. There will be plenty more of those, for starters,' he replies. 'I think it's sweet she wants everyone to celebrate you.' He reaches over and squeezes my hand. 'I haven't forgotten your present, by the way, it just needs tweaking.'

'Tweaking?'

'All will be revealed later.'

'Intriguing.'

He pulls into the Inn car park, which is suspiciously empty of cars. I laugh. 'Where the hell did they put them all?'

'There's a blocked up road over there,' he says, jerking his finger. 'I said they should leave some as there would be people staying at the Inn, but I was outvoted. The caterers were pretty annoyed, I can tell you.'

'I bet. Shifting stuff in this weather would not be fun. Okay, let's do this.'

'Have you practised your surprised face?'

I nod and put my hands up to my face, dropping my mouth open dramatically. 'Is this okay?' I joke, knowing I look ridiculous.

'Maybe open your eyes wider, like this,' he says, pulling a face that makes him look like a fish.

I burst out laughing.

'What?'

'Come on, loser.' I climb out and shiver immediately. We hurry into the lobby and make our way to the restaurant, hand in hand. The open fire and Christmas decorations are a welcome sight after being outside, even for only a couple of minutes, and I feel warmer already.

We walk through the door into the dark dining room, which suddenly lights up. The faces of friends are before me, all shouting 'surprise!' and waving their drinks. I try to do a good job of looking surprised and gasp – probably a bit too melodramatically – as I hear Robert chuckle under his breath, but actually it's not that easy to pretend to be surprised when you're not an actress. I think everyone is too pleased with themselves to notice, though.

Emma jumps on me, pulling me into a big hug.

'Happy birthday, lovely,' she cries, thrusting a glass of champagne into my hand and somehow pulling my coat off at the same time. She gives it to Robert and pulls me further into the room. The usual tables and chairs have been taken away and there's just a table at the end with food and drink piled on it with a big banner with gold letters saying 'Happy

Birthday Rose' draped above it. There are gold balloons touching the ceiling and lights draped across the doors that lead on to the terrace. The town is all dressed up and the room looks both elegant and festive. Christmas music plays softly from the speakers by the doors and the room smells of warm spices from scented candles in each corner.

'This place looks amazing,' I say to Emma.

'I'm glad you like it. Look,' she says, pointing to the corner where a pile of presents waits for me.

'I said no presents,' I hiss, but she just shrugs and leads me over to her parents standing with Gloria and Graham.

I lose sight of Robert as I greet everyone and try not to get too emotional at being surrounded by everyone I love. The champagne is not helping with this. My last birthday was a quiet one as I struggled to enjoy it without Lucas – he always made a big deal out of my birthdays – but I'm glad Emma did this for me this year; it really feels like a new beginning. For all of us.

Emma's mum comes over to hug me. 'You and Robert must come for dinner soon with Emma and John,' she says, giving me a warm smile.

'We will, I promise,' I reply. I've always suspected Mum asked her to watch out for me and, even though I'm all grown up now, she still always lives up to her promise.

'Right, I won't hold you hostage,' Sue says, looking over her shoulder as a woman makes her way to us.

'Happy birthday, Rose.'

'Heather,' I cry, kissing her on the cheek. 'Thanks for coming.' I spot Robert then, in the corner talking to Mick. He's out of hospital and is doing okay but Joan hovers close by him, eyeing him anxiously. Robert senses my gaze and smiles across at me. He looks like he's planning something.

'I wouldn't have missed it. Are you working on anything new yet?'

I smile at her mind always being on business. 'No, but I have a couple of ideas.'

'Well, I can't wait to see them.'

'Well, well, my two favourite ladies,' Dan says, coming over to stand between us. He's wearing a leather jacket indoors and looks comical standing next to Heather in her elegant black dress. They would certainly be an unconventional couple, but something tells me they would work.

'You again?' I joke, leaning over to kiss him on the cheek.

'What can I say? This place is growing on me.'

'Maybe you can hold a retreat here one day.'

'You know, I might have to come along on one of these retreats myself after hearing so much about them,' Heather tells him.

'I would love that,' he says. She looks a bit stunned that he seems serious and I edge away, hoping the festive season might encourage something to blossom.

Emma pushes her way through a group to find me. 'Are you having a good time?'

'It's great, thank you.'

'What are best friends for? Okay, I have something to tell you,' she says, hissing into my ear. 'I was going to wait but I really can't.'

'What is it?'

'Let's go outside.'

'It's snowing.'

She waves a gold-wrapped box. 'You'll get your present out of it.'

'Okay, fine.' I grab my coat and follow her out of the door and on to the terrace. The snow has died down but it's still icy cold and the breeze floating from the water takes my breath away. The noise and the warmth of the party fades as Emma pulls the door shut behind us.

'Okay, here you go. Happy birthday,' she says, passing me the box. 'Oh, and I'm pregnant.'

Chapter Forty-Three

I give Emma a big squeeze. 'I'm so happy for you.'

She leads us over to a table and we perch on a seat, making sure our coats provide a barrier between us and the cold iron. 'You know, I was wondering today about when it was exactly that I first thought about having children. I couldn't remember, because it was something I always wanted. I can't even really explain why. It was just this feeling inside me, this need to be a mum. I know it doesn't make sense . . . I just can't give up something I've always wanted. I'm scared, though, after what happened. I just hope that this time . . .'

I give her hand a gentle squeeze. 'I know.'

'I just need to believe that everything will work out okay.'

'You both deserve this. I have everything crossed for you.'

She smiles. 'I'm going to wait to tell anyone else, though, until I have the three-month scan. I want to be sure this time. But I had to tell you.'

'I'm glad you did.'

'Now, open your gift.'

I smile and carefully tear open the silver paper to reveal a photo in a distressed cream frame of Emma, John, Robert and me at Joe's.

'Oh Em, it's lovely. Thank you.'

'I like him, Rose, and he makes you happy. You used to have all those photos on your mantelpiece, remember? Maybe you can put this one there. Start a collection again.'

I think about all the photos I locked away and the ones hidden on my phone and computer. It would be nice to have photos on show again. The idea of it doesn't scare me anymore. Memories shouldn't be something to be scared of; they should be treasured. They made you who you are and what your life is. Good and bad. They are part of you. 'I think I will.'

'It feels like a fresh start for all of us, doesn't it?' Emma says, reading my mind.

The door behind us opens, flooding the terrace with sudden light. We turn around and see Robert leaning out of the door. 'I don't want to interrupt . . .'

'It's fine,' Emma says. 'I need to get something ready,' she adds with a wink.

I wonder what cake she has got. It always feels strange eating cake I haven't made myself. She gets up and gives me a kiss on the cheek, then does the same to Robert.

'You two are my favourites,' she says and disappears back into the party, shutting us outside.

Robert comes over and sits down next to me.

'So, it seems to be present time then?'

'It's a tough cross for me to bear,' I reply.

'Mine is perhaps an unconventional gift,' he says, reaching into his shirt pocket and pulling out a small silver key. He lays it across my palm. 'Happy birthday, Rose.'

I narrow my eyes suspiciously. 'This isn't for handcuffs, is it? You don't have some fetish you're going to tell me about, do you?'

Robert bursts out laughing and gives me a quick kiss. 'You will never stop surprising me, Ms Walker. And no, it's not for handcuffs, but if you want to get some, I won't object. No, I'll tell you what's going on.' He swivels in his seat so he's facing me and holds my hand. 'I've been thinking ever since I told my dad that I wanted to leave the firm about what to do next. All I knew was that I wanted to be with you, but then I made myself think about what else I wanted and I came up with this place. The summer here was amazing, and not just because of you – I love this town. It's peaceful but fun, and everyone is kind of crazy, but it's also a community. It's a place I can see myself growing old in. And then I thought about the night of the tree lighting. It was so horrible seeing Mick like that and everyone being so happy one minute and panicked the next, but I realised I had done something. I had helped out with the Inn and I had enjoyed it. I liked the problem solving, talking to the guests, helping, managing the staff, organising things.'

I wonder where he is going with this but I nod in complete agreement. 'You did a great job.'

'When Mick came back, he was really grateful but he was also worried. The heart attack was a real scare but it had been building for a while. He was finding it hard to run the Inn with Joan. It was getting busier during the summer and at a time when they wanted to slow down, it wasn't letting them. He admitted he had thought about retiring but he was too worried about who might buy the place. None of their children were interested in taking it on, and he wanted to keep it as a hotel for the town and didn't want some corporate company to come in and bulldoze the place or something.'

I look down at the key, things clicking into place. 'That wouldn't be good for the town.'

'I agree, so I asked him if someone came forward who promised to keep it as a hotel, who wanted it to remain part of the town, would he sell it? And he said yes.'

'You bought Talting Inn?' I say, my voice barely audible.

'He drove a hard bargain and I had to practically hand over my soul, but yes, he agreed to sell it to me. And selling my flat has meant I had enough to convince the bank to lend me the rest to buy it and renovate it too.'

I let the news sink in for a moment. 'So, you'll be staying here? For good?'

'Yes. That's what I want.' He curls his hand around mine holding the key. 'I bought this place because I fell in love with it this summer and this is where I want to be. But Rose, I'd be lying if I didn't tell you that I also bought it because of you. I want to be here with you. There are cottages out the back they don't currently use; I thought they might make a great art studio for you.'

My lips curve into a smile. 'Really? This is so exciting. But will you be able to run it on your own? Mick and Joan were always a team.' I look down at the key. 'I'd love to help you, if that's something you'd want?'

His face lights up. 'Of course it is. I'd never want your art to be sacrificed, but I can see us working together,' he says, his hand covering mine and squeezing the key between us.

'Me too,' I agree. We'll make a good team, I know it. I reach for him and we embrace. Robert pulls back to give me a slow, lingering kiss. I don't feel cold at all anymore.

'I know that I didn't do things right when we first met but I'll spend my life making it up to you, Rose. I love you with all my heart.' Robert says then, speaking in a low voice close to my ear. He wraps an arm around my shoulders and we look out to sea, watching the dark waves roll over the sand. 'There's one more thing . . .' he whispers.

He leads me through the party into the lounge and over to the crackling log fire that we sat by the night of the tree-lighting. The painting of horses has been removed and in its place hangs my heart painting, *Without winter, there would be no spring*.

Robert takes my hand in his and I squeeze it, looking up at my painting, which looks as if it was always meant to be here.

I wonder if Lucas is out there somewhere watching us and I wonder what he thinks. He always said that love was a gift and if you're lucky to have it you should always fight for it. He always fought for us, and now I want to fight for this new love with Robert. I'll never forget Lucas, though; he will always be in my heart.

Out of a tragedy has sprung something beautiful. I didn't know that I needed Robert and he didn't know that he needed me, but we both found what we didn't know we were looking for.

'It belongs here,' Robert murmurs, pulling me closer.

'Like us. Let's never leave,' I say, turning to smile at him.

'Deal,' he replies, bringing his lips to mine again. He kisses me deeply, sending warmth through my body and branding himself alongside Lucas forever in my heart.

Epilogue

Eighteen months later

Hand in hand, we enter the church on a warm June day, surrounded by pretty much everyone in town. We take our seats in the front pew and I smile over at Emma standing up at the front with John and the vicar and their baby boy wriggling in her arms.

Today, Lucas Smith is being christened, and Robert and I will be his godparents. I was so touched when Emma and John told me the name they'd chosen for their first baby. I know that Lucas would have been too. I hope he gets to see this, wherever he is. The happiness radiating from them can be felt at the back of the church and beyond. And boy, do they deserve it.

'Is everything ready?' I whisper to Robert, fretting about the arrangements for the party afterwards.

'Don't worry, they'll love it,' he says back, touching my thigh reassuringly.

We both love running the Inn together. We redecorated it and put our own stamp on it, and were relieved to have it fully booked for our first summer as co-managers. Some of my paintings now hang in the rooms, and the income I get from selling my work still amazes me. I work in the cottages

Robert had renovated for me at the back of the hotel, whenever I feel inspired, and have actually become a bit of a tourist attraction myself. Dan has even booked to hold his next artists' retreat with us.

We wanted to keep work and home separate, though, so we are expanding my cottage to make it work for two, well, three, including Taylor.

I glance across at Gloria and Graham, who now come to the hotel for their weekly Sunday lunch and always get the best table with a view of the sea. They've welcomed Robert more than I could ever have hoped for and they'll always be part of my life. It's been trickier with Robert's family, but we're getting there slowly. His mum comes to the Inn for dinner when his dad is away on business. His father has kept his distance, but I know that Robert would like them to be reconciled one day. Jeremy is living in London, training to be a teacher, and is slowly but surely turning his life around. He has been to see us at the Inn a couple of times. Robert is proud of his progress and I'm pleased to see him sticking to the promise he made us, and to himself.

After the service finishes, I slip out of the back of the church. The small graveyard is hidden by trees and I walk towards his grave slowly, letting the peace of the setting sink into my skin.

All I can hear are the birds circling in the light blue sky dotted with fluffy white clouds. I always feel that nothing can touch you here – it seems so removed from the world, as though it has its own place in the universe, not tainted by anything else.

Lucas actually didn't want to be buried. He told me that he wanted his ashes scattered at sea but his parents couldn't bear to do that, and I guess sometimes death is about the people you leave behind, so I didn't fight them over it. I will always think of him out there in the sea instead of here in the ground, though.

That's why I have resisted coming here for so long. I look at the gravestone with his name on and hate that it reduces him to something so cold and lifeless, but I refuse to believe this is where he really is. I want him to hear me, though, and maybe this will connect me to him somehow.

I sit down cross-legged in front of him on the slightly damp grass. I clear my throat and speak to him out loud.

'I was thinking this morning about the time we rowed and didn't speak for a week. It was before we moved in together and I'd seen you chatting with some girl at school. I can't even remember who she was; I think she moved to London. But at the time, I was convinced you were flirting with her, that you fancied her. And I didn't believe you when you said you didn't. I realised that week how insecure love can make you. I was afraid that we'd break up, but I was too scared to tell you that.

'Then you turned up at Emma's parents' house with that scrapbook. It had taken you ages to cut out pictures of women from magazines – models, actresses, singers. Hundreds of them. And you said it didn't matter if any of them turned up in Talting, you'd still pick me because you loved me. I still have that book. It was silly but romantic, a bit like you.

'I've never met a celebrity, but I have met a man, and at first, I felt so guilty. Because you never loved anyone but me. You kept that promise you made when we were young enough not to know any better. You never met any woman that you wanted to love more than me. And I didn't think I'd ever love anyone but you.' I pause for breath and for a tear to roll down my cheek. 'The only way I can let my heart move on from us is to love somebody worthy. I want to love someone who deserves it like you deserved it, and someone who loves me back like you loved me. I guess I want you to be happy with the person I choose to love. Because even if I can't keep the same promise you did, I can keep this one. So, I promise, Lucas, that Robert is someone that I wish you could know. That sounds crazy, but I think you would like him. You would respect him. And that keeps me going.'

I pick up the rings around my neck. 'I will always wear your rings, Lucas, even though I also wear one that he gave me.' I glance down at the sapphire engagement ring that Robert gave to me on Valentine's Day. The proposal was perfect for Robert and me. We went for a walk on the beach at dawn, and we sat on the sand to have the coffee and croissants that Robert had brought and then, as we watched the sunrise together, he asked me to spend the rest of my life with him. He instinctively knew I wouldn't want to replace the diamond ring Lucas had given me, so he gave me some-thing unique to match us. We want to have a small wedding on the beach. That place will always be special to us.

'Thank you for all those years you loved me, Lucas, I loved you back even more.' I scoop myself up and look up at the sky as a group of birds fly overhead, out towards the sea. 'I hope, wherever you are, you are happy,' I tell him. I look at his grave one last time and blow him a kiss before walking back towards the church where Robert is waiting for me.

I had a love that I grew up with and now I have a love that I will grow old with.

And I will forever be grateful for both.

Acknowledgements

Thank you to my agent Hannah Ferguson for believing in this story, and me, and for making my dream of being able to hold this book in my hands come true.

Thank you to my editor Emily Griffin for helping me to make this book the best it could be, and for bringing me to Headline! Much love to the whole team at Headline. Special thanks to my fab publicist Frances Gough, Sara Adams for all your hard work, and Siobhan Hooper for the gorgeous cover.

This novel, like all, went through many drafts before it became the story you're reading now so thank you to Juliet Mushens, Sarah Bryars and Elizabeth Arroyo for reading early drafts and giving me such helpful notes.

Thanks to Emma Capron and The Hot Bed team for choosing my short story to win their competition and giving me a taste of being a published writer.

Writing has never been lonely thanks to all the support I've had from fellow bloggers and writers so thanks to everyone I know online and IRL who have given me feedback on my writing, liked my many pictures of Harry (sorry, not sorry), supported this book and generally boosted me when the self-doubt monster swooped in. That's everyone on Wordpress, Twitter, Facebook and Instagram – wish I could list you all but think of the trees!

Special thanks to George Lester for always being so supportive and lovely and replying to my endless cries for help. The best cheerleader and friend a writer could ask for.

Thank you to Harry for letting me use his likeness for Rose's cat Taylor – I'll give you extra treats, I promise.

Thank you to my family and friends for all your support and for not laughing at me when I said I was giving up my job to try to be an author – in my presence anyway.

Special thanks, and lots of love, to my mum for encouraging me to follow my dream and supporting me all the way.

And finally, thanks to everyone who is reading this book. If you can dream it, you can do it!

An Exclusive Q & A with
Victoria Walters

The Second Love of My Life is your heart-warming and touching debut novel. What inspired you to write Rose's story?

Rose, as a character, came to me pretty fully formed – I knew from the start she had lost someone special. I was curious about what might happen after losing someone you love so young and so suddenly. Dealing with grief is something we all have to face at some point and I've read a lot of romances that end with the death of the love interest, so I thought it would be interesting to begin with it instead.

Rose is a passionate painter and eventually works through her emotions in her art. What hobbies are you passionate about?

For me, books have always been a special part of my life as art has been for Rose. Reading and writing are my favourite hobbies, and the things I am most passionate about. I can't believe I'm lucky enough to have turned my hobby into my career, which is how Rose feels about her art.

What is your favourite writing spot?

I have tried to write in public but I just can't do it! I like writing at home, either at the dining-room table or curled up in an armchair under a blanket in winter. I always have to have music playing when I write and often I have my cat Harry curled up with me keeping an eye on what I'm writing.

The novel is set in a picturesque fictitious town in Cornwall, called Talting. Why did you choose to set your novel in Cornwall?

I wanted to create a small, quirky town and was inspired by the town in the TV show *Gilmore Girls*. I thought the stunning scenery of Cornwall would make a perfect setting for the town. I wanted to make it very difficult for Rose to want to live anywhere else.

What was the most difficult part about writing your novel? And what did you enjoy the most?

It was tricky writing from Rose's perspective when she's so lost in grief. I wanted people to connect with her so I think getting the beginning of the book right was the hardest part. I needed glimpses of Rose to come through so readers would root for her. The part I enjoyed the most was creating Talting and all the characters in the town – it was fun creating a special place for Rose to live and I'd quite happily live there too!

In the novel, Rose not only finds love but she also finds herself again. Why was this important to you?

I seem to naturally write stories that way. I enjoy reading coming-of-age stories and I think that has fed into my own writing. I like seeing a character blossom and learn to love themselves alongside falling in love with someone. I didn't want the story to be about Robert 'saving' Rose – they save each other. They have to each find out what they want from life before they can be together.

You have also written the digital short story prequel, *The Summer I Met You*. What else do we learn about the characters of Talting?

The short story is set before the novel and its main focus is on how Emma and John met and fell in love, two of my favourite characters in the novel. We do see Rose though, and Lucas too, and I think we gain more perspective on their relationship and the friendship between the four of them. In a way, it was sad writing it and knowing what happens next but everyone will hopefully understand even more about how and why Lucas's death affected all the characters as much as it did.